Nathan Malone stole her breath away.

Never in her life had she felt like this.

Sean's smile deepened at his gesture. "Is that so?"

Nathan's head bobbed, and those sun-bleached curls fell around his face, his lips curving into the sexiest of grins. "Yes, ma'am, it is."

Sean felt a blush steal up her throat. She didn't even know what to say to that.

"Shy? No, can't be shy," Nathan teased, playing with the shell of her ear. "I think we've just kissed those days goodbye."

Sean giggled as Nathan tickled her ear. "Not hardly," she confessed. "I'll probably be eternally shy."

"Well. Even better," Nathan confessed, continuing to explore her face with his fingertip. "It will be my ongoing pleasure to attempt to break you from eternal shyness."

"Good luck," Sean advised. "I'm a hard nut to crack."

"That sounds like a challenge," Nathan said with a grin, then nodded. "I accept."

Together, they smiled, and a joy sank deep into Sean, a feeling that had been vacant from her life in...forever. She felt protected.

Dear Reader,

About That Kiss introduces the eldest of the Malone brothers, Nathan, and a stranger—an off islander—along with her whimsical five-year-old daughter, who not only steals, but mends, his broken heart. Sean Jacobs is fearful that a past she'd rather leave behind is about to catch up to her and her little girl, Willa. But what's even more terrifying is not only falling for the somber, stoic boat captain, but falling for his entire family. Unbeknownst to Nathan or Sean, though, is that fate has stepped in, and both need each other—and the unique quirkiness of a five-year-old girl—like they need air to breathe.

This third book of The Malone Brothers will once again capture the unique flavors from the first book, *Those Cassabaw Days*, as well as the second book, *At First Touch*. Unforgettable, quirky characters and the idyllic setting of the South Carolina barrier island return, as do the childhood memories the setting encapsulates for me. From the salt marshes to the 1930s beach cottages, having grown up on the southeast coast all it takes is a certain taste, a particular song or the faint recollection of a scent to remind you of true happiness.

Cindy

CINDY MILES

About That Kiss

Recycling programs for this product may not exist in your area.

ISBN-13: 978-0-373-64038-6

About That Kiss

This edition published by arrangement with Harlequin Books S.A.

For questions and comments about the quality of this book, please contact us at CustomerService@Harlequin.com.

Printed in U.S.A.

Cindy Miles grew up on the salt marshes and back rivers of Savannah, Georgia. Moody, sultry and mossy, with its ancient cobblestones and Georgian and Gothic architecture, the city inspired her to write twelve adult novels, one anthology, three short stories and one young-adult novel. When Cindy is not writing, she loves traveling, photography, baking, classic rock and the vintage, tinny music of *The Great Gatsby* era. To learn more about her books, visit her at cindy-miles.com.

Books by Cindy Miles

HARLEQUIN SUPERROMANCE

The Malone Brothers

Those Cassabaw Days
At First Touch
About That Kiss

For Macy Harden, my sweet little cousin, who has the courage of a lion and the fierce determination of her great-grandfather and my grandfather, Wimpy.

For Bonnie Heller, my lovely up-north auntie, who reads all my books and who birthed my crazy cousin, Henry, who shot me with a BB gun one time. It still hurts when it rains (kidding!).

For my Harden family, who gave me so many cherished memories of growing up on the salt marsh, crabbing the river and just general lifelong love. Gosh, I miss Frances and Wimpy!

And for my mom and dad, who always encouraged imagination. I love you guys!

PROLOGUE

Off the coast of Alaska
Bering Sea
Three years earlier

"SWIMMER AWAY, SWIMMER'S OKAY!"

Lt. Commander Jales's call was the last thing Petty Officer Nathan Malone heard as he leaped from the Jayhawk and plunged into the livid sea below. His body shot through the frigid water like a torpedo. He immediately resurfaced, the blade wash from the chopper beating him in the face, the torso. Adrenaline surged through him. Fear propelled him through the water, waves crashing against him. Over him. The sky was nearly as pitch-black as the water. Visibility zilch.

Addie.

He pushed toward the *Zany Moe*, swimming hard, fighting the roaring squall. His fiancée's fishing boat lay on her starboard side, sinking below the dark water. Nathan scanned the boat, his eyes fastening on Addie's red slicker. *Not* her guppy suit. Her arm lifted, waved, then she clutched the rail she was desperately holding on to as another wave swamped her.

Her first mate, Chip, was nowhere. Nathan scanned the choppy water and peered through the rain, looking for the inflatable Zodiac. Like Chip, it was nowhere.

Nathan swam closer to the *Zany Moe*, throwing arm over arm, pushing his weight against the stone-like waves. He shouted at Addie to jump, motioned with his hands. The roar of the storm deafened him, rang through his ears. She couldn't hear him. But she'd understood. Addie nodded and slowly let go of the rail. Their eyes locked for a moment, and she took a step back then broke for the edge.

A wave crashed over the boat, over Addie, washing over Nathan's head. When he bobbed up and cleared the water, he scanned the boat. The water.

Addie had disappeared.

Panic squeezed his throat, and with frantic desperation, he kicked out, swam hard to the bow that was slowly slipping beneath the black water.

"Addie!" he shouted, over and over. His eyes searched. He swam. Looking for just a piece of that red slicker. He ducked under, then back up. Nothing.

The *Zany Moe* was sinking down fast now, and with no captain manning the wheel, the violent, angry sea propelled the boat like a rubber toy in a bathtub. Nathan could feel the tug of the current as the steel plunged under the water. He pushed hard, refusing to give up. She was here. He hadn't lost her.

"Addeline!" he shouted until his voice cracked. He swallowed seawater. He swallowed air. He darted his eyes everywhere as he panicked but saw nothing except gray, black and the white froth kicked up by the crashing waves. The waves grew, like being in rolling hills, and Addie was nowhere to be found.

He turned his eyes skyward and noticed the Jayhawk hovering overhead. His captain signaled and dropped the line. Nathan turned away, scanning frantically the gray swells and bursts of foam as the sea churned. No sign of Addeline. Not…anywhere. He screamed into the wind, until he had no air left, and his throat scorched from swallowing too much salt water. The sea spray from the blade wash as the chopper dropped closer blinded him. With his lungs burning, he swam to his line, and the chopper pulled him up. Nathan kept his eyes fastened on the angry waters below. He couldn't see from down there, bobbing in the storm, being tossed around. They'd find her. From the Jayhawk, he'd be able to see that red coat. Just over that next hill of water. That next wave. She'd be there, waiting. He'd find Addie.

He wasn't leaving until he did.

Nathan clung to the edge of the open door of the Jayhawk as they searched for hours. Dread filled his insides with each ticking moment that passed. She'd not been wearing her guppy suit. The damn thing he'd told her more than once to put on at the first sign of any trouble. It was insulated. It'd keep her warm if she ended up in the icy water.

She'd been wearing only that damned red rubber coat.

Four hours passed before they found Chip, dead. Wearing the guppy suit. And about a half mile away, the inflatable Zodiac.

For three days they searched the wreck site, and even though the waters had somewhat calmed with the passing of the storm, there was never a sign of Addie. Nathan couldn't eat. Couldn't sleep. Wouldn't leave the station, much less his post. Hope fled, turning into a clawing, painful desperation to get Addie back. It left a hole in his gut.

"You did everything you could, Nathan," Lt. Commander Jales said. The Jayhawk's pilot put his hand on Nathan's shoulder and squeezed. "You did, son. That was…a helluva storm, I'm afraid. I'm sorry."

The words reverberated in Nathan's head, bounced off his skull and fell flat. The sea had swallowed her up. Over and over in his head, he saw her standing there, waving at him. He'd never see her again. Pain tore at his insides. He'd not done everything. He'd had eyes on Addie. Had told her to jump. He'd been *right there.*

It'd not been enough.

He'd not been enough.

CHAPTER ONE

Cassabaw Station
Carolina barrier island
Late June
Present day

THE ALARM'S SCREECH broke through the room and Nathan's sleep, and he pushed off his stomach to sit on the edge of the bed. He tapped the alarm off and pushed his fingers through his hair.

Four a.m., and it was opening day of shrimping season. They were going to get an extra-early start.

Running through his morning ritual, Nathan put on a T-shirt and shorts, then pulled his hair back. Quickly washing his face and brushing his teeth, he then jogged downstairs, the smell of bacon and coffee wafting up the stairwell.

"'Bout damn time you dragged yourself out

of bed," his grandpa, Jep, grumbled from the stove. "You goin' for a haircut later?"

Nathan's dad, Owen, was sitting at the table, and he threw his son a grin.

"Jep, enough about the hair," Nathan said, pouring coffee into an insulated thermos. "It's getting old."

"Well, I'm old, dammit, and I'm tired of lookin' at my eldest grandson with long, girlie hair." He swore under his breath. "Ponytail and such. Like a pirate or some such nonsense. Or a hippie! Godalmighty damn."

Nathan chuckled. "Chicks dig it."

Jep snorted. "Sure they do, boy. I can tell by how they're lining the drive each weekend. Now quit arguing and eat up."

Nathan gave his grandpa a quick peck on the cheek then jumped out of the way before the old guy one-twoed him. Grabbing a bacon-and-egg biscuit from the pan on the stove, he joined his dad at the table. Jep sat with them, sipping on a coffee mug surely older than Nathan himself. Tradition, Jep always said. It's a good thing to have. Just then, a quick knock sounded at the back door, before it opened. Nathan's middle brother, Matt, stepped over the threshold.

"'Bout time you got your sorry backside outta bed," Jep grumbled.

Matt ruffled Jep's thick white hair, grabbed a biscuit then sat with them.

"Good to have your help on opening day," Owen said.

Matt gave a lopsided grin. "You almost had two helpers. I had to convince Em that she really shouldn't be on a trawler in the Atlantic in her condition."

"Did she smack you for that?" Nathan asked.

"Yep." Matt shoved the rest of his biscuit into his mouth.

Nathan figured his sister-in-law, now six months pregnant with his first-ever niece or nephew, had a head of concrete. It wouldn't surprise him at all to find she'd stowed away on the *Tiger Lily*.

They quickly finished breakfast, grabbed their gear and set out. The early-morning Carolina air was still and warm and humid as they walked down to the dock. The night birds still called, and cicadas and frogs rivaled their choruses. A typical low-country morning. Tradition. Home. Family.

Living the dream.

Almost, anyway.

Living on the Back River, the water was deep enough to berth their thirty-foot trawler, so while Owen took the wheel and began to ease along, Nathan and Matt both perched at the bow in silence, studying the water ahead as the *Tiger Lily* sliced through the calm darkness. Nathan inhaled, holding the briny air in his lungs before letting his breath out slowly. It was going to be a damn good day. The weather conditions were perfect. Warm air, warmer waters. Nathan knew, though, that the calm blue-gray of the Atlantic could churn and cough and consume any and everything in its path, all in the blink of an eye. The sea? She was never, ever to be trusted. But for now, he'd gladly accept the bounty she'd offered up.

As they cleared the river and entered the sound, Nathan and Matt dropped the trawler's outriggers and they headed out to sea. As morning broke, other trawlers dotted the horizon, but the *Tiger Lily* was in an optimal spot, where the waters were moving in the same direction. They rode the shifting tides, avoided slack-water time. After baiting the nets, Nathan and Matt dropped the doors, and after just one drag they raised both nets filled with Atlantic brown shrimp. Nathan let out a holler, and Matt threw his head back and laughed. Owen simply shook his head, a grin on his weathered face.

The nets dropped load after load, and they filled the coolers to the gills with shrimp. It'd been a good haul for opening day—more than an average haul. By the time they'd dropped the load at the docks and the *Tiger Lily* began chugging home, the sun had peaked. Three o'clock on a June day. Hot as all holy hell.

"Hope that sets the pace for the season," Owen said from the wheel.

"It'd be nice," Nathan called back. Since they shrimped almost year-round, even a slow season wasn't terrible. Last year had been a big improvement from the year before. Same with crabs, which they tended to run commercial traps for in the summer months leading into early fall, just to make the extra money. Even the infamous Carolina blue crabs were heading farther out, away from the riverbeds and into deeper waters. Hell, the entire ecosystem had gone squirrely. They even had a few great whites show up from time to time. One local white that showed up three years running, Lucy, had found herself on the news more than once. Way different from when he and his brothers were growing up, when they could drop lines off the floating dock and pull in an easy half bushel of crabs in no time flat. Still, things had been good for the Malone family.

They were blessed, to say the very least. Nathan glanced skyward once more, noticed the cerulean sky, felt the sun's warmth on his face. Yeah, this year would be good for shrimping.

Owen slowed the motors and eased the *Tiger Lily* into the river leading home. The sun beat down on Nathan's bare back, and he was half tempted to jump in.

"You got new neighbors?" Matt asked.

Nathan glanced at his brother, and Matt inclined his head. Nathan followed his brother's gaze. He lifted the shades from his eyes. At the end of Morgan's old dock sat a girl. A woman, rather. A little girl sat next to her, and their feet were dangling over the floating dock and into the water. The little girl had on a neon pink bathing suit that could probably be seen for miles around. Both had short dark hair, and that was about all Nathan could tell from where he stood. What were they doing there? The little girl leaped to her feet as they passed, waving her skinny little arms. Nathan lifted his hand and waved back.

"No one's lived at old Morgan's place for nearly ten years," Owen called from the wheel. "Far as I know, the old man didn't have kin except his cousin, Bartholomew."

"That doesn't look much like Cousin Bartholomew," Matt muttered.

"Nope," Nathan agreed as he slipped his shades over his eyes and watched as the young woman—no doubt the girl's mother—grasped her daughter's hand and they hurried along the rickety old dock, toward the house. The whole time, the little girl was hopping from foot to foot, looking over her shoulder as the trawler eased up the river. By the time the *Tiger Lily* hit the bend, the pair had disappeared into the swath of live oaks that all but consumed Morgan's place.

"Maybe they've bought the house," Owen remarked. "Shame to see that place just sit. It'd be nice to have new neighbors." He cleared his throat. "Maybe you should run over later and introduce yourself."

"Dad, you are such a social butterfly," Nathan accused, and Matt laughed. "Why don't you go introduce *yourself*? Anyway, you just like having a bunch of kids around."

"I am, I might and I do," Owen readily agreed to all accusations.

Nathan glanced once more at the now-empty dock. Again, he shaded his eyes.

Probably just some summer renters. That was a regular occurrence on Cassabaw. Renters came. Renters left. End of story. Owen was simply too damned nosy for his own good.

As his father eased the trawler toward the Malones' dock, Nathan and Matt jumped out and tied up. Emily, Matt's wife, hurried toward them. She wore a kerchief on her head to keep her hair back, and a pair of big, white-rimmed sunglasses. Her baby belly was just starting to show beneath the white tank and pair of knee-length cutoff jeans she wore. Em preferred the days of old. As they all had grown up on Ella Fitzgerald, Louis Armstrong and the big bands of the thirties and forties, Emily hadn't strayed too far in terms of her taste in music—or style. If it was older than, say, seventy-five years, she loved it. She even dressed in vintage clothing—hats, dresses, shoes. Kerchiefs. Kind of added to her charm, he supposed. Em had a wide arm of culture, however. She could belt out all the words to just about any Aerosmith song. One of kind, his sister-in-law was.

Old Jep, moving a bit slower than Em, followed, wearing his iconic baby-blue cotton overalls.

"Hey!" Emily called cheerfully. "How'd you guys do?"

"Girl, would you quit all that jumpin' around? You're gonna scramble my great-grandson's innards," Jep called after her.

"Or great-granddaughter," Emily corrected over her shoulder.

Jep just grumbled.

"We capped out," Owen said, stepping onto the dock. "Got top dollar at the docks. Better than last year, even."

"Good, good," Jep said. His thick white hair, mostly buried beneath a USCG—United States Coast Guard—cap, flipped up on the ends. "Hope to God you brought some home."

"Dad," Owen chided.

"Jep, you could eat shrimp every day of your life," Matt said, wrapping his arms around his wife and placing his hands over her belly. Nathan watched as his little brother kissed Em on the top of her head, and her arms went around his waist. They both fit. Clicked. Like they were made for each other. He'd had that once.

And he'd lost it.

The grief had dulled somewhat over time, but not enough. If his thoughts lingered too long on it—on Addie, on what they'd had—his stomach would hurt, and he'd feel the hole her death had left in his chest widen a little more. It'd been nearly three years since that day in the Bering, when Nathan had been right there, ready for her. Then, she'd disappeared. The sea had, in fact, swallowed her up. If his thoughts went there too much, the memories and guilt would consume him. Being home with his family had saved his life. The void was still there, though, silently digging in when he wasn't looking. Staying busy helped.

Nathan liked seeing his younger brother so happy. Matt's stoic and hardened ex-marine demeanor had changed the moment he'd admitted that he'd fallen in love with his childhood friend. Well, he'd fought it for a while, and he'd been a pain in the ass to live with until he'd finally given in. Still, he damn well deserved the happiness.

"Well, of course I would," Jep agreed. "Jewels of the sea, that's what they are. The most perfect edible sea creatures God ever created, if you ask me."

They all laughed. Jep had a one-track mind: his stomach. Might be why he was closing in on ninety and still going stronger than a mule.

The rest of the evening passed as it usually did once the summer shrimping season started. Early to bed, early to rise. A day in the trawler. Home-cooked meals on the back porch. And thanks to the longer days of sunlight, Nathan squeezed in a run almost every evening. Sometimes Matt joined him, but lately he'd spent more of his evenings with Em remodeling one of the rooms in the old river house where they lived—Emily's childhood home, which was next door—into the nursery. Emily called it nesting, and Nathan guessed she was probably right. So he set out alone in the late evening; gray running shorts, black Nikes and a neon yellow handkerchief tied around his head to keep the sweat from running into his eyes. And, according to Jep, to keep his long girlie locks from flying all over the place.

"Stop by the beauty parlor on your way home," Jep called from his rocker on the front porch as Nathan took off down the drive. "And watch out for cars!"

Another reason why Nathan wore the neon yellow headband. Jep was full of bark, but that old man loved his family like no one's business.

It was probably the one thing that kept Nathan grounded since Alaska. The one thing he had left.

"Yes, sir." Nathan threw his hand up and waved, hearing Jep grumble something about the mosquitoes, then headed out to the coastal road.

"MA-MUH, COME ON! Just a little walk. Just long enough to kick a pinecone until the pointy things all fall off. I want to see lightning bugs! Pleeeeeease?"

"Willa, quit all that whining," Sean Jacobs gently scolded her five-year-old daughter. "It's unbecoming."

"But I can't help it," Willa said, and looked up at Sean with those wide, endless pools of blue eyes. "It just falls out of my throat and rolls right on past my lips. I can't stop it! I want to go so bad!"

A smile tugged at Sean's mouth, and she gave her small daughter a critical eye. She wore a blue-and-white-striped tank top and white shorts, and her skinny little legs and knobby knees seemed to hang straight from her ears. "Well," Sean said thoughtfully, and smoothed Willa's almost-black hair—cut bluntly in the most adorable of short bobs—behind her tiny ear. "Okay. Get your sneakers on."

Willa made a dash for the mudroom. "Why do you call them sneakers, Mama? Are we gonna be busy sneakin' around or something? It's a funny name, Mama. Did your mama call them sneakers, too?"

Sean's insides turned, just a little, at the irony of Willa's words. *Sneakin' around.* She inhaled. Exhaled to brush the jolted feeling away. "That's just what we called them when I was your age, is all." She joined her daughter in the mudroom, pulled on her navy Keds. Willa set in her lap something that seemed to be becoming a more frequent part of her wardrobe. Sean gingerly fingered the costume fairy wings she'd picked up last Halloween.

"Willa, seriously?"

"Yes, Mama! We have to be fairies *all the time*!" Willa argued. Rather, crooned.

Sean sighed, shoved her arms through the thin elastic bands that went around her shoulders to keep the wings in place, then helped

Willa into hers. She imagined if something as simple as wearing a pair of sparkly fairy wings made her daughter happy, she'd gladly do it. They set out, with Willa nonstop chattering about everything her eyes lit upon, her little wings flapping up and down with her movements.

"Now go find a superior pinecone, Willa Jane. One that will withstand a good kicking."

"Okay, I will!" Willa exclaimed, and took off into the dense yard of pines, scrub oaks and palms. She'd bend, retrieve a pinecone then inspect every single inch of it. Only the most perfect one would do.

Sean stared out at the saltwater property they'd leased for the summer. She liked it. A little worn down, perhaps. Unkempt. The windows needed washing. The grass needed cutting. The inside was a little musty from being closed up for so long. But she felt safe. The furniture was old but sturdy, and the refrigerator kept things icy cold. Perfect, in her eyes.

The small river house nestled in the shade beneath mammoth oak trees drenched in long, wispy Spanish moss. It looked like a picture straight out of a travel magazine. A fairly decent-size porch overlooked the back of the property, which meandered through tall magnolias and scrub palms, leading down to a single wooden dock that jutted out over the marsh and stopped at the river. At high tide, she and Willa could sit on the small wooden landing and dangle their feet into the water. This would be a nice retreat for a while.

"Mama, you're being so slow," Willa called ahead of her. "I found the most *stuperior* pinecone. C'mon! I wanna walk through the graveyard."

"Willa, again?" Sean replied, catching up to her daughter. They crossed the small two-lane river road and headed down a worn dirt path scattered with bits of seashells that led to an old cemetery they'd come across a few days earlier. "Don't you think it's kinda scary?"

"Nope!" Willa announced cheerfully, and having found the perfect pinecone, dropped it on the ground. She gave it a kick, then waited for Sean to take a turn. "It's the place where all the lightning bugs go. Probably so the ghosts can see at night."

"It's also a place where all the mosquitoes go," Sean replied. "We're going to get eaten up again."

"So? Just scratch it!" Will answered. "It's

fun, Mama. Hurry! Use your wings, why don't ya? You'll be faster that way!"

Willa always had an answer. *For everything.* Her five-year-old mind never rested. And she feared nothing.

Completely unlike Sean herself. Afraid of everything.

As she and Willa took turns kicking the pinecone, Sean noticed the sun had disappeared beneath the horizon now, leaving the sky a grayish purple streaked with marigold. The light surrounding them was nothing more than a haze, and she could smell the salty sea. Even with Willa's chatter and the occasional gull's screech, Sean heard hundreds of night bugs begin to chirp. Cassabaw Station was a pretty place, a hidden gem that seemed to have wedged itself into another time and not budged. Ahead, Willa waited at the cemetery's old rusty gate, hopping from foot to foot impatiently. Sean stepped clear of the path, met her daughter at the gate, lifted the old latch and they walked inside.

"There's one, Mama!" Willa cried out almost immediately. Sean looked, and sure enough, she'd already found a lightning bug. Then another, and another. Willa leaped and giggled as she chased the blinking insects, flitting around like a little firefly herself. Sean stood back and grinned. Savored the small moment of joy in their lives.

"Careful not to step on the graves, Willa," Sean called.

"I'm careful!" Willa answered. "Come on, chase them with me!"

Sean joined her daughter, and together, they raced, jumped and squealed as they cupped their hands together to capture the illuminated creatures, then peeked through the cracks of their fingers to see each little bug's bottom light up. She watched Willa and thought how beautiful her daughter was; so young, innocent, carefree and full of love and laughter. Sean suddenly regretted not having a camera to photograph Willa, to catch her with the light just right, making her truly seem like a little woodland sprite. Sean prayed Willa would never know cruelty, possessiveness. Or evil. Only love. Joy.

It was then that Sean heard heavy footsteps on the path. She stopped and whipped around. A dark figure jogged toward them, a neon yellow band around his head the only thing standing out. For a moment, fear strangled her insides, and her gaze darted to her daughter. To the figure, growing closer, then to her daughter again.

He was big—much bigger than she was—and probably faster, too. Even from where she stood, and in the low light of dusk, she could tell he was muscular, fit. Sean didn't know him, or anyone else on the island. And they were about as isolated as they could be. He was right between her and her daughter.

"Willa, come here!" Sean called out. "We have to go. It's getting dark fast."

"Mama, I'm busy!" Willa replied, annoyed. "Just a few more minutes."

"Willa, now!" Sean demanded, and broke into a run toward her. Sean had to reach Willa. She couldn't let the jogger get close to her daughter.

As the figure jogged past the cemetery, he spoke. "Evening," he said in a low voice, with a short nod and a slight Carolina drawl. His longish hair was pulled back, and a beard covered his lower jaw.

He kept on jogging.

Sean kept her eyes on the man but didn't reply. He ran in the direction she and Willa would return, then disappeared from sight.

Sean's tension slowly eased, and she turned to Willa. "Just a few more minutes, then."

"Thanks, Mama," she cried, and continued chasing the lightning bugs and talking to the ghosts, as if they were all sitting around watching her.

Sean let out a long sigh and turned her stare in the direction the stranger had disappeared. She hated that she allowed such terror. He'd been merely jogging, nothing more. The hazy light fell faster by each passing second, and she wondered briefly if she'd ever, ever stop looking over her shoulder. If the fear would ever leave her alone.

CHAPTER TWO

"MAMA! CAN WE get an ice cream cone? Please?"

Sean shielded her eyes against the sun beaming down as they ambled along Cassabaw's boardwalk. She shook her head. "You haven't had dinner yet, Willa."

"How about a hot dog?" Willa, dressed in a blue tank top and white shorts and sneakers, pointed toward the pier. "From that man with the cart?"

Sean squinted as she glanced at the hot dog vendor and his pushcart with a broad, red-and-white-striped umbrella. "But you need veggies, sweetie."

Willa crossed her skinny little arms over her chest. "Mama, you don't get veggies at a hot dog cart." She clasped her hands together and jumped up and down. "Pleeeeeease?"

"Okay, but double veggies tomorrow night."

Willa took off toward the vendor, and Sean

followed. "Two, please," she requested. "And a bottle of water."

"Put lots of ketchup and mustard on mine, please," Willa requested.

"No onions?" a low voice said from behind.

Sean turned and came face-to-face with the bearded jogger from the cemetery. Well, face-to-face only after she looked way up. He was tall—at least six foot one or two. He wore a kerchief tied around his head, and dark shades covered his eyes. She couldn't help but notice the size of his biceps, and the sun-kissed color of his skin. He was every bit as mammoth as she'd thought the night before. A force she would be unable to stop, if the situation came down to that. She pushed herself to her full height, edging herself between the stranger and her daughter. In a way, she felt silly. They were in public. Just a small coastal town. More than likely, everyone within a hundred-yard radius knew him. Yet, he unsettled her. So she took caution.

Willa, though, peered around Sean and looked at him, too, and made a face. "Those are stinky," she said. "Mama, why are you in my way?"

"Willa," Sean warned. Suddenly, she wanted

to be...away. Not in this place. Not with attention drawn to them. It was the last thing she wanted.

"Yeah, but good on a dog," the stranger said, continuing his conversation with Willa. His voice had a slight rasp. A slightly lilted Carolina accent. "You should try it." One corner of his mouth lifted, and Sean noticed full lips and straight white teeth. "Best dogs on the Eastern Seaboard."

"What is an Eastern Seaboard?" Willa asked.

"Pah! Eastern Seaboard. Best dogs of anywhere in world!" the vendor cried out in a broken accent. He seemed like a friendly guy, and clearly was a regular on the beachfront.

"Sorry, Hendrik. Best dogs of anywhere in the world," the stranger agreed.

"For the lady?" Hendrik asked Sean. She noticed he was polite, too. Respectful. She liked that.

"Just mustard for me, thanks," she answered the vendor, watching his dark brown eyes assess her closely.

"Are you gonna get stinky onions all over yours?" Willa asked the stranger.

"I am," he replied. "You?"

"Nah," Willa replied.

"Willa, what have I told you?" Sean needed to stop the exchange. Willa would talk to a goat if she'd let her. Her daughter had no fear, and that alone put terror into Sean's heart.

Willa sighed. "Never talk to strangers," she answered, then looked at the stranger, squinting against the sun. "Mama says child abductors and serial killers and just plain ole weirdos lurk everywhere and that I should be extra extremely careful."

"Willa," Sean growled. She glanced at the stranger, wishing she could at least see his eyes. You could tell a lot in a person's eyes, she'd learned. That grin remained on his face.

"It's true," Hendrik added. "Must be careful at all times, little one. Many weirdos." He handed her the hot dogs, wrapped in red-and-white-checkered waxed paper, and pulled an icy-cold bottle of water from a cooler. "That's seven American dollars," he said.

Sean handed him a ten-dollar bill. "Thanks, and keep the change." She handed Willa her hot dog, and they headed out onto the pier. As they passed the stranger, her daughter, with mouth crammed full of hot dog, gave him a curious eye.

"Bye," Willa mumbled around the bite she'd just taken.

He merely waved.

Perhaps Sean had misjudged the stranger. In all sincerity, he was obviously a local and friendly with the townspeople. The exchange he'd had with Willa had been…harmless. He was just making casual conversation. Wasn't he?

As she and Willa wandered the pier filled with locals and tourists fishing along the sides, Sean felt the stranger's eyes on her. She'd been so…aware of him. Of his presence looming beside her. Yet she hadn't felt that threat of fear that usually accompanied her initial internal terror. The vendor had seemed to like him. And, for that matter, so had Willa. Still, Sean and her daughter were not locals. They were summer tourists. She had zero plans to get to know anyone on a personal level.

But when Sean turned, the stranger wasn't lurking and staring at her, as she'd thought. He was gone, and Hendrik had a new set of customers at his cart.

That probably wouldn't be the last she saw of the stranger, though. This was a small island. They couldn't stay cooped up in their river house all summer long. And despite her repeated warnings to Willa, her opinionated daughter would undoubtedly make some sort of conversation with the stranger. Who, while somewhat reserved, would converse back. If not him, another stranger. Willa was…verbose in the most charming of ways, to say the very least. People couldn't help but engage with her. It was nearly unavoidable. But Sean would again try to caution her daughter.

"Willa, sweetie," she began, as they walked. The sun's rays warmed her bare arms and legs, and made Willa's hair shine. "You can't just talk to any and everybody. You never know who a person really is."

Willa's tongue darted out to catch a glob of ketchup on her chin. "That's why you talk to people, Mama. Then you know who they really are."

Sean sighed. Willa was too smart for her own good sometimes. "I mean," she began again, "you never know about people. Sometimes, they could be… I don't know. Hiding something."

Willa squinted as she looked at her. "You mean, like hiding candy in their pocket?"

Sean shook her head. They reached the end

of the pier. "No, honey. Like…that man you were chatting with. He could be, I don't know. A stalker!" She knelt down to look Willa eye-to-eye. "He probably isn't, but that's the thing. You never know. So you have to be really, really careful about who you talk to. Understand?"

"Yes, ma'am," Willa said slowly. She turned to the water then, chewing on her hot dog, and by the quizzical expression on her face, Willa was turning everything Sean had said over and over in her mind.

Sean could only hope her daughter retained some of her advice.

A FEW DAYS later Sean and Willa drove into the next town—over the marsh, past the Coast Guard station and over the drawbridge—to shop at the larger grocery store. Sean wanted to stock up so she wouldn't have to make another trip in for at least a month. Since it was just her and Willa, they didn't need a lot, but still—certain foods disappeared fast. They walked in through the automatic doors, a blast of cold air greeting them, and Willa raced straight to the produce section. There weren't too many people in the store, which was fine with Sean. She and Willa mulled over a large display of peaches.

"What, no fairy wings?" a husky voice said from behind her.

Startled, Sean turned, and there he was again. The ponytailed, bearded stranger with a killer smile and a taste for stinky onions. For the first time she noticed his stunning eyes, which, until now, had always been covered by a pair of aviator sunglasses. His eyes were a stormy sea green and filled with caution. And a little amusement. Maybe even curiosity. They seemed honest, those eyes. That much, she could tell.

Willa looked up from her peach selecting. "Mama has to wash them on account that she says they smell funny. She says you're a stalker."

Sean muttered under her breath, then flashed the man a nervous smile. Mortification struck Sean at Willa's inadvertent tattletale of their previous conversation. But what if he really was a stalker? She didn't know the first thing about him, other than he was a runner who ate hot dogs. "Sorry, we're in a bit of a hurry."

"That's right, a big giant hurry," Willa added. "We are having a picnic at the end of the dock tonight." She sniffed a peach. "Mama says we're dining alfresco. With the dolphins."

The man's gaze moved over Sean's face. He seemed to study her for a moment, intense and inquisitive. "I see. Well, then," he drawled, "I don't want to keep you. You two ladies have a good day."

Sean watched him walk away, pushing a grocery cart, a very male and slightly bow-legged swagger. She noticed he never lingered too long. He said what it was he wanted to say then left. He had noticed their fairy wings, though. Sean pondered that as he wandered down an aisle and out of sight.

Who wouldn't notice the fairy wings? Maybe she was spending way too much time wondering about it. Quickly, she and Willa picked out their fruits and vegetables. As luck would have it, once they started wandering the aisles, they ran into him again and again. He'd smile each time, give a slight nod, but didn't say another word. Only watched with those mysterious eyes.

Perhaps he hadn't liked the fact that she'd warned her daughter he could be a stalker.

Stalkers, though, came in many forms. Many shapes and sizes. Including handsome islanders. They could be poor, or filthy rich. They could have dazzling smiles, kind sea-green eyes or piercing blue ones. They could even have extra-butter movie popcorn in their grocery carts. Or a gallon of chocolate milk. Danger knew no boundaries. It was not prejudiced, either.

Yet, he hadn't taken a threatening stance. Hadn't stared too long, or made any comments or gestures that had truly made her uncomfortable. Had he?

Still, one could never be too cautious. And she wasn't taking any more chances. She'd made that mistake in the past. Never again. Willa was all she had, and she'd keep her safe at all costs.

Even if the stranger really, truly didn't seem all that dangerous.

Once Sean and Willa reached the river house, unloaded all the groceries and put them away then did their daily reading lesson, Willa watched cartoons while Sean started their dinner. They'd decided on meat loaf, mashed potatoes and peas. After mixing the meat, spices, egg, milk and bread crumbs, Sean shaped the loaf, placed it in one of the new pans they'd purchased and popped it in the oven. She'd started peeling the potatoes when a sudden knock sounded at the door.

They've found us!

Panic flashed through her, and she dropped a potato on the floor.

"I'll get it!" Willa cried out, running to the front door.

"Willa, no!" Sean called out, but too late. Willa had the door open.

And there stood the stranger with startling green eyes.

"Mama! It's the stalker! How did you know where we lived?" Willa asked him.

He eyed Sean over Willa's head then looked at her daughter with a serious expression, drawing sun-bleached eyebrows together. "I'm your neighbor," he said, and jerked a thumb over his shoulder. "I live up the river a ways."

"That was you on the shrimping boat," Sean stated, rather than asked. She felt a bit foolish now, when she reflected on her immediate reaction when she'd first seen him on the boat. Drug runners or some other kind of criminal. She and Willa had been sitting on the dock, their toes in the warm salt water, when the big boat appeared around the bend. Fight or flight was her immediate response, and she'd chosen to fly. She'd expected…something else. Not a shrimp fisherman.

He gave a half nod. "With my dad."

Correction. A *family* shrimper.

"Are you a pirate?" Willa asked.

One corner of his mouth tipped up. "Do I look like a pirate?"

Willa cocked her head, her dark hair hugging her jaw. "I think you look like a pretend pirate."

The man met Sean's gaze. Amusement danced in his eyes. "Is that so?"

Willa's head bobbed. "Yes, because you have long hair and a beard and your skin is brown. But you don't have a patch on one eye. Or a parrot on your shoulder." She sniffed. "Or the right hat."

"Willa, honestly," Sean muttered.

He merely smiled. "A parrot and an eye patch, huh?"

"I'm not supposed to talk to strangers," Willa blurted.

The man stuck out his hand. "Well, that's good advice, then. I'm Nathan Malone. Now we won't be strangers anymore."

Willa looked at Sean, and she nodded her

approval. Willa shook his hand. “My name is Willa Jane Jacobs, and I’m five and a half.”

“Nice to meet you, Willa,” Nathan said. He glanced again at Sean. Waiting.

“Uh, sorry. Sean. Jacobs,” she said hastily. She could use her manners even though she had no intentions of getting to know her neighbors, or anyone else on the island. She and Willa were here for a short time. Nothing more. The very last thing she wanted was to become friendly. With anyone.

When Nathan held out his hand, she accepted it and gave a hesitant shake. She didn’t hold his hand for long. But enough time, though, to notice how rough it was. Strong. Definitely the hand of a working man. Or a pirate. “Sorry, we were just— I’m in the middle of cooking.” She glanced behind her, to where her potatoes awaited her, then looked back at Nathan.

“Right,” Nathan answered in a slow drawl. “Dining alfresco with the dolphins.” He reached for a foil-covered plate that he’d set on the top step and handed it to Sean. “Since we’re neighbors, my granddad insisted on sending over these cheddar biscuits. He swears they go with anything." Nathan shoved his hands into his pockets. "Welcome to Cassabaw."

Sean gave a nervous smile. *Oh, God. Hope he's not waiting around for an invitation to eat with us!*

"Hey, Nathan. You wanna dine alfresco with us and the dolphins? Mama, can he?"

Ugh! Willa Jane! Panic nearly choked Sean at Willa's casual invitation. She didn't want him—or anyone else—to join them. The less Nathan Malone knew about her and Willa, the better off they would all be. To have dinner with him? That would lead to questions. Answers. Neither of which was Sean willing to do.

NATHAN WATCHED SEAN'S wide hazel eyes. She all but scrambled to give her daughter an answer. He decided to end her misery.

"Thanks, but I can't," he said to Willa. Then he glanced at Sean. He couldn't help but wonder what her deal was. Had he done something she hadn't liked? Maybe she was socially awkward. Either way, her eyes had glazed over with what he perceived to be pure panic at the possibility of him sticking around for supper. "I've got to head out." He inclined his head toward the foil-covered plate Sean now gripped so tightly her knuckles were white. "I'll let you girls get back to it, then." He threw a smile at Willa. "No longer strangers, right?"

"Right!" Willa said excitedly. "Bye, Nathan!"

Nathan gave a wave and made his way down the narrow, shell-and-sand path that led to the road. He ran the half mile home. As his lungs expanded, contracted and the salty low-tide marsh seeped into his nostrils, his thoughts stayed on the woman and her daughter. He recalled how he'd happened upon them wearing fairy wings, jumping around the cemetery catching fireflies. That image didn't fit the way she'd panicked at the thought of him eating supper with them. Not that he would have accepted anyway. Even before Willa's impromptu invitation, it had been pretty evident Sean didn't want him there.

This newcomer seemed edgy—not usually a characteristic of an off-islander. Typically, they wanted to be involved. Almost...like they wanted to become a local, he guessed. But this pair was different. Cautious. At least, Sean was. Willa, on the other hand, seemed like she was ready to take on any and everything that came her way. What a funny kid. And those fairy wings were… Damn, they were adorable. He couldn't help but wonder where Willa's father was. Deadbeat? Or just dead? Had to be, not to take part in their lives. Some men had it made and just didn't realize it.

Regardless, it wasn't his place to wonder. Or worry. He'd done his duty. He'd delivered the biscuits and he'd been neighborly.

Jep was waiting for him on the front porch.

Nathan inwardly groaned as he took the steps and sat on the last one, leaning against the pillar. He hadn't wanted to approach Sean and Willa. Hadn't wanted to go to their home. He hadn't wanted to take them those damned biscuits. It'd all been Jep's idea. *It's the neighborly thing to do, son.* Yet despite his reluctance to visit the Jacobses, Nathan's desire not to cross Jep Malone superseded his desire to keep a distance from women in general. He was polite when he encountered any woman. Speaking to them when they ran into one another in public was one thing. Specifically delivering homemade biscuits to a woman's home was altogether different. That went beyond politeness and into some murky area that led to connections and relationships. Thing was, his grandfather knew it. Knew it well, too.

"You gonna let me sit here all day, or are you gonna tell me what's what with them two?" Jep asked.

Nathan met his grandfather's always-fiery gaze. "I wasn't exactly welcome."

Jep blinked, pushed his USCG cap farther back onto his head and rubbed a particular spot with his thumb. "Huh. Go figure. Probably your sunshine personality." He furrowed his white eyebrows. "What does that mean, boy?"

Nathan watched a dragonfly land on the top of Jep's cap. "She seems scared of something, maybe. Eyes all wide, always looking around. Like she was expecting to see someone she didn't want to see. Didn't have much to say at all. I could tell she wanted me gone ASAP." Nathan picked up a pebble on the step then tossed it into the yard. "You should've seen her face when her kid asked me to eat with them." Nathan shook his head and looked at his grandfather. "Pure terror."

"Huh." Jep's eyes narrowed as he inspected Nathan. "Might be that bushy appearance you keep, son. You look like some crazed killer."

Nathan grinned. "Yeah, maybe I do. Her kid ratted her out. Told me her mama said I could be a stalker. The kid said I looked more like a pirate."

"She's right about that," Jep agreed with a croaky laugh. "Well. Guess we'll have to try harder. No sense in letting them two little gals sit over there in that musty old house with only the ghosts, gulls and fiddler crabs for company."

Nathan studied Jep's profile. "Why are you always trying to play matchmaker, Gramps? Can't you leave well enough alone?"

Jep guffawed. "Youth. Wasted on the young, I tell ya! In my day, a man would see a pretty girl and take it upon himself to make the first move. You, on the other hand, seem not to have caught on to that." Jep leaned forward in his rocker, and his expression, with those big eyebrows stretched upward and eyes rounded, nearly made Nathan burst out laughing. "It's called courtin'! Look it up in the dictionary."

Nathan fought a smile. "We have Google now, Jep."

"Bah! Google, schmoogle. Them two gals are all alone over there."

"Might be how they want it," Nathan argued. "The mama seems set on being left alone. I myself kind of like it that way, too."

Jep pushed up from his rocker, and the bones in his knees crackled and popped. "Like I said. Try harder." He paused and eyeballed Nathan. "And it don't matter what you want, boy. You're as lost as they sound. You at least got a name, didn't you?"

Nathan nodded. "Sean and Willa Jacobs."

Jep headed toward the door. "Willa, you say? Never heard that before. Well. At least all your good sense hasn't left you fully yet, boy. There's hope yet. I'll see you tonight."

Nathan watched his grandfather disappear into the house, and he shook his head. "Yep. Least I still have my good sense. The good sense to keep to myself."

Before Nathan had any more time to ponder on Jep's words, his father called out. "Nathan? You ready?"

"Yes, sir," Nathan replied, and jogged around back and down to the dock, where his father waited to sail out for a late-day cast. Nathan leaped onto the *Tiger Lily*'s deck, then his father steered up the river at a slow chug. With such agreeable currents, the shrimp would be running, and Nathan hoped they'd cast a good second haul for the day.

They soon slowly passed Sean and Willa on

their dock, dining alfresco as planned. Willa jumped to her feet and started waving.

"Hey, Captain Nathan!" she yelled in that little-kid voice. She had on her fairy wings, and so did her mama. Every time the little girl jumped, the wings flapped as though she would take off flying.

With the late-afternoon sun pressing against his skin, Nathan found it hard not to smile at Willa's enthusiasm. He waved back. "Hey, Willa!"

Owen waved, too.

Sean, on the other hand, busied herself with something on the bright pink blanket spread over the dock. She kept that dark head down, her long, slender legs still showcasing the same faded cutoffs she'd been wearing earlier. The same white tank exposed skin unused to the sun. Unlike Willa's pink wings, Sean wore white ones that sparkled when the sun caught them just right. It made Nathan wonder about the reserved woman. Fairy wings seemed completely at odds with the serious, aloof side he'd witnessed. A thought caught him off guard. *Something kinda sweet about a mother who'd wear wings to indulge her little girl.*

As Nathan turned his gaze away, they eased

out of the river and into the sound. He kept his eyes trained on the horizon. His thoughts, though, strayed back to Sean. Again, he wondered if there was something about him in particular that made her keep her distance. She was reserved and definitely not encouraging toward him. Twice, she'd actually shown what he perceived to be panic at his presence. Did he make her nervous? Or, was there actually a man in the picture? Hell, that could be it. How many off-islanders had come to Cassabaw for the summer, only to be joined by their significant other at a later date? Loads.

And now he was not only being ridiculous for thinking about it, but he was spending too much time turning scenarios over in his head. Wasn't his business. Quickly, he pushed it from his brain. Wasn't his problem. He didn't care.

Couldn't care.

Not now. Not ever again.

CHAPTER THREE

THERE WAS A certain stillness to the early morning that Sean rather liked. Before the sun rose, when the world was still quiet, or before the clouds began shifting from ominous gray and white to shades of orange and purple as they did when the sun tried to push its way through. A new day. For a long, long time, Sean believed hope came with each new day. She wished she believed it now.

This morning, Willa still slept; Sean had awakened long ago, when the chug of a boat heading downriver had drifted through her partially opened bedroom window. It was strangely peaceful, that lonesome noise. Ghostly, in a way. As if she floated in some dream world. A place where, maybe, she'd always existed and danger didn't. It even felt somewhat safe. Normal. Rather, what she perceived normal to be. Family. Neighborly neighbors hand-delivering scrumptious cheddar biscuits.

And maybe it was safe. Normal. Slightly. Perhaps.

Not that she'd let her guard down for one solid second.

The captain of the *Tiger Lily* probably saw her as a grade-A nut job. Or at the very least, a snob. She'd purposely kept her head down last night as Nathan and his father had passed by on the river. Part of that was because her daughter had convinced her that the dolphins would be friendlier if they thought the two of them were fairies instead of regular people, so Sean had once again donned a pair of wings, too.

Willa, of course, had made a big production of calling out to Captain Nathan. Sean had allowed it. But she wouldn't fall into the habit of becoming too friendly with the green-eyed shrimp boat sailor. Having as little contact as possible made the transition of leaving a little easier. It wasn't easy, though, because of Willa's exuberance and propensity to talk to everyone she encountered. Getting to know people meant those very people would want to know more about Sean and Willa. That was where things got tricky for Sean. Parts of her life simply defied explanation, and yet she loathed lying. And the older Willa became, the more observant she was—which made it more challenging for Sean to tell people something about her and Willa that wasn't precisely accurate. Truly, it was much, much easier to avoid interactions with locals altogether.

Yet, even the very innocent interactions with Nathan Malone had made Sean pause. Already, the sound of his trawler made her heart quicken. She imagined him at the wheel, those steely hands gripping it with ease and confidence. A sure stare out over the sea, unafraid. Fearless.

More intimate thoughts invaded her, somewhat unwillingly. The way she felt heat rise to her cheeks at his voice, or the very thought of that intense, curious stare. She admitted only to herself that he affected her. She tried to banish that unwanted feeling. It'd do no good to confess. To him or anybody. She and Willa would be gone at the close of summer.

She couldn't help where her thoughts wandered, though. And after Willa went to bed, or in the early mornings when Sean was alone, she pondered it. Thought about...*before*. Before they had to run. Before they had to hide. When she had simply been…herself. What she had looked like. Who she'd been. She sought her brain's memory vault; dug through events, pictures, until she'd found a few. Long blond hair. Hazel eyes that most folks said smiled all on their own. It seemed surreal now, that time in her life. Before Houston. Like a dream that had occurred—the events never truly had happened. Yet, they had. And it seemed that years separated that Sean from the Sean she was now.

So back to the question—whom did Nathan see? She most definitely wasn't a snob. And, for pride's sake, she hoped she didn't seem like a nut job. In all truth, she couldn't be sure what she was anymore. She'd been running for so long; somewhere along the back roads, mom-and-pop diners and one-horse towns between Kansas and Tennessee, up to Boston and down to South Carolina, she'd lost herself. She knew it.

And couldn't do a single thing about it.

Sean sat on the back porch steps facing the dock and river, with acres of marsh on each side. It moved like wheat, she thought, when a breeze caught it just right, and the willowy little stalks all shifted and swayed in sync with the cicadas and crickets' song. Salt infiltrated her lungs with each breath; in this short time she'd grown to actually like the tangy taste it left on her tongue. She took a sip of the coffee while her mind continued to be rebellious…

Those stormy green eyes belonging to Nathan Malone kept intruding. She'd tried not to notice, but he'd trapped her with that curious gaze more than once. It'd been unavoidable.

And the easy, amused smile he had for Willa? Sean had noticed that, too. The look he'd given Willa had come fast, easy. Natural. Sean couldn't help but find Nathan's indulgence in Willa's buoyancy and constant inquisitiveness more than charming. Almost… bewitching. He'd taken to Willa almost immediately, and she with him.

But the look Nathan had for Sean herself? That was somewhat guarded. Curious. Wary.

She'd also noticed how the sun had turned his hair so many shades of blond, and that even the darker colors were lightened by hours of being on the sea. His skin had bronzed—so different from her own pale skin and dark hair. The sun felt good, though. Perhaps she'd end up with a little tan after all.

"Mama?"

Sean turned to see a sleepy-eyed Willa standing in the doorway, clutching the stuffed whale Sean had bought for her in Newport News when her daughter had begged to stop at some mariners' museum. "Good morning, baby," Sean said, and held out her arms for her daughter.

Willa padded over and sat beside her, snuggling against Sean's side. Sean reveled in the warmth of Willa's small body, the clean scent of her hair, despite it twisting and sticking up every which way. She hugged Willa tightly and kissed her cheek. "What are you doing up so early?"

Willa didn't say anything; she merely shrugged and snuggled closer. The only time of day anyone could catch Willa Jane Jacobs quiet was early in the morning. Still sleep-fogged and groggy, she was a shrugger and a nodder. At least until 8:00 a.m.

"Can we go down by the river and watch Captain Nathan go by in his pirate ship?" Willa mumbled into Sean's shoulder.

"Well, I think they've already headed out this morning," Sean answered.

"Can we be there when they come home?"

Sean pushed down that familiar panic of her daughter growing too fond of, well, anyone. The agony of seeing the confusion and hurt in Willa's big blue eyes when they had to pack up and leave. Leave people she'd grown fond of? Willa's reaction killed Sean every time. "Why, baby?"

Another shrug. "He's nice. And I like his pirate beard. I like to wave at him is all." She peeked up then, her wide eyes staring up at Sean. "Don't you?"

Sean smiled back. How could she not? "I do."

"Well, then, Mama, let's go so we don't miss him. And you gotta be like me and wear your wings."

Sean searched her baby girl's face, so full of hope. Untouched by the ugliness and pain life could dish out. Sean would do anything to protect her daughter from that kind of pain. But already, Willa was getting into a dangerous habit of inserting Nathan Malone into their daily lives. A habit the little girl wasn't even aware of. *I'll cave this time, but I'll have to figure out a way to divert Willa's attention to something other than the pirate next door.*

Sean gave Willa a nod. "Okay, just this once.

But we don't want to become a bother to them. They're working, you know."

Willa cupped Sean's cheeks with her little hands and stared into her eyes. "Mama, you're so silly. They're not working. They're fishing!"

Sean's heart melted at the feel of her daughter's hands on her skin, at the twinkle in Willa's eyes. "Okay, Willa Jane. They're fishing."

"LOOKS LIKE YOU got a fan club," Owen said to Nathan as they guided the *Tiger Lily* up Morgan's Creek and past the new tenants of the old homestead.

Nathan stared through his shades against the bright sunlight. Sure enough, there was little Willa, jumping up and down at the end of the dock, waving frantically as they passed by. And sitting beside her, feet in the water and those white sparkly wings strapped to her back, was Sean. Her wave was not as enthusiastic, but still, there was a wave. Nathan returned the gesture and gave the *Tiger Lily*'s horn two short blasts. Willa turned to her mom, moving excitedly, wings flapping, and waved some more. He couldn't help but wonder what the little girl had said.

And what Sean had replied.

Something about her—both of them—got under his skin. Couldn't shake either one. Just the slight interaction Nathan had had with Sean got to him in a way that surprised him—in a good way. She smelled great. Her hand had been soft in his upon their first shake. And her eyes seemed bottomless. She was a mystery. A tight-lipped, closed-off mystery. She didn't seem to want much conversation. So why did that make him want to find out why she was so closed off? Why did he have the urge to make her smile? Instead, he retreated when she appeared to be uncomfortable in his presence. Hiding from the world, perhaps?

Much like himself.

Yet his thoughts landed on her over and over, and at the most annoying of times. Like after midnight, when he'd been about to drift off to sleep, *bam*. Sean would appear behind his eyelids. That little pixie face and dark, shorn hair and too-wide hazel eyes awakened him. Once awakened, other thoughts drifted in, like her reaction to him the night he'd jogged by the cemetery while she and Willa were catching fireflies. What was she so afraid of? He'd barely spoken to them, just a polite greeting. Then again, they were in a strange place, and he was a bearded jogger. Jep had said he looked like a crazed killer. Maybe Sean had thought the same?

Then there was Willa. Oozing more confidence than any five-year-old should have, she was quite the opposite of her mom. She seemed to claim the world as her own, unafraid. He liked the kid. He liked them both.

He didn't like that he liked them, but there it was. Unavoidable.

Yet Sean Jacobs had made it somewhat clear that she didn't want to be bothered. Not by him. Not by anyone.

The thought left him confused, torn between reality and his urges. So he pushed the dilemma behind the locked door where he kept those emotions and went back to living his uncomplicated days as best as he could.

FOR THE NEXT few days, Sean and Willa were at the end of their rickety dock, waiting for the *Tiger Lily* to pass.

Clearly Owen had told Jep about Sean and Willa regularly being on the dock to greet them because Jep took matters into his own nosy, busybody hands.

"Here," Jep said, thrusting his old truck keys into Nathan's hands.

Nathan looked at his grandfather. "What're these for?"

Jep's eyebrows clashed together into a formidable scowl. "Take my truck and drive over to those gals' house and invite them over for supper."

Nathan blinked. "When?"

"Tonight. I want to meet them."

Nathan glanced at the clock on the wall—2:00 p.m. "Kind of a late notice, don't you think?"

Jep's frown deepened. "Of course it's not. Now hurry up, will ya?" Jep turned and started shuffling pots and pans onto the stovetop. He threw one last glare over his shoulder. "Don't come home without them, boy."

"Jep, quit playing matchmaker, will ya?"

Jep scowled at Nathan. "Now, what makes you think I'm matchmakin'? I want to meet them, is all. Neighborly thing to do, so go get 'em."

Nathan searched his father's and his brother Matt's faces, both sitting at the kitchen table. Both wore similar smirks. With a long sigh, Nathan headed out. "Yes, sir."

Having just showered after finishing their shrimping for the day, Nathan went upstairs, pulled on a clean black T-shirt, a pair of well-worn khaki shorts and the cleaner of two pairs of Chucks then headed downstairs, out the door and straight to Jep's truck.

During the drive, Nathan imagined every scenario that could possibly play out with his appearance at Sean's. She wouldn't want to come. She'd politely refuse. Willa might well beg to go. Sean would give her daughter what she probably thought would be a discreet stink-eye, but he'd see it. Of course, she might even refuse to answer his knock.

By the time Nathan pulled up in front of Sean's house, he felt like a complete horse's ass. How could he force her and Willa over to the Malones' for food? Jep and his damned busybody self! With a deep breath, Nathan climbed out of the truck, the creaking metal and iron of the door echoing through the trees. Before he made it to the porch steps, the screen door flung open and Willa came running out.

"Hey, Captain Nathan, whatcha doin' over here?" Willa asked. She wrapped her arm around the pillar of the porch, swinging her body on a pivoted foot. She wore a silver tiara with big purple gems embedded in it.

Sean joined her on the porch, her guarded expression holding surprise. She waited for Nathan to answer Willa.

"Well, my grandfather is kind of the king of our castle over there." Nathan indicated upriver with a jerk of his thumb. "And what he says goes." He shoved his hands into his pockets and shifted his gaze to meet Sean's. "You ladies are cordially invited to come over to our house for supper. Tonight." He waited for Sean's refusal.

"Mama, can we please?" Willa crooned.

"Well, I mean..." Sean's hesitantly nervous smile and shy demeanor caught Nathan off guard. She gave her daughter a quick look. "What about our nightly walk?" she asked Willa. "Our search for the ultimate, superior pinecone to kick?"

Willa gave an exaggerated sigh, with her narrow shoulders rising then falling. "Mama. We can do that any ole time. There are one hundred pinecones in the yard. I wanna go see Captain Nathan's grandpa king! Please?" She jumped up and down in place, making her wings flap as though she were trying to take off.

Sean's gaze returned to Nathan's, and he could plainly see she didn't want to accept the invitation. He halfway thought of giving her an out, but he didn't. He instead kept his mouth shut, waiting.

Then Sean sighed. "Okay, sure. Thank you. We, uh…cordially accept. Since your grandfather is king and all."

"Yay!" Willa hollered.

Nathan blinked. He hadn't expected Sean to agree, and now that she had…what was he going to do? It was bad enough how often he found her in his thoughts. Constantly. And that was with very little contact. But now? She would be in the cab of the truck. With him. And then at the house.

"What's *cordially* mean anyway?" Willa asked Sean. Then she looked at him. "Is your grandpa really a king?"

Nathan chuckled, relieved that Willa's chatter eased his apprehension. He wondered briefly if Sean could sense his unease. "You'll have to see for yourself." He looked at Sean. "I'll drive you over. If that's okay?"

"Oh." Sean looked at her bare feet and cutoff jean shorts. “Uh, okay. Do you…want to come in and wait while we change?”

Willa didn’t give Nathan one solid second to decide. She bounded down the steps and grabbed his hand. “Come on inside, Captain Nathan,” she said, tugging his arm.

The little girl pulled him to a love seat and pushed him into it. “You can wait in here.” She threw him a grin then disappeared up the hallway. Sean hesitated.

“We’ll, uh…” she started to say. “We’ll only be a second.”

Then she, too, disappeared, but mother and daughter’s muffled conversation continued in another room.

Nathan rested his hands on his knees and looked around. *Who are you, Sean Jacobs?* Sparsely furnished, the old house reeked of spick-and-span clean. He should know; living in a house filled with present and past USCGs, where cleanliness and order ruled the roost, he recognized the tinge of lemon in the air. He wouldn’t say *too* clean, but…something along those lines.

A few unpacked boxes still remained, pushed against the walls. Through the archway, a kitchen faced the marsh and the dock beyond. Nothing hung on the walls. No pictures of family set on the one end table between the couch and love seat. The small, box-shaped wooden coffee table held a stack of hardback books, and Nathan leaned forward and lifted the first one. *The Adventures of Tom Sawyer.* The next, *Treasure Island.* Classics, and well used given the worn-out and dog-eared pages. On the inside flap, a neat cursive hand had written *For my baby Willa with the wild imagination. Love, Mama.*

It was, Nathan noted, the only personable item in the entire room.

He suddenly felt like an intruder. Someone…unwanted. A threat, maybe? Despite her acceptance of Jep's dinner invitation, Sean's hesitancy etched lines around her eyes, and those eyes flashed concern. Maybe after being around his loud, friendly family a time or two, she'd relax. *Hell, maybe I will, too.*

Just then, a thundering of footfall burst from the hallway, and Willa came to a screeching halt before him. The little girl wore what appeared to be an old-fashioned dress, a faded, old cream-colored thing with lace and ribbons. And the sparkly fairy wings, of course, accompanied by a pair of cowboy boots. He lifted one eyebrow.

"Nice dress," he stated.

Willa's grin exposed all of her straight little teeth. "My mama got it for me in a special shop that sells only really old things," she informed Nathan. "That's why it looks so yellow. And it cost ten whole dollars."

Nathan cocked his head and inspected the aged material. "Hmm. That's a pretty good deal. It looks at least a hundred years old."

Willa's grin widened. "You think so? Mama, did you hear that?" She turned as Sean walked into the room. "Captain Nathan says my fairy dress is at least a hundred years old!"

Nathan rose and his eyes rested on Sean's. "That's why it looks yellow," he added, and threw her a grin. It felt awkward. Mainly because the look on her face spoke volumes. As in, she seriously didn't want to be going with him to supper. A house full of strangers. He didn't blame her, though. He imagined she'd rather stay out here, alone with her daughter, and kick around some ultimate pinecone. Whatever that meant.

Nathan then noticed that Sean had changed into a sleeveless sundress, white with little flowers all over it, falling to just above her knees and tied at the waist. On her feet she wore brown sandals. He realized how slender she was. And with her short dark hair and wide hazel eyes, she kind of looked like a pixie. A very pretty pixie. He'd keep that to himself, though.

"All right, well," he said. "Let's go meet the king."

CHAPTER FOUR

HAD SHE LOST all her good sense? Why on earth had she caved to Willa's pleas?

She knew why. It wasn't as big of a mystery as she tried to make herself believe. Willa's happiness, the desire to stretch out her daughter's carefree childhood for as long as she could. That was why. And, she admitted only to herself, Nathan connected with Willa. And Willa responded to that connection in such a positive way. Those big blue eyes lit up when Nathan came around, or when he passed their dock on his pirate ship. Despite the knowledge that, at some point, she and Willa would have to leave Cassabaw, Sean just didn't feel like disappointing a five-year-old. Of depriving her of a little bit of normalcy, like a backyard barbecue with nice people. The fact that facing a handful of strangers clawed at her stomach in familiar way that usually meant *back off, keep your distance.*

Yet here she was with her daughter, sitting in an old pickup truck heading to supper. Not backing off. Not keeping her distance. With *strangers*.

Sean listened to Willa's nonstop chatter with Nathan as he maneuvered down the crushed-shell-and-dirt path of their drive. At the end, he turned left onto the little coastal road, shrouded in oaks and Spanish moss, and shifted, metal grating and the truck giving a good jolt each and every time it went into a higher gear. Willa laughed, thinking it hugely hilarious. Sean's head banged twice against the window.

Quietly, she observed.

Looked. Listened. And observed.

Classic rock played on the radio. The interior of the truck held an aged smell, but was clean. From the corner of her eye, Sean noticed the black T-shirt Nathan wore snugged tightly around his biceps as he held the truck's wheel. Thick veins snaked over his hands, around his golden-skinned arms. She also noticed that around his neck he wore a leather cord with a medallion of...something. Made of silver. And his hair, bleached and weathered by the sun, pulled snuggly back from his face in a ponytail. Dark shades covered his unusual green eyes. Cautiously, she turned her head, ever so slightly, to get a better view of his profile, and when she did she noticed a silver scar jutting through his top lip.

Suddenly, those lips turned up at the corners, and on closer inspection she noticed Nathan had glanced her way.

"Taking inventory?" he asked.

"What's inventory?" Willa echoed.

Nathan's grin widened. "It means your mama was studying me," he said.

Embarrassment heated Sean's cheeks. "I was not."

That only made Nathan chuckle.

"My mama studies everybody," Willa said. "To make sure they're not serial killers or anything." Willa glanced at her. "Right, Mama?"

"Willa," Sean scolded softly. "You don't have to tell everyone our secrets, do you?"

Willa squinted as she gave that some thought. "Nope. I guess not. Just Captain Nathan."

Sean's gaze darted toward Nathan, whose attention was fixed straight ahead on the road, but his lips twitched.

He might be amused by Willa, but her exuberance and openness presented a real issue for Sean. Her mind raced. No doubt Nathan's family—Nathan himself, more than likely—would ask questions. She'd become quite good at firing off appropriate answers without looking like she was totally making them up. But the older Willa got, the harder it was to bat off personal questions. Her daughter had eyes like a hawk and a sharp mind that missed absolutely nothing. Just like she had with Nathan, Willa would call Sean out on anything she believed to be untrue. Despite Sean's attempts at coaching and teaching, her daughter seemed to be without filter. One never knew what would emerge from the little girl's too-mature-for-her-age mind and mouth.

Sean needed to be extra careful. Despite the challenge presented by Willa's increasing awareness, Sean could not afford to relax her vigilance. Which brought her mind back to the question: Why on earth had she agreed to accompany Nathan to a strange place with strange people and a million innocent yet detrimental questions?

Sean glanced at Willa, who chattered about the fireflies that came out at night. Her daughter looked up suddenly, her blue eyes soft as she grinned. Sean smiled back.

That's why. Her precious daughter. It was the

one thing Sean had done right in her life. She wanted to somehow, someway keep a shred of balance alive in Willa. To allow her gracious memories of a magical childhood that she could look back on later in life, fond recollections that could bring a smile or make her heart feel glad. Things Sean could only imagine.

She prayed she could keep it up.

Nathan slowed the truck and turned into a long drive that led back to the river—much like at her and Willa's place. It made sense, she thought, seeing how they were river neighbors. A large, stilted river house with a wide wraparound porch sat within an opening among the trees.

"Whoa," Willa said in a low voice. "You live here?"

"Yep. Grew up here," Nathan answered. "Come on," he continued, and climbed out of the truck. "Let's go meet everyone."

"Come on, Mama!" Willa yelled, and followed Nathan out of his side of the truck.

With a deep breath to steady her nerves, Sean climbed out. Giant oaks laden with long Spanish moss formed a canopy over the house and yard. A large metal building stood off to one side farther back. And an arbor of some sorts sat to the left of the porch. Big blooms of hydrangea graced each side of the porch steps. On the porch an old man was sitting in a rocking chair, then stood slowly.

Like some Norman Rockwell picture.

Walking around the front of the truck, Sean joined Nathan and Willa. He watched her closely. Crickets and cicadas chirped, filling the air with bug-song. Somewhere close, the saw grass rustled as a breeze rushed through the salt marsh. In the distance, oyster shoals bubbled in the low-tide mud.

Noises that, only recently, had become familiar to her.

Oddly, Sean found she liked it.

"Will you all quit lingering around the yard and get over here?" the old man called. "I'm tired of waitin'."

"Who is that?" Willa asked.

"That's the king," Nathan said with a grin. "He's been dying to meet you both."

With that, Nathan inclined his head to Sean, a motion to follow, and Willa bound ahead of them both, wings flapping, her skinny legs eating up the ground as she headed for the elderly stranger. This was a side of Willa that

Sean admired and also feared: she didn't meet a stranger. Ever.

Sean glanced at Nathan. "Sure hope your grandpa is up for Willa's energy."

Nathan grinned. "I have a feeling they're going to get along pretty good."

As they made their way to the porch, even though Nathan walked beside her, he definitely kept his distance. She had to admit that the rugged shrimp boat captain made her curious. While his looks appeared a bit rough—even his walk had a certain swagger to it—Sean felt there was something solid in Nathan. Safety, perhaps? No, not that. Maybe she simply recognized the same reserve she had. He'd been polite but never pushy. He seemed to respect her boundaries. Maybe his reserve was personally motivated. In a way, he seemed to want to keep distance between them, the very same as she did.

Nathan cleared his throat, and a sheepish grin stretched the scar in his lip. "I'm going to apologize right now for anything uncouth my grandfather says. He is sort of lacking a filter. There's no stopping him, I'm afraid."

A nervous laugh escaped Sean. Strangely enough, Nathan's hesitancy put her at ease.

Somewhat, anyway. "It's okay. He may have met his match in my daughter. Also filterless."

Nathan gave a soft laugh. "So I've noticed."

By the time they reached the porch, Willa and the older man were already deep in conversation, which worried Sean. But as they joined them, their banter eased her mind.

"They aren't real wings," Willa said. "See? I put my arms through here." She demonstrated the removal of her costume wings while the old man watched intently.

His bushy white eyebrows lifted, raising the bill of his USCG cap. "Huh." Then he rose from his bent-at-the-waist stance and crossed his arms over his chest. "I ain't buyin' it. Fairies are known to be pranksters. You might be pullin' my leg right now."

Willa's brow scrunched up. "What's a prankster, King Jep?"

"Well, you know, child," Jep remarked, "a trickster. A mischief-maker. Someone who tries to play tricks on old folk."

Willa's already-wide eyes stretched even wider at the accusation. "I wouldn't do that!"

A smile tipped Jep's mouth. "Well, that's good to know, Willa." His glance moved to

Sean, and his brow furrowed as he gave her a thorough and silent inspection.

"This is Sean Jacobs, Willa's mom. This is, uh—" Nathan chuckled "—King Jep."

"Yeah, Mama, he's the King of Sea Diamonds, he told me so," Willa added.

"Nice to meet you, darlin'," King Jep said, offering his hand. Sean took it and he squeezed, not too hard but firm. She did the same. "Sean, eh? Good, stout Irish name." He threw Sean a curious glance. "Usually reserved for the menfolk. No matter. Welcome to our home, darlin'."

"Thank you for inviting us for dinner," Sean said, trying not to sound nervous. "Sea diamonds?"

Jep dropped his hand. "Shrimp, darlin'. Shrimp! The most perfect creature God created, just ahead of the chicken." His head cocked sideways as he considered her, giving her a head-to-toe glance. "You're a skinny thing. You ain't got worms, do you?" He winked. "I'll put some meat on your bones."

"Jeez, Jep," Nathan chided, then shrugged and looked at Sean. "See? No filter. Sorry."

"Hey, why do your blue pants go all the way up to your neck?" Willa asked Jep.

Nathan laughed, and Sean gave him and Jep a sheepish grin as she felt her cheeks turn red. "I'm kinda used to no filter, as you can see."

"Filters are overrated anyway," Jep stated bluntly, then looked at Willa. "Well, I imagine it's because I don't like wearin' a belt, and these stay up." He grasped one strap, showing it to Willa. "Overalls, darlin'. Keeps my britches up!"

Willa giggled then followed Jep as he shuffled down the steps. "Come on, then," he called over his shoulder. "Supper won't cook itself now, will it?"

"King Jep, is your kitchen outside?" Willa asked.

"One of them is," he replied.

Nathan inclined his head. "After you."

Sean gave another hesitant smile as she watched her young daughter bounce up and down as she accompanied a man almost a century old. "Willa has found a new buddy, so it seems."

Nathan shoved his hands into his shorts pockets. "Might be a recipe for disaster."

"It might," she said as they followed Jep and Willa.

Just then, the breeze brought with it the

sound of very old music, like maybe from the World War II era, or older.

"Jep, my middle brother and his wife all love the old tunes," he stated. "From the twenties and thirties, mostly. My little brother is in love with seventies classic rock. The result is a cluster of strange and great music. You'll get used to it." He nodded before she could reply. "Speak of the devil."

A pregnant woman rounded the corner of the stilt house, making her way toward them. Tall and lanky, she had only a delicate baby bump. With long reddish-brown hair piled atop her head, a wide, genuine smile exposed white teeth. A natural beauty—even from a distance Sean could tell that.

"Um, warning, she's a hugger," Nathan said softly moments before the woman pulled Sean into a tight embrace.

"Hi! I'm Emily!" the pregnant woman exclaimed. "I'm Nathan's sister-in-law, married to the middle Malone boy. It's so nice to meet you!" She pulled back, her hands still gripping Sean's upper arms, and inspected her. "I really love your eyes. They remind me of extra-big almonds."

"Oh," Sean said with surprise. "Thank you."

Another filter-less soul.

Yet...Sean found she liked her. She sensed a sincerity in her that oftentimes wasn't present in others. Emily didn't seem shy, either—qualities that Willa had, Sean noted. Maybe that was why she immediately liked Emily.

Emily slipped her arm through Sean's and pulled her along. "Is this gruff-looking guy behaving himself?" she asked Sean.

"Sis, I'm not that bad," Nathan said, and gave Sean a raised-eyebrow, innocent look. "Besides, I'm a pirate. Just ask Willa. I have to look gruff. It's in the Pirates Handbook of Rules."

Emily snorted. "Good Lord! I'll just bet it is." She gave her head a shake at Sean, a gesture that seemed to link them as conspirators. "Now he thinks he's a pirate. And your little girl is absolutely adorable."

"Thank you." Sean just smiled. She didn't know what else to say. She was in Friendly Overload with Emily. Never had she met such...nice people.

When they rounded the corner of the house, the yard opened up, with a dock leading to the river. Across the river, a lone white water bird stood in the muck edging the marsh, its long orange beak stark against the green-and-brown reeds. The sharp, pungent scent of salt hung in the air. Nathan's shrimp boat sat at the end of the dock, the outriggers jutting skyward.

A small red-tin-roofed house was farther down the dock. And where the grass ended and the river bank began, beneath looming oak trees, several white Adirondack chairs sat facing the water. There were two occupants—a handsome dark-haired guy and a lovely blonde woman. Behind them was a picnic table covered with a checkered tablecloth. Close by, a small enclave stood, apparently the outdoor kitchen. Jep, Willa and another man—Nathan's father, perhaps—stood over a large cooler, peering inside. Emily led Sean to the couple in the chairs.

"I'll just go help Dad, Jep and Willa," Nathan said, and left Sean to Emily's caretaking.

"Hey, guys," Emily said to the couple. The dark-haired guy leaped to his feet and grasped Sean's hand in a firm shake.

He smiled wide, and the very same green eyes that Nathan had twinkled. "I'm Eric Malone, the baby of the family and obviously the better-looking one." He dropped his hand and moved to stand behind the other chair, enveloping the young woman who sat in it. "This is my gorgeous fiancée, and Emily's baby sister, Reagan." He kissed the top of her head.

"Nice to meet you both," Sean answered. "I'm...Sean Jacobs. My daughter, Willa—" she glanced over to where her daughter was helping the men "—has found a new friend. We live just up the river." Sean noticed Reagan wasn't exactly meeting her gaze. Not precisely, anyway. It was then she saw the walking stick propped against the chair.

Wow. Blind. At such a young age.

She briefly wondered how it happened.

"I was an airman once upon a time," Reagan offered with eerie intuition, as though she'd seen the question in Sean's eyes. "An explosion on the tarmac and...voilà! Now I'm a blind artist engaged to a crazy rescue swimmer."

"Oh, I'm...sorry," Sean stammered. "I mean, I didn't intend to stare."

"I stare all the time," Eric stated with a smirk.

Reagan nodded. "He does." She grinned, and Sean noticed how much she looked like Emily. Yet different. Beautiful in a different way. "And it's fine. Life is good," she said, and slipped a hand up and grasped Eric by the neck, caressing his cheek.

The look on his face was absolute and pure love.

"Mama! Come over here and look at these sea diamonds!" Willa hollered from the cookery.

"Ha! Old Jep's pulling that sea diamond stuff with the kid," Eric exclaimed. "He did the same to us when we were growing up."

Emily laughed. "I remember." She shook her head. "The years have left that old sea biscuit unchanged."

As a group, they made their way to the cookery, and Sean stood back and noticed what a large, grand cluster of family they were. Never had she been around such engaging people. They all seemed so close. So fond of one another. The brothers teased each other, and King Jep seemed to be the instigator of most of it. She'd gathered that Emily and Reagan had grown up with the boys, and the sense of family bond was strong. Stronger than Sean had ever seen in her life. And the way Eric looked at Reagan? The protective arm he had around her?

She briefly wondered what that would be like to have.

For the fifth time, Nathan turned his gaze toward Sean and his brother and sisters-in-law. What were they talking about? Now that they were all walking to the dock kitchen, he busied himself, making sure he didn't appear to be the least interested in what they had been discussing.

"Hey, Captain Nathan, whatcha keep lookin' at my mama for?" Willa said loud enough for everyone to hear.

Just that quickly Nathan learned how perceptive and intuitive Willa Jane Jacobs was.

Eric, that irritating jackass, threw back his head and laughed. "Dang, brother." He clapped Nathan on the back. "That was a clear bust-out." Eric held up his hand to Willa, who, without hesitation, gave him a high five.

Nathan had no reply. There was no getting out of a Willa observation. That was a fact he'd come to realize, just as clearly as Sean knew she couldn't pull one over on her daughter. So, the fact he'd been staring at Sean had been flatly called out by a five-year-old. Hell, he couldn't help it. But now he'd make a conscious effort not to. The last thing he needed was to be the butt of his brothers' ribbing. That would only make him want to punch them in the face.

Besides, he didn't want to make Sean more uncomfortable than she probably already was. He briefly wondered what she thought. Her expression seemed closed, so he didn't even try to guess what might be going through her mind. He merely turned around and continued deveining the pile of shrimp he'd been working on. Hoped it wasn't obvious that he wanted to knock Eric on his ass.

"Ah, the mysterious girl on the dock," Owen said to Sean as she joined them. "Nice to finally meet you."

Sean gave a shy nod. "You, too, sir."

"Young lady." Jep inclined his head, beckoning Sean to join him. She did. "Know how to make hush puppies?"

Out of the corner of his eye, Nathan watched Sean peer over Jep's ingredients. Then she looked at his grandfather with those enormous hazel eyes.

"Teach me?" she said.

Was it the way she said it? Or the sincerity in her quiet voice that caught Nathan so completely off guard? Whatever it was, it had affected poor Jep, as well. The old man's cheeks turned red and splotchy and he sputtered, cleared his throat, then gave Sean an affectionate pat on the shoulder.

"Of course, gal," he said, and she stepped closer to him, and so began Jep's lesson in the art of making hush puppies.

Nathan watched the interaction further, and found it more than curious. He was astounded to find himself almost mesmerized by the way Sean's innocent acceptance of Jep had not only made the old man stammer, but slip into his Irish accent. Jep Malone did that only when he was absolutely furious, or completely enamored.

The way Sean responded to Jep touched Nathan's heart in a way he wasn't expecting. It made him sit up, take notice. Not just the fact that she was beautiful. She was and, despite Nathan's determination not to notice, he had. He'd been unable to help it. No, his attention went beyond the recognition of the beauty that resided beneath her bewitching eyes or the love he saw in those very same eyes whenever she looked at her daughter. It was something about those two small words, *teach me*, that Nathan found so humbling. So damned enchanting. It made his earlier determination not to get close to her just that much more difficult.

He watched her now, seemingly at ease with his grandfather, allowing the old man to show her how to combine the ingredients for his secret hush puppy recipe. Whatever clever thing Jep was saying to her was rewarded with a smile—one that was entirely different from any Nathan had seen on her yet. It was intriguing. It was baffling.

He suddenly realized it wouldn't be quite so bad being the one who coaxed such a smile from Sean Jacobs.

When Nathan looked away, it was his father's eye he caught.

And Owen simply smiled.

CHAPTER FIVE

IT HAD BEEN over an hour since they'd arrived at the Malones', and for the first time in…well, a long, long time, Sean felt at ease.

"Sean, this is my husband, soon-to-be father of this bundle of sweetness," Emily stated, then linked her arm through his. "Matt."

Matt Malone was a beast. As big as Nathan was, but with an edge. Sharp. Maybe even dangerous. Not to his family, though. That much Sean could tell. He had the same eyes that all the Malones had—a furious, sea-storm green. His hair was clipped short. Not buzzed, but close. Military? Police? There was an intenseness about him that gave Sean pause, made her almost want to move away from him. The way he'd measured and weighed her. He wasn't trying to hide his scrutiny. Not at all. Could he tell she was keeping secrets?

The moment that she saw him soften as his wife leaned her head against him, and Matt's hand went to her belly, Sean relaxed. He was curious about her, was all. A small part of her still wondered, though, if he could see through her. If he could see just why she wanted to keep to herself.

"All right, now everyone knows everyone, and I'm starved. Let's eat!" Jep called out.

Everyone gathered at the mammoth-size picnic table beneath the oak trees, and Sean found herself seated between Nathan and Eric. Willa had found her place right beside her new best friend, Jep. Next to her, Nathan's dad.

"Let's bow and give grace," Jep barked.

"Who's Grace?" Willa asked.

"Willa," Sean said, telling her daughter to shush with a finger over her lips.

Jep glanced at Willa. "You know. Prayer. A thank-you to the good Lord for our blessings."

"Oh!" Willa exclaimed. Then she obediently closed her eyes and folded her hands before her.

"Dear Lord, we thank you for this bounty, and for the folks who prepared it. Mainly, me. And thank you for our new neighbors, and for finally getting them over here. Amen."

Sean's gaze met Jep's, and his mouth twitched into a slight grin. She liked him. There was nothing pretentious about the elder Malone. He said exactly what he meant, no matter the outcome. Honesty. Integrity. Filter or no filter.

Chatter broke out as everyone began passing platters of fried shrimp, mashed potatoes, corn on the cob and the hush puppies that Jep had shown her how to prepare. Large plastic glasses held iced and sweet tea garnished with lemon slices. She felt as though she were in a travel magazine for the coastal south.

"So where are you from, Sean?" Owen asked.

Sean, prepared for the question, offered him a smile. From the corner of her eye, she noticed Nathan had paused and seemed interested in her answer. "Originally, a small town just outside Dallas," she stated. "But I moved around a good bit as a child. Lately, we were in Norfolk, Virginia."

"Makes for a well-rounded youngster," Owen offered. "I was stationed once at Virginia Beach. Nice place."

"Tell us what you do," Emily asked, her head cocked to the side as she studied Sean. Too closely. "No, wait. Don't tell me. If I had to guess, I'd say…an elementary school teacher."

"No way," Eric said, rubbing his jaw and eyeing Sean. "Nurse."

Panic began to seize Sean's ability to hold a straight face. Her eyes shifted around the table. Everyone watched, waiting for her answer. "Well, I've had a myriad of occupations over the years," she began. "Freelance writing being one." A nervous smile edged its way onto her face. It felt cagey and fake, and she couldn't help it. Not one bit. Usually, she had standard answers to offer polite conversationalists when they asked about her occupation. But this nice family? Suddenly, the lies tasted bitter on her tongue.

"My mama takes care of me," Willa piped up, not looking at anyone in particular as she seemed focused on shoveling in fried shrimp. "Mama says that's a full-time job, don't ya, Mama?"

Internally, Sean sighed with relief. She had nothing to offer these people by way of personal information. Not anything they'd like to hear, anyway. Besides…two souls with zero filter—Jep and Willa—could be disastrous if they had access to too much of Sean's history. Who knew which people they'd accidentally share the wrong information with?

She noticed the others around the table now had their attention on her daughter, and that caginess eased out of her. Not all, but some.

"Not only is that a full-time job, but it's an important job," Nathan replied. "So Willa, tell me what your favorite thing is about Cassabaw so far."

Sean shifted her gaze to Nathan. He was completely engrossed in Willa's response. He'd intentionally diverted further questions away from her. She'd have to thank him later.

"Well," Willa answered, "I like dining alfresco with the dolphins. But I wanna jump in the water and Mama says there are sharks and stingrays and flesh-eating amoebas and that I can't. I like eating ice cream on the pier, too. And riding the Ferris wheel."

"Ah," Nathan said, nodding. "The old sharks-and-stingray-and-dreaded-amoebas fear." He leaned toward Sean, keeping his voice low. "Sharks won't wander this far inland, and the rays, well—" his voice dropped lower "—they won't bother you."

"Swum here my whole life, darlin'," Jep said. "Not once have I seen a shark out there." He nodded toward the river. "Ain't no amoebas, neither."

"Well, I ain't afraid of sharks," Willa piped up. She shoved a hush puppy into her mouth. "Mama's scared of everything."

"Willa," Sean scolded. "Don't talk with your mouth full."

"Yes, ma'am," her daughter answered around the hush puppy.

She *was* scared. Of nearly everything. While her fear was justified, she hated that her daughter now saw it. Until recently, Sean had been able to hide that personality flaw. "Well, if Jep and Nathan say it's safe, then—" she inhaled "—we'll give it a try."

"Yay!" Willa cried, then continued eating.

The rest of the meal went by as any other ordinary outdoor meal, she supposed, with light chatter of weddings, soon-to-be baby births and nursery renovations. No one else asked her anything personal, and for that she was grateful. She learned all of the Malones except Matt, who was, until recently, in the Marine Corps, were at one time or another US Coast Guard rescue swimmers. Eric still was and worked at the local base on Cassabaw. Sean noticed how quickly the conversation shifted away from that topic of Nathan's tenure as a rescue swimmer. She found herself wanting to know more, and wasn't too sure she liked that feeling…

When they finished eating, the men began cleaning off the table and carrying dishes into the house. Everyone had a job to do, and they seemingly did it without a single thought. She'd never seen anything like it.

"Trust me," Emily said, patting her arm. "I grew up around them and this cleanup still fascinates me." She fondly glanced at the men as they worked. "Military and Coast Guard life has them moving like a well-oiled machine, don't you think? I'd get up and help but would be rushed right back to my seat."

Sean rose and lifted the near-empty bowl of hush puppies. "I'll just take this in," she said, and Emily simply smiled.

Sean crossed the yard, and just as she reached for the screened door leading into the kitchen, it was opened by Nathan. His frame all but filled the entrance, and those green eyes met hers. He smiled, reaching for the bowl. "I'll take that, thanks," he said, then inclined his head and pushed the door open wider with his shoulder. "Come in. I'll show you around the oldest bachelor pad on Cassabaw."

Sean glanced over her shoulder and saw

Willa standing in front of Emily and Reagan. Her entire body appeared in movement as she enthusiastically told her story. God only knew what that story was. With a deep breath, Sean turned to Nathan. "I'd like that."

"This way."

Inside, the fresh scent of lemon hit her. The level of tidiness and cleanliness either meant they hired a housekeeper, or they were all neat freaks…or Emily was correct and their military-based upbringing left them preferring things to be in order. It was nice. The decor favored a nautical theme at its most basic—it was straight out of an old copy of *Moby Dick*. On the walls of the living room, an old cast net filled with sun-bleached shells, starfish and sand dollars clung to the ropes, and faded blue-and-white wooden oars were nailed crossways above the brick fireplace.

"The fishing gear once belonged to my great-granddad, Patrick Malone." Nathan moved across the room to a wall covered with framed pictures and pointed to one. Sean moved closer and peered at the black-and-white photo of a handsome, happy young couple. A small boy wearing black stockings, suspenders, dark knickers with a white billowy shirt stood between them overlooking the sea. The boy's hands were in the air and slightly blurred, as if he'd moved them just as the shutter on the camera had closed.

"They came from Galway, Ireland. This was taken the day they left on a steamer bound for America. Patrick and his wife, Annie, brought little Jep to Cassabaw when he was only seven." He chuckled. "Even in that picture there you can tell Jep was a handful, just like he is now. If you listen closely, you can sometimes hear the Irish lilt in Jep's voice."

"Yeah, the madder he gets, the heavier the accent gets," Matt said from behind them. He joined them at the picture. Eric, with Reagan by his side, and Emily also wandered in and joined them.

"Aye, boyo, you'd best get your arse outta that river right now!" Eric imitated Jep, with a heavy Irish accent. "I'll skin ya, boyo! I'll do it!"

Everyone laughed.

Sean wondered what it would be like to know your own heritage reaching back more than a century. It completely fascinated her, and as she peered at the black-and-white images of little Jep, his parents and old Cassabaw, she found she wanted to be a part of that. Not the Malone family per se, but a family tradition that extended further than herself, generations. She allowed the briefest of thoughts to linger about her own heritage, of where she actually came from. Perhaps, one day, she could find out. For Willa's sake.

Willa. So engaged in the Malone history, she'd very briefly forgotten her daughter was in the care of someone else. Sean glanced out the large picture window facing the marsh, searching for Willa.

"If you're looking for Willa, she's with Jep and Owen," Matt offered. "She's fine."

Sean met Matt's gaze. The ease of his smile and the assurance in his eyes made her believe him.

"Hey, Sean," Emily piped up. "You'll have to bring Willa to the big Fourth of July celebration. Food, music and lots of fun all along the pier."

"All the businesses turn out," Eric added. "And there's a huge fireworks show after dark."

Sean smiled and gave a nod. "I…will. It sounds great. Thank you."

"Mama! Look what King Jep and Prince Owen gave me!" Willa came flying inside.

The Malones all laughed at her names for the elders.

In her small hands Willa clutched a piece of PVC pipe about six inches long, with a long cord wrapped around it. At the end was a triangular-shaped weight. She also had a plastic bag containing what seemed to be a piece of raw chicken. Sean looked at her daughter.

"What in the world is that for?" she asked.

"Well, King Jep says if I tie this chicken to the end of the string, then tie the other end with the pipe to our dock at low tide then drop it in the water until it hits bottom, I can pull it up very, very, very slowly and a crab will be on the end!" Willa's large eyes widened even more as she explained. "Only if I have patience, though. Prince Owen told me that." She jumped, making her wings flap. "Can we go and tie it off now? Please?"

Nathan bent and looked at Willa. "I think the tide is just about right. I'll give you a hand." He glanced at Sean. "If that's okay with your mama."

Nathan coming over to their home. Giving her daughter a small bit of normalcy and happiness by tying a piece of chicken to a string to catch a crab. Such a simple thing. Why not?

Although what in the world would they do with the crab once they caught it?

Sean nodded. “That’s fine.”

They said their goodbyes then, and Sean thanked Jep and Owen for tending to Willa in such a kind way. Jep followed them to the porch.

“You bake, young lady?” he asked Sean.

She smiled. “Some.”

He scratched his head. “Hmm. You do anything else?”

Sean thought about it. “I knit.”

Jep’s eyes lit up. “I like them little blankets that go across your lap.”

Sean couldn’t help but grin. “That sounds like a request.”

“That’s exactly what it is. Good night. And don’t be a stranger over here.”

Sean waved goodbye and followed Nathan to the truck.

The Malones certainly were a unique family, with a known—and celebrated—history that went back more than a century. She was surprised to find herself at ease with them. Then Nathan placed his hand at the small of her back as she climbed into the passenger side of the truck, and her insides gave a quickening. Butterflies? Shivers? Nerves? She'd packed those sensations away long, long ago.

Yet, the longer she spent in Nathan's company, the more relaxed she became. Made her look forward to the next time he stood close to her. Looked at her. Touched her. Maybe she was just now realizing all of these things because, for the first time in a very, very long time, she was allowing it. It frightened her.

And it thrilled her at the same time.

In the truck, they listened to Willa's excited chatter. She clutched the plastic bag of raw chicken in one hand, and the pipe and weighted cord in the other, and every so often Nathan would glance over Willa's head and offer Sean a slight smile. It made her uncomfortable—the intimacy of two adults connecting over a child. It made her want it more.

And it confirmed just how screwed up her life presently was. Actually, had been for one hell of a long time. But for now, they were here, in this place. With these people. And it all made her daughter happy, and, if she was being perfectly honest with herself, it made her feel...normal. And for that, Sean was grateful.

Unfortunately, by the end of summer, it would all be over.

Nathan pulled into their drive, and Willa headed straight for the dock.

"Willa, be careful!" Sean called out.

As Nathan walked beside her, his presence crowded her, almost as if he took up all the space and air around her. When she looked up, his gaze rested on hers.

"She's a great kid," he said in that deep, slightly lilted voice. "I'm glad you both came over today."

The butterflies kicked up in Sean's stomach again, and she gave a hesitant smile. "I am, too, Nathan. I… We had a good time." Surprisingly, she had. It shocked her, and scared her at the same time. Getting involved with the Malones meant having to say goodbye, and she knew that would hurt Willa. It was one of the reasons she feared even simply going to dinner. Getting to know Nathan's sisters-in-law, his dad, grandpa. His brothers. *And him.*

The fact that Sean had enjoyed herself stunned her. In a way, she felt that she'd known the Malones her whole life, instead of having just met them. They'd made her feel so *at home*. It was a new sensation for her. She liked it. And she was scared to like it. *Why do I have to be so complicated?*

The sun had lowered in the sky, and the night bugs chirped in the marsh grass as they started across the dock. A slight breeze brushed Sean's cheek, and the sky had begun to turn into a palette of reds, purples and burnt orange.

"I, uh, well, I thought maybe you and Willa could, or would want to keep me company on the Fourth," Nathan blurted out. His gaze held hers, so much that Sean couldn't look away. "Maybe?"

And then she did something that completely baffled her.

"We would," she accepted. "Yes. Thank you."

A slow smile lifted the corners of Nathan's full mouth, stretching tight the silver scar that slashed through his lip. "Yeah?" he asked. As if he hadn't heard her correctly.

She wondered the same thing. When had she kept company with a man? It had been… a very long time. Where had the fear she had been clinging to so steadfastly gone? Was it the sincerity Sean saw in Nathan's eyes? Or was it the doubt, the hesitancy she'd noticed in his request? He'd been as startled by her acceptance as she had been. Sean hung her head and felt the blush stain her cheeks. "Yeah," she agreed.

"Right on, right on," Nathan said, nodding, and he didn't stop smiling until they reached the end of the dock, where Willa bounced from foot to foot, waiting.

"Come on, guys!" she called out, waving her chicken and cord in the air. "I wanna catch a crab."

Sean sat on the edge of the dock as the sun crept lower and lower, and the shadows reached closer. The night birds emerged and glided over the glassy river water, and she watched a hulking pirate of a shrimp boat captain show her fairy daughter how to drop a crab line.

The worry returned, though, and began to creep over her, submerge her in the darkness she'd lived with for what seemed like years. She inhaled. Exhaled. Inhaled again. Slowly pushed the breath out through pursed lips. She watched Nathan, bent on one knee as Willa leaned in close to soak in his every word, his every move.

This time, Sean pushed it all away. Shoved aside the fear, the worry, out of sight, out of mind. At least for now.

What could it hurt to pretend that she was normal, that she'd stay on Cassabaw, and that this cute guy who was completely sweet and funny with her daughter was all real and would last?

For now, for this split second in time, she'd allow it.

Any misgivings would certainly surface later, and only then would she deal with it. And the moment the thought entered her brain, she all but gasped. So used to dodging, hiding and escaping was she that the thought of merely allowing a little normalcy in her life took her aback. Could it really be so easy? Surely not.

But for the very first time since Willa was born, she was willing to give it a try.

"Mama! I got one," Willa hollered. "Come here! Look!"

Sean watched her daughter hop from one foot to the other with excitement as Nathan scooped a crab up with a net. Nathan's grin widened as he glanced her way, and Sean found she had a hard time looking away.

She'd worry about that later, too.

CHAPTER SIX

Houston, Texas
Several weeks before

"KARA, HOLD MY CALLS."

The timid young blonde at the desk gave a short nod. "Yes, Mr. Black."

Chase Black strode into his office and closed the door behind him. He was surprised Kara had lasted as long as she had. Two full weeks. She jumped at her own damn shadow, much less the sound of his voice. Any day now he expected to find her packed up and gone. Or a resignation letter sitting in his in-box. Didn't matter to him, there were always more temps where she came from. Shrugging out of his suit jacket, he draped it across the chair opposite his desk then flung himself into the posh leather of his own chair. Midmorning conference meetings exhausted him, and he'd just as soon hire someone to stand in his place. Too bad he didn't trust anyone to take care of his business. The moment he closed his eyes, the intercom squawked.

"Mr. Black?" came Kara's small voice.

Chase inhaled and let it out slowly. "What?"

"I'm sorry, sir, I know you said to hold your calls." She paused, apparently awaiting Chase's approval. He remained silent then she continued. "There's an Adam Mitchell on the phone and—"

Chase's eyes popped open and he bolted up in his chair. *Jesus.* "Put him through. And this time, do hold my calls, Kara."

"Yes, sir," she answered.

"Mitchell," Chase said to his caller. "I hope you have something for me."

There was a pause on the line. "I found her."

Chase's pulse quickened. "Are you sure?"

"I'm sure," Mitchell returned then went silent.

"Jesus Christ, I can't believe it," Chase muttered. "After all this time."

"She's not alone," Mitchell said. "She's got a kid."

Confusion crossed Chase's brain. A kid? What the hell?

"I lost her in Virginia Beach," Mitchell admitted. "But I'm on it."

"Damn, Mitchell," Chase growled. "You'd better be on it. When you find her again, I want to know right away."

"You got it."

The call ended, and he leaned back in his chair. Opening a drawer, he pulled out a framed photograph, and he swiped it with his finger. Taken a week before their wedding. He'd begged her not to leave, but that hardheaded girl had left anyway. And with no family, she'd been untraceable. For five damn years.

She was on the East Coast. Mitchell would find her. And the kid. He'd forgotten to ask how old the kid was. Not that it mattered. He was after her, not some runaway brat she'd picked up along the way.

He smiled at the photo and grazed his finger along the woman's face once more. "I always said you can take the girl out of the streets, but you can't take the streets out of the girl." He slipped the photo back inside the drawer. "Doesn't matter. You and your secrets will soon be back here where you belong. With me."

Cassabaw Station
Present day

"SON, IT'S ONE in the morning. What's wrong?"

Nathan sat on the back deck in a metal-and-cushioned glider that was older than he was. The moon had risen over the water and beamed a silvery path across the black surface. The ever-present brine of the river rose to Nathan's nostrils, and he inhaled slowly.

"Do you remember when we were all little, and Jep used to tell us that when the moon's shine left a path across the water that it was the wee Irish fairy folk's walkway to America?"

Owen chuckled and dropped into the chair beside Nathan. "I do. He told the same story to me as a boy." He paused. "Fairies and moonbeams aren't the things keeping you up all hours of the night, son."

Nathan scrubbed his jaw then pushed his thumbs into his eye sockets. "What if the moonbeams are pathways for our lost loved ones? Mom? Grams? Addie?" Nathan sighed. "I don't want to like her so much, Dad," he admitted. "And that kid." He shook his head. "I don't want to like either one of them so much."

Another soft chuckle from Owen. "And why is that?"

His dad had the calmest of voices—deep, even, soothing. No matter how bad a situation, as kids or as adults, Owen's voice was like magic. It could lull a person into believing...hell, almost anything.

Nathan inhaled again, and pushed out a frustrated breath. He sat forward, resting his elbows against his knees. "I asked Sean if she and Willa wanted to go to the Fourth of July festival with me, and Sean said yes. Now I'm not sure I should have asked. I don't get the impression she's staying here for long. She still has unpacked boxes in her living room, and I'm pretty sure it's all they have." He looked at Owen. "At first, I thought she just didn't like me. She'd act so...indifferent when I came around. As if she couldn't get rid of me fast enough. But then when she came over and met everyone? It seemed...better. I guess."

He was frustrated at his inability to accurately say what he wanted to say. Maybe because he wasn't sure about what he was feeling. "I think she's going to leave. And to be honest, I'm not exactly sure I can get involved with someone who is temporary." He locked his fingers together, studied them. “I almost don’t want to get involved with anyone. It’s not fair, Dad.” He swallowed around the knot that tightened his throat. “It’s not fair to Addie.”

Owen leaned forward and placed his large hand on Nathan’s shoulder. He squeezed, just like he had so many times in Nathan’s life when things had turned upside down. The gesture comforted.

“Nathaniel,” Owen said in his even, calm voice. “I know it’s not fair, what happened with Addie. But she wouldn’t want you to go through life unhappy. You’ve beaten yourself up over her death for far too long, son.” He gave Nathan’s shoulder a firm shake. “It wasn’t your fault, boy. The sea took her. It was one of the risks Addie took, taking on the Bering. You know that.”

The memory of that awful day closed in once again on Nathan, piercing his brain as if someone had jammed a knife blade into it. “Yeah, I know,” he admitted. “But she was *right there*, Dad. I lost her. And I can’t seem to let it go.” He swallowed hard. “Let Addie go.”

They sat in silence for a moment, and a chorus of cicadas rose on the night air. The sticky-hot coastal breeze clung to Nathan’s bared arms and chest, and his mind raced with possibilities, with should-haves and with regrets. And with fear.

All things he'd rather no one else know about. But Owen had a perceptive radar like nobody's business. Nathan had not been able to fool his father as a boy, or as a teenager. And not as a grown man, either.

"Son, when I lost your mother there were only three things that made me want to wake up in the morning. You and your brothers. But it's something you have to find—" he tapped his own chest "—inside of here. It can't be taught. And it can't be coerced. It has to be decided. By you."

Nathan nodded. "I haven't known Sean long. Hell, I've only known her for a couple weeks, and not really the good kind of knowing at that." He looked at Owen. "But I can feel it, Dad. I can feel a draw to her and Willa. It's a pull that I can't help, and I find myself up all hours of the night worrying about it. Wondering if I should just leave them both the hell alone. Wondering how I can pull a smile from her. Fearing I won't see them again. Scared to death I'm doing wrong by Addie." Nathan gave a soft laugh. "It all scares the hell out of me, Dad."

Owen rose, his knees making a popping sound as he straightened. He placed a hand on Nathan's shoulder once more and squeezed. "Well, boy," he said, and gave him a firm pat on the back. The moonlight made his weathered skin look silver. "That's where you're going to have to come to terms with yourself. Ask yourself what you really want, and if it's worth it. And even if Sean and Willa weren't in the picture—if you'd never even met them—you'd have to deal with this. It's been too long. You're going to have to let Addie go. Not discard her, you see. Let her rest—" he tapped first his temple, then his heart "—in here and inside of here. You loved her, boy, and there's no shame in keeping that love tucked away. You're a Malone, after all. We Irishmen have a—"

"Bottomless heart, with room for lots of love," Nathan finished for him. "So Jep's said forever."

Owen smiled. "That he has. Now, get some sleep, son. See you in a few hours." He gave a half nod, then stepped into the darkened house, leaving Nathan alone.

He sat back then, resting his head against the glider, his gaze locked on that beam of moonlight stretching across the river. A smile pulled at his lips as Willa's expressive face came to mind. She'd get a kick out of that old Irish tale for sure.

What would Sean think?

Sean Jacobs. She kinda looked like a fairy herself, with that short dark hair, those narrow features and wide eyes. She had curves, too—just slight ones, and he'd thought they were… perfect. Those eyes, though…when he looked into them, they seemed to turn from hazel to a rowdy storm of grayish blue, tinged with uncertainty, suspicion and something else undetermined. He could read her body language, see the stain of blush on her cheeks when he'd asked her to join him on the Fourth of July. Maybe she was battling the same things he was inside.

Maybe she'd even be willing to let him in.

CHAPTER SEVEN

FIVE DAYS HAD passed since Nathan had invited Sean and Willa to join him for the Independence Day celebrations. Sean had thought of very little since.

"Mama, how many more days until the fireworks day with Captain Nathan?"

Sean pushed the hair away from Willa's forehead and smiled as her daughter lay tucked beneath the covers. "Five. Why? Are you excited?"

Willa's head bobbed up and down. "I am! Captain Nathan says there'll be fireworks over the ocean sky. And cotton candy. And other stuff."

Sean laughed. Willa was one big sugaroholic. "That does sound pretty fun." Sean bent and brushed a kiss against Willa's forehead. "Sweet dreams, my fairy princess."

Willa's eyes glowed as she gave Sean that lopsided grin. "Sweet dreams, fairy queen."

Sean crossed the room and turned off the light then, as she looked back, she saw her daughter turn her face to the stream of moonlight falling through the window. She said nothing—just let Willa think magical thoughts—and wandered down the hall. With a second thought, she slipped out onto the porch, and the screened door creaked as she gently closed it. Having not bothered with purchasing any porch furniture, Sean eased onto the wide step and leaned back against the pillar. Even if she went to bed now, sleep wouldn't come anytime soon. It never did. She'd lie there, staring at the ceiling. Wondering. Worrying. Contemplating.

She'd rather do all that sitting outside. Something about the moonlight, and the way it turned everything in its path silver, comforted her. Almost…made her believe in magic. Or miracles. Or both.

She'd take either one.

Sean inhaled. She liked the way the air felt damp and heavy in her lungs, the way it clung to her skin. It made her feel…present. Alive. The mournful song of a night bird crooned over the marsh, and it was joined by crickets and whatever other river bugs woke in the dark, and it almost seemed to be a wave, conducted by a maestro of the marsh as it started downriver and, in a uniformed upsurge, made its way to her. Almost as if it was meant just for her ears, at this time, this night.

Money. She had enough to last through to the first of the year. The balance of her savings account had grown to quite a healthy amount. Eventually, though, she'd need to add to it. She'd been planning to work on a new project since arriving in Cassabaw, but other things had superseded her intentions. Namely, Nathan Malone. She wondered briefly what he'd think of her bricf cxplanation of how she made her income. It was something she kept even from Willa, for fear her daughter would inadvertently let her secret out—especially if Willa knew that she was the subject of her projects.

Sean wrote, under a pseudonym, a series of children's books. The young heroine, whose name was Darling, was a fearless faerie from the kingdom of Netherdreams who attended Mrs. Froggenhall's School for Slightly Misguided Young Faeries. Darling always seemed to find herself in the utmost pickle of all pickles, only to cleverly save the day. The books provided a nice income, and she was not only able to be home with Willa daily, but also could easily work anywhere incognito. The day would come, though, when Willa would have to be told. Sean hated keeping it from her daughter—especially since she'd given Willa each book in the series. Willa loved them. Sean wondered if her daughter would understand when she told her, one day, that she'd had to keep it a secret. She hoped Willa would.

That led to more thoughts. Soon, Willa would be school age. She'd turn six in September. Kindergarten. And Willa had been begging to go to school. She would thrive in that environment. Sean knew that. Wanted it for her. But would it be safe?

The good thing with Sean's current occupation was that her identity was completely veiled. Everything was done via the internet. Her pseudonym was completely random. She was untraceable.

At least, she prayed she was.

It'd been five years. She'd been running, dodging, keeping a low profile for five damn years. She and Willa both. Her daughter had more perception than most kids her age. Willa now asked questions. Wondering why they had to always move. Wondering why other kids got to have pets. Wondering why they couldn't just find a home and stay. And…asking if she had any other family. It was heartbreaking. It was…exhausting.

And not fair at all to her daughter.

Yet, selfishly, Sean wouldn't have changed a thing. Not if it meant never having that sweet child to call her own. Willa was all she had. She was her heart. The reason she lived. She'd do everything to keep her happy, and safe. Which was why they'd always been on the move—

"You're up. Is…this too late?"

Sean nearly jumped out of her skin as Nathan's deep voice broke through the darkness. Then he emerged from the shadows of the wood, and the moonlight fell over him. Not for the first time, she thought he looked like a swarthy pirate from another time, another place.

"It's not too late," she said. "Do you always creep around other people's property at night?"

He moved closer; slow, easy, as though making sure she'd allow it. He shrugged. "Not just at night." He inclined his head toward her. "Want some company?"

There went those butterflies again. "Sure,"

she answered quietly, trying her best to not sound like he affected her. But he did. He really, really did.

Nathan sank to the step beside her; not too close, but close enough that she felt his presence. The brush of his shoulder against hers as he shifted. His scent—something clean, something subtle—whispering by her nostrils. She wanted him to go away. To stop bothering her, to leave her and Willa alone.

She wanted to know everything about him.

Ever since that evening on the dock, when Nathan had taught Willa how to drop a crab line, she'd been curious about him.

He hadn't left her mind since.

"So," she began, taking control of her voice. "What brings you out into the night?" Eyeing his profile in the shadows, she again noticed his rugged features, straight nose, revealed by the hair he'd pulled back. She had no doubt that beneath that beard lay a sharp, strong jaw, as both his brothers, his father and even Jep had the same. Muscles in Nathan's chest, his biceps, pulled at the black T-shirt he wore. Sean's fingers dug into her thighs, and she waited for him to answer.

"Well," he said in that ever-so-slight Carolina drawl. He stared down at first, seemingly at his hands as they rested against his jeans-clad legs. Hesitation. A little shy, maybe?

Then he turned to her, and Nathan's gaze found hers. "To tell you the truth, ma'am, I can't quite seem to get you off my mind."

Scratch that. Definitely not shy.

"I'd like to take you out. On a date." He cleared his throat. "Just me and you, if you'd like to."

Sean felt heat blaze to her cheeks, and she was thankful for the darkness. Fear also scorched her, leaving her unsure and uncertain. Part of her—she wasn't quite sure which part—was flattered. She wanted to go. Wanted to bask in his strength, his quiet masculinity. Wanted to feel special.

The other part—the part that kept her moving from town to town, from one part of the country to the other—stalled. His request confused her. It excited her. It flustered her.

"I— That's nice of you, but I have Willa," she stuttered. Great. Now she was stuttering. No one had made her react so crazily in a long, long time. That fight-or-flight reaction was overtaking her, even though she wasn't sure which path to take.

Nathan held up a hand. "Don't get me wrong—I'm not trying to ditch Willa. Honest to God, you have the cutest kid I've ever met," he said with a chuckle. "And I plan on showing her a big time on the Fourth. Besides, Emily and Jep have all but been fighting over who gets to spend more time with her." He smiled. "Jep wants to teach her to play chess. And Em wants a baking buddy." He ducked his head, looked at the step beneath him, then lifted his gaze to hers. It was solemn. Fathomless. Fearful. Fearless. All of those emotions flashed in his green eyes.

"I'd just like to take a pretty girl on a picnic," he finally said. "Would you? Go with me?"

Sean couldn't tear her gaze from Nathan's. She didn't know him. She hadn't been on a date in…she couldn't recall. So many years—a lifetime ago. She hadn't left Willa's side since her birth, either.

No, Sean didn't know Nathan. Not really. Yet somehow, she sensed it had taken quite a lot for him to come to this place. To ask her out on a date. She speculated briefly if he didn't do it often—go on dates, that is. She didn't know for sure, but he wasn't behaving the way guys who routinely ask women out typically did. Nathan rose from his place on the step, shifted his stance and shoved his hands in his pockets. He seemed about as nervous as she felt.

She'd been so reserved with him in his company—even the very thought of spending any time with him was something Sean had vehemently pushed from her mind. Yet, somehow, he had broken through that wall she'd built around herself. That protective wall that forbade any and all trespassers. Before, she'd been concerned about Willa's safety. After spending time with the Malones, she'd come to realize that the only danger there would be their breaking hearts when she and Willa would have to say goodbye. Perhaps Nathan could be her one exception. Even if for just a little while.

He definitely was a solid male figure in Willa's life. And that was something she'd been missing out on. Perhaps Sean's rationale all this time had been off. Willa needed more than her mother. She needed someone strong. Someone with integrity. That someone might be Nathan.

And, of course, there were those butterflies. The first Sean had had in forever.

Strangely, she found herself smiling. Her rebellious lips tugged at her face, without her permission. And then her head bobbed. Actually nodded an answer before words left her lips.

"I will," she answered softly. "I'll go with you."

Nathan grinned—a wide, true smile that pulled at the corners of his eyes. "Yeah?"

Again, Sean nodded. "Yeah," she replied, repeating his word of enthusiasm. "You're sure Willa won't be any trouble? Other than a big talker, she's a good girl."

"I know she is," he stated. "And no—no trouble at all. She'll meet her talking match with old Jep." He looked at her then, and his eyes softened, and Sean felt something she hadn't felt for so very long. Trust. Which terrified her, since she barely knew him.

Yet Nathan put her at ease with that simple, humble admission that he'd been unable to get her off his mind. Honest. He was definitely that.

"I'm really glad you said yes, Sean Jacobs."

"You might not think so later. I'm...a little rusty at this dating thing," she admitted.

"That makes two of us," Nathan answered,

then he rose. "Does tomorrow sound too pushy?" he said with a chuckle.

Sean stood, and although Nathan was a step below her, he still stood taller. She looked up. "A little," she teased. *Teased?* "Tomorrow's fine," she said hurriedly, when something that seemed like fear or doubt passed over his gaze. "What time?"

His stare didn't leave hers. "How's four sound?"

"Four o'clock is fine."

Nathan gave a short nod. "Great. I'll pick you and Willa up." He started down the steps then paused to look over his shoulder. "Shorts and sneakers are fine. But bring a long-sleeved shirt if you have one."

"Ah," she said as he slipped into the shadows. "A shorts-and-sneakers kind of picnic date."

"Yep," he said from the darkness. "You won't be sorry!"

Sean stood there in silence, beneath the moonlight and the magnolias, amid the crickets and night bugs, and everything Cassabaw, and smiled.

Yeah, she knew what would come later. The worry. The guilt. The fear. And the disappointment. It always did. But for now? She'd have a tiny slice of normal.

She'd worry about the later, well, later.

"GODALMIGHTY, SON, YOU look like an escapee of some sort. I can't believe that pretty girl even said yes to you. Why don't you shave that beard off? Maybe cut some of that hair?"

"Jep, I'll give you a hundred bucks if he shaves that beard and cuts that hair," Eric, Nathan's youngest brother, said. He slipped Nathan a conspirator's grin. "Make it two hundred."

"I'm not shaving or cutting anything," Nathan said. Nerves had his stomach in knots. He hadn't slept a wink all night long. The last thing he was going to do was…shave and cut.

"I can't believe she said yes," Jep repeated.

"Dad," Owen chided. "Leave the boy alone."

"What? He used to wear it high and tight," Jep complained, referring to the military-style haircut they'd all sported while they served. "Looked presentable. Like a decent young man. Now he looks like a miscreant."

"Ha! A miscreant. Jep, yours isn't high and tight," Eric added, biting into a sandwich. He perched against the counter, pointing with his sandwich. "Look at all that white hair, sticking out all over the place. You look like Einstein."

"When you're ninety, you can do what you want, look like you want," Jep remarked, then took off his USCG hat and ran his fingers through his hair. It stuck up every which way. "Besides, the ladies like it this way."

Eric burst out laughing, and Nathan just shook his head. "I'll be back." He started for the door then glanced over his shoulder. "When they get here, don't," he warned, giving his sibling and grandfather a scowl.

"Don't what?" Eric asked.

"Just…don't," Nathan said, and walked out the door. Behind him, his grandfather and brother both chuckled. He pointed at Jep. "You look like you just escaped from the asylum."

Eric and Jep laughed harder.

They were plotting against him, and he knew it.

He didn't care.

She had said yes. Unbelievably.

No amount of hacking would sour his mood.

He was closing in on thirty years of age. He wasn't afraid of a date.

He most definitely wasn't afraid of some family ribbing.

The moment Nathan drove into Sean's drive, his stomach snarled. He almost stopped the truck. Then, he did. Putting it in Park, he stared down the lane. What in God's name had he been thinking? Where did he think this date would go? With her boxes still packed in the living room, and him knowing virtually nothing about her, it was probably going nowhere except…a picnic. A mom and her kid and him, along with his guilt over Addie. He'd thought to talk to Sean about Addie. Nothing heavy, just…talk. He had a feeling he was stepping right into it, as Jep would say.

Nathan took a deep, calming breath. "Let it go, Malone. Man up. Don't be a chickenshit." He took another deep breath. Blew it out slowly. "Just step in it."

With that self-criticism and pep talk, he put the old truck in gear and started toward Sean's house. The lane opened up and the house with its wide porch appeared before him. Sean and Willa both sat on the steps, waiting. Both wore white shorts and little blue sneakers. Willa had on a pink shirt and her wings, while Sean had on a blue tank top. Willa leaned over and kissed her mama on the cheek.

That knot sitting in his stomach leaped to his throat.

He'd never seen anything sweeter in his life.

Yup. He was stepping into it, all right.

Stopping the truck, he put it in Park and jumped out. "You girls ready?" He hoped he pulled off nonchalant as well as he thought he did.

"We are!" exclaimed Willa, and she bounded off the porch. She skidded to a halt inches in front of him, and looked up. She had one big blue eye pinched shut, as if in serious, intense concentration. "What did you say King Jep was going to teach me?"

Nathan grinned. "Chess." He squatted down on one knee so he could be eye level with her. "Willa, if you're unsure about staying with King Jep and Miss Emily, you can come with me and your mom." He winked at her. "I won't mind a bit."

Willa studied him, as though weighing his offer someplace deep in her mind. Then she placed her little hand on his shoulder and gave him a gentle pat. "Thanks, but I'm okay. I like King Jep. He's funny. Besides—" she leaned closer, to keep the words only for Nathan's ears "—my mom never has any fun." Her dark eyebrows furrowed. "Make her have some fun, Captain Nathan."

Nathan returned her serious expression. "Yes, ma'am."

When he rose, Nathan's gaze met Sean's. She watched him closely then smiled and silently mouthed the words *thank you*. He returned a single nod.

The girls piled into the cab of the truck, and Nathan made his way down the drive. Willa sat in the middle and chattered the entire way to the Malone house. About everything from fairies to cemetery ghosts to eating spaghetti to swimming off the dock to flesh-eating amoebas. Each subject bled right into the next one.

His grandfather was waiting on the front porch, sitting in his favorite rocker. When Nathan pulled the truck up, Jep rose. He adjusted the bill of his cap and pulled it down, then tilted his head up to look at them.

"'Bout time you got here," he called out. "My chessboard is getting cold."

Willa jumped from the truck and ran up the porch steps. She tilted her head back as Jep looked down. Neither said a word for a moment, both just…staring. Studying. Weighing. Finally, Jep broke.

"What're you looking at, fairy girl?" he asked.

The five-year-old stared a moment longer. "I'm trying to see behind your eyeballs and into your brain, King Jep. To see what you're thinking."

"Huh. Is that so? What do you see?"

Willa put her hands on her narrow little hips. "I can't tell you. It's a secret."

"I hate secrets," Jep muttered. "Well, come on, then. Let's go set the chess table up." Halfway to the door, he glanced over his shoulder. "We're playing alfresco, down by the river."

"Yay! Did you hear that, Mama?" Willa squealed. She ran down the steps and threw her arms around Sean's waist. "I love you, Mama," she said.

Sean hugged her tightly and kissed her cheek. "I love you, too, baby. Be kind to King Jep, okay?"

"I will!"

Then Willa grabbed Nathan in a similar hug, tightly around the waist. "Bye, Captain Nathan!"

Nathan swallowed hard and patted Willa's head. "See ya, fairy princess."

Willa took off and bound up the porch, and

she and Jep then entered their own world, effectively ignoring Nathan and Sean.

Nathan grinned. "Looks like a recipe for disaster to me," he said.

Sean laughed softly, and Nathan found he liked the sound. "I think Jep will need a big nap after we get back."

She was probably right.

Nathan inclined his head toward the house. "Ready?"

An expression of confusion passed through Sean's large eyes. "So…not in the truck?"

"Not in the truck."

"So where?"

Nathan indicated toward the house. Rather, the side of the house. That led around to the dock. "You'll see."

She smiled at him. Hesitant. A little unsure. And her cheeks stained red.

In that moment, Nathan thought he'd never seen anything more endearing. It'd been the right thing to ask Sean out on a date.

It felt right. For the first time in a long, damn while, *he* felt right.

CHAPTER EIGHT

AS HER HANDSOME, charming neighbor led the way toward the dock, Sean felt a myriad emotions. Fear, of course. Excitement. Curiosity.

Guilt. For leaving Willa, although she seemed completely content being left with Jep.

For keeping secrets. Although she'd never told Nathan that she and Willa were staying on Cassabaw, the omission still gnawed at her. While she hadn't dated in ages, she wasn't ignorant of how things worked. A man asked a woman out when he was interested. Interest led to...other things. For some, perhaps, there were no strings attached. But she had Willa. And they were leaving. And part of her wanted to blurt it out right away, just to keep from harboring information from Nathan or his family. They were so genuine, and had opened their home to her and Willa. It bothered her to keep secrets now.

She and Willa wouldn't stay beyond summer's end. She knew it was unfair to Nathan to accept his offer of a mysterious date. Yet, for the first time in a really, really long time, Sean felt incapable of saying no. Of running. Hiding. Slipping further into her invisible world. She was tired and wanted to just…feel. But was it right to do so, all the while knowing she'd be gone in a couple of months? Before, she had no problem moving. No problem keeping her and Willa private. Not getting involved. Not reaching out.

This time, Nathan had changed her mind.

And she'd said yes.

And it terrified her. Now she could see why. It scared her to think she might make an emotional connection with Nathan, with his family, only to disappear at summer's end. She didn't like feeling vulnerable, and she hated even more for someone else to see that vulnerability. Nathan at once frightened her and soothed her fears. It was…beyond confusing. Selfishly, she didn't want all of those consuming thoughts to ruin the first date she'd had in forever with such a nice guy.

"Okay, watch your step," Nathan said, drawing Sean from her thoughts. She lifted her gaze to see him watching her closely. He'd already climbed onto the deck of the *Tiger Lily*, and he leaned forward, hand outstretched, a smile tugging at his mouth as he waited for her to take it.

Sean placed her hand in Nathan's, and he pulled her on board.

"Thank you," she said shyly, and then looked around. The *Tiger Lily* was a well-used trawler, smelling slightly salty, slightly sea-ish, yet the decks were scrubbed clean, and the wheel shone in the afternoon sunlight. A smile touched her lips. *A pirate's ship.*

"What's so funny?" Nathan asked, leading her to the bow of the boat.

Sean looked into Nathan's striking eyes. They twinkled, as though amused by something. She gave a nonchalant shrug. "Nothing, really. Other than it's my first time on a pirate's ship."

Nathan laughed. "Anchor away!" he hollered with a pirate's accent.

As they pulled away from the dock, Jep and Willa stood close to the bank, waving. Sean waved back and watched her daughter grab the old man's hand to help him over to the chess table, set up on the dock.

How had this family already infiltrated their lives? Willa's openness and enthusiasm to connect with people was both heartwarming and heartstopping for Sean. Heartwarming in that her daughter lacked fear. She was bold, brave and had an abundance of affection for people. At the same time, she was capable of stopping Sean's heart because Willa might not recognize people she shouldn't connect with. Not everyone was like the Malone family. The very thing that made Willa Jacobs happy could be the very thing that brought danger on them both. At times, it left Sean with such a heavy heart, she could feel the weight of it, like an anvil, pressing hard, pressing down.

She turned and watched Nathan at the wheel. He wore a faded blue T-shirt and pair of dark khaki shorts. His hair was pulled back, and his shades now covered his eyes. Arms corded with muscle gripped the wheel as though he'd been doing it all of his life. Like he belonged here, to this place. To the sea.

She wondered what that would feel like. *Belonging.*

Sean noticed the small covered docks with faded red and blue tin roofs leading out of the river and old wooden pillars sticking out of the water. Enormous oaks stretched close, their branches draped with wispy gray moss. Rays of sun poked holes through the canopy, like peering through a kaleidoscope. The brine of the river rose to her nostrils, and Sean inhaled.

Was any of this real? A month ago, she wouldn't have even considered taking Willa in public without holding fast to her little hand. The thought of a date had *never* crossed her mind. Now, here she was, in a picturesque little coastal town she'd found by literally closing her eyes and letting her finger drop on the map. Cassabaw seemed to be right out of the 1930s.

And somehow she'd become immersed in the tableau. Here she was on a date with a handsome sea captain. She'd left her daughter in the care of a witty old Irishman. It didn't seem real.

Yet it was.

Salty spray from the Atlantic grazed her cheeks as Nathan picked up speed, navigating out of the river and into the sound. The late-afternoon sun warmed her skin, and Sean gripped the side of the trawler. Wood smoothed by so many hands before her felt warm beneath her palms.

"Where are we going?" she called over the growl of the motor.

A smile curved Nathan's mouth, and the wind whipped at his hair, his T-shirt. He looked completely at home on the sea as his strong hands gripped the wheel. "You'll see."

Sean nodded and stared at the open water ahead. The gray-blue ocean lapped at the *Tiger Lily*, and frothy white caps dotted the horizon as wind stirred up waves. Seagulls screeched overhead, and Sean turned her gaze heavenward, shading her eyes as a bird's shadow fell over the deck. When she glanced over her shoulder, beyond Nathan, the docks and tin roofs and the jetty leading out of the sound were mere pinpoints. She could barely see them. Where was Nathan taking her?

Soon, something appeared on the horizon. Nothing more than a dot at first. Nathan guided them straight toward it, and as the dot grew larger, Sean realized it was a small island. An uneven strip of gray-white sand curved around the patch of land, and mossy trees gathered in its center. Although they were still a bit away from the shore, the *Tiger Lily*'s engine was silenced, and Nathan left the wheel.

"Anchor away," he called, and a big *kersplunk* sounded as the heavy iron dropped into the water. He grabbed a large cooler and another canvas bag. "Ready?"

Sean looked from Nathan to the water, then back to Nathan. "We— You want to swim to shore?" Her gaze scanned the water. "I'm not sure."

Nathan chuckled, and she noticed it was a jovial, manly sound that she rather liked. "Sharks?"

Sean nodded. "They're there. They're everywhere. You just can't see them."

Nathan gave a lopsided grin. "I won't lie to you, you're absolutely right." He inclined his head to the side of the boat. "Guess I'm so used to them not bothering me and me not bothering them that I don't even think about it. But we'll take the raft."

Relief washed over Sean. "Oh. Phew. Okay." She let out a breath. "Thanks."

Again, Nathan chuckled, and he settled the cooler and bag into the raft, lowered it then climbed overboard.

Sean peered over the edge of the boat, and Nathan grinned up at her, extending a hand. "Can you make it?"

Sean nodded, threw first one leg over the edge, then the other, and climbed down the ladder she hadn't known was there. She reached for Nathan's hand, and he helped her board the rocking raft. She settled onto a small seat in front of Nathan, and they took off for the shore.

"Hold on," Nathan called out, and Sean followed his instructions as the raft bucked and pushed against the waves.

Then, the sandy shore was there, and Nathan ran the raft right up onto it. They both hopped out, and Nathan tossed a small anchor out and dragged the small craft farther onto the shore.

Sean stood and glanced around. The mossy trees. The driftwood that had settled into the sand. Snowy-white egrets, with their long beaks, flew among the trees—one or two close by. "Wow. This place..."

"Pretty spectacular, eh?" Nathan said. "Me, Matt and Eric camped out here as kids with Dad and Jep." Sean tried to imagine what a youthful Nathan looked like. He laughed softly, and the sound blended with the tide lapping at the shore. "We pretended it was Neverland," he admitted. "And we were Lost Boys."

"That is so cute," she said. *Peter Pan* was one of her most favorite novels of all time. "Who was Pan? Jep or Owen?"

Nathan laughed. "Who do you think? Jep

insisted on being Pan. Every time. And Owen would always be Hook."

She smiled. "Is that why your trawler is named the *Tiger Lily*?"

Nathan nodded as he set down the cooler and canvas bag then withdrew from the bag a dark-blue-and-red-plaid blanket and spread it out. "Partly. Come on," he said and inclined his head toward the trees. "I'll show you something."

Sean followed Nathan toward the trees then along a thin trail beaten down by foot tread. Almost immediately they were out of the sun and beneath a shady canopy. Small palm shrubs and larger pine trees filled the maritime forest. Nathan led them to an enormous oak tree in the center of the island. Squatting near the trunk's base, he pushed back the fronds of a shrub palm, swept away some moss.

Sean walked closer and peered over Nathan's shoulder. The bark had been scraped away, and carved into the smooth, aged wood were three names, barely visible, scrawled in choppy, childlike font. *Nathaniel. Matthew. Eric.*

"You did that?" Sean asked. She found it whimsical. Adorable. Unique.

Nathan traced the names with his fingertips. "Yep. I was nine."

Sean knelt beside him, running her fingers over the scratched letters. "Were you here with your dad?"

He quieted then looked at her. "My mom. It was the last time she was here. She died a year later. Cancer."

"Oh," Sean said. She'd wondered why Owen's wife hadn't been present but hadn't wanted to ask. "I'm sorry."

"It was a long time ago, but I remember her more than my brothers do. She was…the best." A smile touched his lips. "Matt and Eric and I used to pile up in a fort made of chairs and blankets and pillows and our mom would settle in there with us and read to us." He rose and searched the mammoth treetop. "*Peter Pan* was always our favorite. She always loved Tiger Lily in the book. When she died, and Dad and Jep bought the trawler, we decided to name it *Tiger Lily* in her honor."

"I think it's perfect," Sean commented, then glanced upward into the branches of the oak. The sunlight dappled through small holes in the branches and leaves, and when her gaze returned to Nathan, he was already looking at her. She noticed the spots of sunlight scattering on his skin.

"We would call this our secret Lost Boys hideout tree," he said, and his voice was raspy, gruff with old memory. "We would climb all over it—well, at first, Eric didn't. He was too young. Instead, he'd stay below us on the ground and yell." He stepped back, to get a better view of the tree, perhaps. "We'd play out our favorite scenes from *Peter Pan*." Nathan grinned, and the green of his eyes seemed to shimmer, brighten. "Good times."

Sean smiled back. She hardly knew what to say to such a sad, bittersweet tale. She imagined him as a child, heartbroken over the loss of his mother.

She knew the feeling. Sort of.

Inhaling, she glanced around. "Do you come here often?"

Nathan started down the path, and Sean followed through the woods. "Sometimes. It's quiet. I camp out here when I need some time to myself. Most people don't even know it's here. Tourists stopped coming around since we put the signs up."

"Wait. This is *your* island?" Sean asked.

Nathan chuckled. "Well, it's the Malones'. Jep purchased it when Dad was a kid."

The path wound to the beach and they made their way to their blanket, and Nathan kicked off his shoes and stuck his toes in the sand. He held his hand up to Sean. "Sit with me?"

Sean hesitantly placed her hand in his—it was rough, warm, secure. Nathan tugged at her, and she took a place on the blanket beside him. She, too, kicked off her Keds and dug her feet into the sand. She gazed out to the sea, and the shade from the trees fell upon them as the sun began its descent.

Nathan rested his forearms on his bent knees, and his presence beside her felt heavy. Different.

Good.

"So, Sean Jacobs," he said, bumping her with his shoulder. "Let's play a game. I've already taken a turn." He looked at her and smiled. "Tell me something about you." He busied himself digging into the cooler, pulling out the supper he'd packed. "Here," he said, handing her a sub-like sandwich wrapped in wax paper. "Jep is famous for these."

"Thanks," she said, accepting the sandwich that smelled like heavenly spicy shrimp salad.

Pulling back the wrapper, she took a bite. Flavors burst onto her tongue. "Wow. I see why he's famous for it."

"Good, huh?" Nathan agreed, biting into his. "So. Your turn."

This was the thing Sean had feared most. She had to be careful here with this man and this family. They mustn't know too much.

And she mustn't get too attached.

And she mustn't allow her fears to show. Not only would she hate for the Malones—Nathan in particular—to know just what sort of life she'd once led, the things she'd done, but also what if, somehow, her past came looking for her in Cassabaw? The thought of any one of the Malones getting hurt because of her kept her on her toes, as far as revealing information went.

Tucking her hair behind her ear, she finished chewing and focused on the sand between her feet. Dug her toes in deeper. "Oh, there isn't much to tell," she began. "I grew up in a dusty little town just outside Dallas." She gave a dismissive laugh. "You know, where everybody knows everybody." She inhaled, exhaled. "I eventually left for the big city with stars in my eyes." She wiggled the sand between her toes, took another bite, finished it. Her gaze lifted to meet Nathan's, and he watched her closely, those eyes as profound as any she'd ever seen. She shrugged and looked away. It was hard to look at Nathan when she was leaving so many truths of her story out. Truths that, if he knew, surely he would change his mind about her. A vague memory, one she'd pushed away long ago, surfaced, of living on the streets, digging through Dumpsters behind restaurants to find food. And other acts she'd rather soon forget. "Well, the rest is kind of clichéd. I met a boy, thought he loved me." Again, she gave a soft laugh. "Turns out he didn't."

Nathan said nothing. He simply watched. Ate. He pulled out two sodas, handing her one without a word. She guessed he wanted more.

"Thank you. So, nine months later and my life changed…wholly. And in the very best way possible," she said, taking a sip of soda. "It's been just me and Willa ever since. She is—" her gaze met Nathan's, trying to communicate the sincerity of her words "—everything that matters to me in this world." The statement hung heavily, awkwardly. Unsure of what to say that would lighten the moment, she did what she always did: turned the focus around, away from her. "So, what about you?"

HE KNEW SEAN held back. There were years, experiences, she'd purposely skipped, and although he wanted mightily to push, he didn't. Not on the first date. But he wondered about her hesitancy. Was she hiding something embarrassing? Something she wanted to keep buried. For now, he would give her space. Time to get to know him.

Hopefully, in time, she'd learn to trust him.

Nathan considered her question then nodded. "So, when we were younger—I'd say Eric was six, Matt was eight and I was ten—we went on a hunt." He wiggled his brows. "For Bigfoot."

Sean laughed. "Did you find him?"

Nathan held her gaze. "I swear as I sit here, I saw something. Something big ran across the road at the north end of the island." Nathan stirred his memory, and it made him smile. "We were on our bikes, the sun was fast dropping. Long shadows fell across the road and into the marsh. I— We all swear to this day that we saw a tall, hairy creature, walking upright, lumber across that road."

Sean giggled. He rather liked the sound. "Wow. Sasquatch on Cassabaw. What would you have done, had you caught him?"

"In our young minds, we wanted him for a pet," he admitted, as he recalled that night. "We wanted to lure him to the river house with chunks of biscuit. We dropped those chunks all the way down the road and up our drive." He laughed. "But there was no Bigfoot. Only a fire-mad Jep, because we'd used a whole batch of biscuits as bait."

Sean smiled, shaking her head. "No doubt you had several woodland creatures following those chunks."

"Raccoons," Nathan admitted. "I still remember Jep chasing them across the back lawn with a broom."

They both chuckled.

They finished their po' boy sandwiches and sipped their drinks before Nathan pushed to know more.

"So, a Texas girl," he teased, then nodded. "I thought it was an underlying rule for Texas women to have—" he held his hand above his head "—really tall, really big hair?"

Sean smoothed her shorn hair behind her

ears. "I guess I didn't get that memo," she said. "I've had mine short for some time now."

Nathan eyed her appreciatively. "I like it. It…suits you."

Sean glanced down, as though bashful. Or embarrassed. "Thank you."

Nathan cleared his throat. "Willa's a pretty great kid. You've done a good job with her."

She nodded. "She's been a very easy child. Even as a baby. She's spoiled me."

Nathan wanted to know where Willa's father was and why it seemed he wasn't in the picture. Those, though, were questions for another time. She'd already avoided the topic, given him the bare-minimum information, and he wasn't about to lose what little ground he'd gained with her.

"Actually, it's the complete opposite," Sean said. "She's done a good job with me."

Nathan studied her. Noticed her small, sharp features. The way her nose fit her face so well, and how curvy her lips were. The wind had picked up, and as it pushed by them Sean's dark, pixie-like hair blew across her forehead, leaving a long hank over her eyes. Without thinking, he lifted his hand and brushed it away, and her cheeks stained crimson.

"I think it's probably pretty even," he said, and clasped his hands together between his bent knees. To keep from touching her. God, he wanted to. For the first time in… Jesus. How long? He wanted to kiss her. He wanted to see trust shine in her eyes. He held back, though. The tension between them felt heavy, and he wasn't sure if it was good tension or the kind that made a person take flight. He dropped his head and caught her gaze. "You two are a perfect match."

Sean smiled. "Thank you. That…means a lot."

Nathan forced his eyes away from her lips, which looked soft and full and turned up just right. "So," he said, steering the conversation away from anything that seemed threatening, "what did you want to be when you grew up?"

Sean pulled her knees up, wrapped her arms around them and gazed up to the sky. "Well, when I was little I remember wanting really badly to be a Jedi Knight."

Nathan laughed.

"What's so funny?" she asked.

He shook his head and ran his hand over his bearded jaw. "*I* wanted to be a Jedi Knight."

Sean's laugh resonated over the waves lapping at the shoreline. "No way!"

Nathan nodded. "It's true. When we weren't being Pan or Lost Boys, anyway. Matt and Eric would pretend to be Stormtroopers and would chase me all around the house. Sometimes, we'd all be Jedi Knights and pretend that Jep was Darth Vader, only Jep wouldn't know it." The memory flashed before his eyes as though through an old projector film. "Jep would turn around and catch us at various posts in the kitchen while he cooked supper, and he'd yell, 'What are you foolish kids up to now?'" Nathan thought how much he really liked a smiling, laughing Sean Jacobs. "So what else did you want to be?" he added, keeping it light. "Since Jedi 101 wasn't available."

A smile remained on Sean's lips, and her eyes moved toward the sky once more. At first, she kept silent, seemingly staring into her past. "I remember at one time wanting to study the stars," she admitted, and her expression softened, as though recalling a time that may have been a really good one in her life. Carefree, perhaps. "The constellations, galaxies—there is so much out there," she said quietly. "I can sit and watch the sky for hours. Willa, too.

We've taken to watching the stars from the floating dock after the sun goes down. She takes pride in finding the first twinkler of the night."

If she liked watching the stars from the dock, he wondered what she'd think of a sky full of them from the sea. He grinned. "Stargazing alfresco."

She said nothing; only smiled, and Nathan couldn't help wondering what lay behind that smile. What secrets, what pain or joy, if any, lay hidden behind those solemn eyes? He was glad he'd been the one to put a smile on her face now, anyway.

Sean's gaze shifted and stared off into the distance, and Nathan didn't have to turn to know what it was she looked at.

"Cassabaw's lighthouse," he informed her, and swiveled to watch the beacon. The sun had fallen fast, and the sky now streaked with fiery colors of red and orange.

"I love lighthouses," Sean admitted, and rested her chin against her knees. "There's something so mysterious about them. Don't you think?" She tracked the lighthouse's beam as it struck through the fading dusk. "I like to imagine what the lighthouse keeper must have looked like way back then."

"Actually," Nathan said, "he looked a lot like me."

Sean's gaze met Nathan's, and she cocked her head. "Really?"

Nathan shrugged. "There are photos hanging in the lighthouse museum. Nearly identical, me and Great-Grandpa Patrick."

She narrowed her eyes. "You're teasing me."

Nathan held up a hand. "Promise." Then he grinned. "Jep's father, my great-grandfather Patrick, was the last lighthouse keeper on Cassabaw. Those photos we looked at the other night? Of Jep in his knickers and suspenders? They left Galway for Patrick to come here and work the lighthouse."

Sean half turned where she sat and looked at Nathan straight on, her eyes wide. Then she looked at the lighthouse. "Seriously?"

"Absolutely." He gave a nonchalant shrug. "We Malones are kind of legendary on Cassabaw."

"You're serious."

"I am completely serious."

Sean pushed to her feet, walked to the edge of the shore and stared out across the water.

"That is so cool!" she exclaimed. She stared a moment longer then looked over her shoulder at Nathan. "Can you show me? The pictures in the lighthouse?"

Nathan rose and walked to stand beside her. The warm July water lapped over his bare feet. "On one condition."

Sean's eyes rounded. "What?"

"You and Willa have to go on another date with me." He shrugged and crossed his arms over his chest, casting his gaze out to sea. "That's the best I can do."

Sean burst into laughter. "Talk about dramatic."

Nathan smiled and looked at her. Noticed the various flecks of green in her hazel eyes, the shape of her eyebrows and how her lips curved up in the corners. "Well?"

Sean's eyes flashed for a moment as she considered.

Nathan ducked his head to get a better look at her. To convince her. "I'll throw in a personal tour of the lighthouse."

The smile started small, just one corner of her mouth. Then, she met his gaze and offered a full-on beaming grin that, this time, reached her eyes.

Nathan felt his heart skip.

"Deal."

"I knew that'd get you."

Sean shyly looked away. "It sure got me, and Willa will be thrilled. So…when?"

Nathan didn't hesitate. "Tomorrow."

Sean laughed. "You don't waste any time, do you?"

Nathan's heart squeezed, and he was sure as hell that at some point he would be terrified at the outcome of all this. But for now, he couldn't seem to help himself. He couldn't keep his eyes off her. "Not when I'm dead set on something."

Sean's face softened and she again cast her gaze down. The sea wind whipped at them, and her dark hair fell over her eyes, and with slender fingers she pushed the strands behind her ear.

Nathan wondered then how it would feel to kiss her.

Hell. He might as well find out.

CHAPTER NINE

GOD, NATHAN WAS going to kiss her.

Wasn't he?

And she wanted him to, right?

Right?

Wait. Yes!

No. Wait! No!

"So! Nathan!" she said in a nervous, laughing voice, and stepped out of the web of electricity that seemed to envelop them both. She knew she sounded like a lunatic, but swear to God, she couldn't help it. "Other than a Jedi Knight or Pan, what did you want to do with your life? Oh! Is this a shark's tooth?" Sean bent over and grabbed the triangular-shaped white-gray shell, and turned it over in her hand. She held it up and peered through it. Why? Heck if she knew. All of a sudden she was panicky. Scared. Flustered. And very, very unsure about what she was doing with a man she'd surely never see again after the summer's end.

She turned just as Nathan bent close and thrust the object at him. "See?"

An intent expression crossed his face, and Sean thought he pretended not to notice how completely awkward she'd become. That he didn't call her out on it was...gentlemanly. Appealing.

Almost as much as a grown man confessing to want to be Peter Pan when he was a boy.

Something she certainly wasn't used to, either.

Nathan lifted the object from her palm and studied it.

"Yep. A shark's tooth." His gaze rose, and the green in his eyes rivaled that of the sea. He didn't look away as he handed the tooth to her. "That's luck of the sea, Sean Jacobs." He drew a deep breath. "I always wanted to be a rescue swimmer. Just like Jep and Dad." He busied himself then, collecting the empty soda cans and shaking out the blanket. She helped him fold it, and his eyes remained on hers as they joined corners. His hair whipped in the wind. That smile lifted a little more. She thought he looked feral, like a wild island animal.

She thought he was possibly the most handsome man she'd ever seen.

Sean felt the space around her close in. Why was he affecting her so much? "Why did you leave? The Coast Guard?" she blurted out. Immediately, she wished she hadn't.

He stood there though, all six-foot-plus of him, a solemn expression etched on his features, replacing the playful one he'd worn earlier. Regret struck Sean like a load of bricks.

"I'm sorry," she said. "You don't have to answer that."

Still, he watched her with that profound stare. "I lost my fiancée to the sea. She drowned. I was there with the chopper and team, and we were going to pull her and her shipmate from the water. Her ship was going down. I saw her one second, the next…" A faraway look lit his eyes, and he was silent for a bit.

"She waved, and then was just gone. She never resurfaced. I was right there and couldn't save her," he admitted, and his deep voice stirred the salty air around them—so much that Sean felt it inside her. "The Guard no longer held the appeal it once did after that." He kneeled, packing the blanket into the canvas bag he'd brought, then stood. "I mean, if I can't save my own fiancée…" He left the sentence open, unforgiving. "Anyway. Yeah. So, I packed it up and headed home to Cassabaw." He gave a short laugh. "Where my poor family members had to put up with a whole lot of hell from me for quite a while."

She should have kept her mouth shut. She, of all people, knew not to ask personal questions. She dodged them to the nth degree. What made her think Nathan would want to drag up the past? Now she felt horrible, because it was quite obvious that the memory pained him greatly. He'd quit the Coast Guard because of it, and she couldn't blame him for that. He must have loved his fiancée a great deal. She wondered what that felt like, being that loved.

She shoved that thought aside and focused on what she knew. She'd done a lot of running in her lifetime, too.

"Nathan, I didn't mean for you to—" Sean let out a sigh, and touched his arm. "I'm really sorry you went through that. And I'm sorry to have made you go back there."

Nathan stood still, his gaze far off, as though revisiting that hurtful memory. The wind tossed his hair, long pieces of sun-bleached blond and caramel strands that had escaped the tie at the nape of his neck. Then he sighed, and looked down at her. And smiled.

"For the first time, Sean Jacobs, it doesn't hurt so much to remember."

Sean couldn't take her eyes off his, that profound stare he had gripped her in a vise right there in the sand. She could hear the tide lapping at the shore. The wind rustling the sea oats and saw grass.

And a silent roar inside of her head. A warning? To run away?

Run toward?

"Now, this is living, huh?" he suddenly said, interrupting her anxiety.

Sean glanced over her shoulder. The sight drew her full attention, and she turned around.

Standing side by side, arms brushing but not invasively so, Sean and Nathan watched the sun as it hovered over Cassabaw. The sky had shifted from blue with white puffy clouds to a palette of red, orange and heathery purple.

Nathan pointed. "See how the sun reflects off the water?" he said. "Jep always told us as kids that the sparkles you see there were sea diamonds, and that mermaid princesses and warriors were tossing them back and forth to one another." He chuckled. "Treasures of the sea."

Sean looked, and the surface of the Atlantic was truly covered in sea diamonds. She imagined mermaids and seahorses frolicking just beneath the water, an entire world hidden from mankind. It struck within her the desire to put the whimsy of Cassabaw, of a boy, his brothers and grandfather to story. It was the first time since arriving that she felt driven to write something new. Perhaps she would now. Briefly, she wondered what Nathan and his family would think of their family tales being put to paper.

"It's breathtaking, Nathan." She shifted her gaze to him, only to find he already had that weighty stare directed at her.

"Yeah," he replied. "Breathtaking."

Sean felt the heat rise to her cheeks, yet she couldn't tear her eyes away from his. She felt drawn to Nathan Malone, and in this moment, in this time, she wanted nothing more than to fall into his arms, to let his strength pull her in tight, shield her from the things she feared every night, and every day. She wanted to forget that she ran, that she hid—and that she pulled Willa right along with her in that fear.

God, she wished it would all go away.

She wished she could just...be. That she and Willa could have a normal life.

Could it even be possible?

Nathan's mouth shifted, and a soft grin tugged at the corners of his lips. "Thank you," he said quietly—as quiet as could be expected over the tide.

Sean cocked her head. "For what?"

By the way he rubbed his bearded jaw and shook his head, he was just as amazed by this moment as she was. "I'm not sure," he confessed. "But it's been a long time since my heart has felt so light," he said, and placed his hand over his chest. Sean's gaze fell on the ring he wore—Coast Guard, maybe?

"It's you," Nathan said, his eyes shimmering like the sea diamonds. "It's because of you."

The air in Sean's lungs caught, and she could only return his smile, unable to speak.

Nathan studied her for a moment; wordlessly, yet his eyes seemed to speak volumes. "Ready to sail?"

"Yes," Sean answered, and it came out breathy, shaky. She cleared her throat. "I am, yes. Of course. Absolutely."

Nathan gave a soft chuckle, shouldered the canvas bag and grabbed the cooler, then they climbed into the raft and he started the small motor. At the *Tiger Lily*, he guided Sean up the ladder then he followed, and by the time everything was loaded and the raft secured, the sun had fallen out of sight, and dusk was fully upon them.

Sean wondered about Nathan as she watched him walk around his vessel; moving with such confidence, as though each thing he touched, he'd done it a thousand times before. It came naturally, so it seemed. As if he hadn't lost faith in himself after his fiancée had drowned. As if he didn't hold himself responsible.

Sean could tell he did. She'd seen it in his eyes, and there'd been pain there. A lot of it.

For the first time, Sean Jacobs, it doesn't hurt so much to remember.

Nathan had said those words to her. Had spoken them with his voice, accompanied by that profound emerald stare. He'd meant it. And Sean was stunned by how happy that fact made her. To watch him now? To see his confidence as a live thing? He did indeed look like a fierce pirate. Maybe one who wasn't feared, but rather one admired.

Her eyes followed him, his movements, and when he caught her staring, she blushed and pretended she hadn't been so engrossed by turning her gaze to the sky.

She didn't miss the sound of his soft laugh.

Sean leaned back, watching the darkening sky and the twinkling stars that were beginning to make an appearance. "How do you think Willa and Jep are doing?"

"We didn't get a distress call on the radio," Nathan commented, "so I imagine they're still knee-deep in the chess game. Jep can play for hours."

"Is that why no one can beat him?" Jep had claimed as much, saying he was, by far, Cassabaw's one and only chess champion.

Nathan nodded. "That's exactly why no one can beat him. No one else has his patience."

The *Tiger Lily* purred to life, and Nathan set sail. As they continued along, seagulls kept pace with the trawler. Sean again glanced skyward. "How can you navigate in the dark?" she asked. "How do you know the way home?"

Nathan pointed upward, and Sean noticed a rather large star blinking in the sky.

"First star to the right, then straight on till morning," he said with a grin as he quoted Peter Pan's directions to Neverland. "Want to take the wheel?"

"Oh," Sean said, shaking her head. "I probably shouldn't."

"Come on," Nathan urged, and beckoned her. "There's nothing to it."

"Really?"

Nathan nodded, his gaze steady. "I give you my word."

Somehow, Sean felt that Nathan's word, no matter in what context it was given, was a big, big deal.

Moving toward Nathan, Sean slid behind the wheel. Behind her, the hulking sea captain of the *Tiger Lily* reached around her, grasped her hands in his large ones and placed them correctly on the ship's wheel. His presence, his body so close to hers, caused her to shiver even in the sweltering Carolina summer evening.

"Just keep your eyes fixed straight ahead," he said, bending close to her ear.

Sean did as he said and watched the water ahead as she gripped the wheel.

"You're doing great," Nathan said, and he ducked around to look at her. "I think you're ready to be promoted to lieutenant."

"Really?" Sean said, chancing a glance at him. "So soon?"

"You catch on pretty fast. Confidence," he replied and leaned closer. "I like that."

Sean couldn't help but wince against the wind. She was anything but confident. How could he not see it? Fear raced through her, even as she gripped the wheel as tightly as she could.

As evening grew hazy and shadowy, Nathan took the wheel, directing them through the sound and up the river. Overhead, more and more stars gathered to twinkle. Before the Malones' dock came into view, a little voice carried over the marsh.

"Captain Nathan! Mama! Is that you?" Willa called out.

Nathan flashed Sean a grin, then reached over and blasted the horn.

When it stopped, Willa's squeals of laughter rang out.

Sean couldn't stop smiling at the sound of it, and when she turned to thank Nathan, he wiggled his eyebrows. Sean shook her head and giggled.

It almost made her breath catch. Giggled? When in God's name had she last done that? Other than with Willa?

She couldn't even remember.

Nathan navigated the *Tiger Lily* close to the dock, and Eric was there to lash the tie-downs. Willa hopped, waving a large…something in the air with one hand. Nathan climbed down then helped Sean over the edge and onto the dock.

"Mama! Look what me and Jep made," Willa said, waving a large cookie that was almost too big for her one little hand. "They got raisins."

"They have raisins," Sean corrected.

"They do!" Willa agreed, and hugged Sean around the waist. She looked up, revealing the cookie crumbs that dusted her chin. "I missed you, Mama. Did you have fun with Captain Nathan?"

"I sure did," Sean confessed, and noticed Nathan grinning as he finished tying down the trawler.

"Mama, can we get a chessboard?" Willa asked. "Jep taught me to play and it's really fun. I beat Mr. Eric at a game."

"Did not!" Eric teased.

"Oh, yes, I did!" Willa called back.

"Everybody beats Mr. Eric," Jep joined in. He turned a gaze to Sean. "She's got a good eye for the game."

"I hope she didn't cause you any trouble," Sean said. She knew Willa minded her manners, but she wanted to check all the same.

"She's fine company," Jep admitted. "Was quite a good help in the kitchen, too. We made oatmeal cookies."

Sean laughed. "So she told me." Placing her hands around Jep's, she gave them a gentle squeeze. "Thank you for watching out for her."

By the beam from the dock lights, Jep's tanned cheeks stained red. "Well. She was no trouble." He eyed her daughter. "I imagine I'd like it if she came and visited some more. Since she can carry a decent conversation and all."

"Can I, Mama?" Willa begged. "King Jep's fun."

Nathan and Eric burst out laughing, and Sean had a hard time not joining them. Instead, she eyed first Jep, then Willa. "Yes, since you were such a good girl and minded your manners, you can come back some time."

"Thanks, Mama! And Mama, do you think we can get King Jep a pair of wings like mine? I think he really likes them."

Sean smiled and slipped a glance at Jep. On his weathered face was the funniest of expressions, with his eyebrows furrowing into a mock frown but the corners of his mouth lifted into an unstoppable grin.

"I like 'em good enough," he agreed.

Sean looked at Willa. "What do you tell King Jep?"

Willa ran to Jep and threw her arms around his waist. "Thank you so much, King Jep, for letting me come over to play chess with you and make cookies."

Jep's expression softened. He gave Willa a firm pat on the back. "Well, you're welcome, missy. You're very welcome. Come again soon, will ya?"

"Yes, sir!" Willa exclaimed.

Sean found Nathan watching the exchange, then suddenly, his eyes shifted to meet hers. For a moment they just...stared, as if everything hung, suspended in midair. What was it about this family? This place. This *guy*? How welcoming and accepting they were of her and Willa. Without really knowing much at all about Sean, they'd accepted what she'd told them, without further questions, without harassment. It made Sean feel almost a part of their very solid and affectionate unit. She knew they were still curious—she'd given them only a handful of half facts. But they hadn't pushed.

She liked that. Respected it. And she loved how they all teased one another. Lovingly so.

Very briefly, she imagined what it would be like to *really* be a part of it.

Of *them*.

CHAPTER TEN

HER PRESENCE IN the cab of the truck almost overwhelmed Nathan.

All at once, he saw Sean Jacobs. Really saw her. Could feel her…everywhere. No longer just a pretty face. She'd let him into her private life. Not all of it—that much was obvious. But some of it. Maybe more than she'd wanted. She'd wanted to be a Jedi Knight, of all things. All the nights he'd lain awake thinking about her became completely clear.

She was unique. Unlike any woman he'd ever known. She was selfless. She put others way before herself. She was a really great mother. The love he saw in her eyes when she looked at Willa stunned him. She'd clearly had a fear of the sea, yet she had put her trust in him. It'd jump-started a bit of confidence he'd thought had long ago left him. And it felt good.

He was drawn to her in ways he'd tried to deny at first. Mainly because of the memory of Addie. He'd somehow felt as though he were betraying his fiancée by merely being attracted to Sean. And he'd been attracted to her since the first time he'd laid eyes on her. But now? He saw so much more than her surface beauty. He suspected she still hid something from him. From the world. He couldn't imagine what it was. Did it have to do with Willa's father? Aside from the revelation she'd thought she loved the guy, she never, ever mentioned him. Perhaps Nathan need never know. It was her past. Just like he had a past.

This? This was now.

And he'd felt something shift in his world. He'd confessed his loss of Addie. And not only had Sean expressed understanding, but also Nathan had felt it. Seen it in her eyes. He liked the way they sparkled when the laugh or smile truly came from within. Her eyes danced. Just as they had as he and she had shared their childhood dreams.

He had no idea where any of this would go, but for the first time in…since the accident, really, he wanted to give it a shot.

The question was, would Sean want to, as well?

He slipped a glance at her, over the top

of Willa's little head. Shadows raced across Sean's features as the moon shot through the trees down their drive, and her eye caught his as it had repeatedly since they'd gotten off the river. Her eyes seemed to shimmer as she looked at him, then she'd turn shyly away.

She was so damned beautiful.

So beautiful, it almost hurt to look at her.

Yet once he did look, and she looked back, he seemed paralyzed. Motionless in a fathomless gaze that called to him. That saying about eyes being the windows to souls? He completely understood the meaning of that now.

What he'd give for her to fully trust him. Nathan knew well that trust wouldn't come easy for Sean. She was alone with her young daughter, doing the very best she could to keep everyone around her at bay. Why? What was she so afraid of? Yeah, he wanted more than anything for Sean to turn loose her fears. To trust his family. To trust *him*.

It was something he was willing to work at to get.

By the time Nathan pulled up in front of Sean's house and put the truck in Park, little Willa had slumped against him and was fast asleep. Without thinking, he unclasped her seat belt and lifted her into his arms. He flashed Sean a grin. "I've got her."

In her slumber, Willa slipped her arms around Nathan's neck and snuggled against him. He patted her back as he climbed the porch steps. What a sweet kid, he thought. Sweet and alert and with a soul much older than her five years. Ahead, Sean opened the door and stepped inside.

"This way," she whispered, and led Nathan down a short dark hallway. At the end, Sean turned into a small room and clicked on the bedside lamp. Nathan laid Willa on the bed decked out with *Beauty and the Beast* bedcovers. She blinked her eyes open, focused on Nathan for just a second before she smiled, closed her eyes again and drifted back to sleep.

Nathan straightened, taken aback. Sean stepped in front of him, bent over and brushed a kiss across Willa's forehead. She whispered into her daughter's ear—something only Willa could have heard. Then Sean rose and smiled at Nathan.

"Ready?" she said.

Nathan nodded, and Sean flipped off the lamp and they left Willa to her dreams.

Silently, he followed Sean through the shadows of the house. At the front door, he paused behind her. Her eyes looked like the river in the moonlight. Shining. Dark. Wet.

"Thank you, Nathan," she said quietly, shyly. As if she wasn't used to being on a date at all. "I haven't had such a nice time in—" she gave a soft laugh "—well, in forever I guess. It's been a long time since I went out. On a date." She glanced away. "With…anyone."

"Well, if it makes you feel any better," Nathan said, trying to keep his voice down, "neither have I."

Sean looked at him again, and this time she studied him. As if she knew a little more about him than Nathan had let on. "Then I'm glad," she finally said.

"Glad?"

She nodded, shifted her weight and leaned slightly against the doorjamb. "Yes. Glad," she said. Cautious. Hesitant. "That you decided to ask me."

He knew he wanted to kiss her. Wanted to damn well stop thinking about it and just do it. When had he become so awkward? Why were his palms all sweaty? He balled his hands into fists. Yep, sweaty. What the hell was that all about?

Something about her. Something about Sean Jacobs made him pause, where in his teenaged years he would have dived right into it. It'd have been the kiss of a lifetime.

Now, with this woman? He waited. Maybe because he could sense she wasn't sure about him at all. The underlying layer of fear that Sean always seemed to have about her almost radiated now. Nathan could feel it in the air like a current of electricity. She wanted to bolt. Wanted him to leave. He should do that.

"Well," Nathan said at last, ready to end his misery. He shoved his hands into his pockets and backed away. "I'll see you tomorrow, then."

Sean kept silent for a moment, and that current grew denser between them. He couldn't help but notice how the light made her eyes look, like puddles in the ground after a nighttime rain. Dark pools, despite her eyes being hazel, but in the dark they seemed fathomless. The current zapped between them, almost as if the air surrounding them pressed inward, and closer.

"Okay," she said quietly. "See you then."

Nathan gave her a nod, turned and jogged down the porch steps. He got to his truck, put his hand on the door handle. And paused. His chest thumped a little harder. A little faster.

Nathan didn't think about anything else except moving faster. He bound up the porch steps and walked straight toward Sean. Her eyes widened just a little as he closed in, grasped her face in both of his hands and lowered his mouth against hers. She gasped, and he swallowed the surprised sound and kissed her. And when her mouth relaxed and she kissed him back, Nathan exhaled, his heart pounding, then kissed her deeper.

He abruptly pushed away, staring at Sean, and her gaze shimmered like a black liquid river in the light.

"I'm sorry," Nathan muttered, trying to shake off the pull he had toward her. It was too fast. It was all too fast. He knew it.

Despite the look of utter surprise, a very slight tilt to Sean's mouth caught him off guard.

"Don't be," she whispered, hesitated, continued. "Don't ever be."

Nathan blinked, and he knew he looked as off-kilter as he felt. But his brain went elsewhere, to a place where nothing else mattered except now. She didn't reject him. He stepped back to her, ducked his head and captured her lips once more, and she let him. The warm night air sifted between them, and to Nathan nothing tasted sweeter, and he kissed her hungrily. Everything about her was soft. Felt perfect. He shook, just trying to control where his hands went.

Sean kissed him back. Nathan's heart skipped.

His hands cupped her jaw, the back of her head, and he tilted her just right to fit his mouth. Her hands slipped to his chest timidly, then caressed his beard, then her fingers sank into his hair. Nathan groaned and kissed her deeper.

Then he forced himself to settle down, slow down, stop. He rested his forehead against hers and breathed, keeping up with her ragged breaths.

Neither said a word—didn't move, only stood there. Recovering.

Slow. This had to go slow. He didn't want to move. Didn't want to break whatever spell they'd both fallen under.

Didn't want Sean to bolt.

Nathan chanced a glance. Sean's eyes were downcast. Her chest rose and fell a little slower now. Her small hands still clung to his neck.

"Hey, you," he said quietly, ducking his head to try to peer into her face.

Sean remained silent. Didn't move an inch, didn't say a word.

Nathan tucked his knuckle under her chin and tilted her gaze to meet his. Her eyes were large, round, shining in the soft light of the porch. "Hey," he repeated again. "Is this okay?"

His gaze focused on her lips, soft, full, as she pulled the bottom one between her teeth.

"I want it to be," she finally said, so quietly Nathan could barely hear her voice as it blended with the still summer night. Crickets and cicadas groaned through the marsh and trees, sounds Nathan knew well. Now they seemed magnified. Everything seemed... clearer.

"Then it will be." He swept her lips with his, a gentle, settling kiss that he really didn't want to walk away from. But he did. For now.

He dropped his hands from Sean's face, giving her a smile. "I'll see you tomorrow."

Sean's hand lifted and she touched her lips with her fingertips then smiled at him. "I'll see you tomorrow."

Nathan climbed in his truck and took off into the dark, down the long drive, farther away from Sean Jacobs. Farther than he wanted to be at the present time. As he turned onto the road that led to his home, moonlight streamed through the windshield, and Nathan stared up at the large, illuminated globe that suspended in a sky so black, it looked like a blanket of ink hanging over Cassabaw.

How had this happened? One minute he was just living day to day. Not thinking anymore of a happy future, with a wife, kids, a family of his own. Things he'd dreamed of with Addie, and those dreams had been crushed right before his eyes. He'd thought he'd never again feel for another woman. Not like how he'd felt with Addie.

Sure, he'd settled into life on Cassabaw. With his family. With the shrimping business. That was all easy stuff. It'd been his life once. A part of him that had never extinguished. But he'd had love with Addie, and had lost it. He'd not put himself into any circumstances that would cause him to cross those boundaries he'd inadvertently set for himself. The hard stuff. He'd submerged into the safety net of the Malones. Of what he knew. It'd been easy, doing that.

This thing that was starting with Sean? It

was different. The draw he felt toward her overwhelmed him. Forced him over those boundaries he'd set. And that kid of hers? She'd had his attention from the moment he'd seen her jumping up and down waving on the dock, fairy wings flapping with each move she'd made. She had his heart, though, running through the cemetery catching fireflies. He may have appeared to have been simply jogging past, but he'd taken notice. It'd been an enchanting scene, Sean and Willa carefree in the dusk, wearing wings and jumping in the air. He now felt an intense desire to care for them both. Protect them.

Protect them from whatever it was that Sean feared.

Hopefully, she'd trust him. Trust him enough to let him in.

Let him protect her.

With one final glance at the moon, Nathan gave it a wink, almost a conspirator's gesture between the two of them. Sean had stirred something fierce in his heart. Something he'd thought had died that day in the Bering Sea with his fiancée. It hadn't died. It'd just been dormant. Hibernating.

Waiting, maybe, for Sean. For them. Sean and Willa.

A smile tugged at Nathan's lips. He pulled out onto the deserted road and headed home. His heart felt lighter tonight. Lighter than it had in years.

Maybe lighter than it had in forever.

Which made him pause and consider. *Everything.*

Nathan turned into his drive, pulled up next to the house and climbed out. Jep was in his usual place on the porch. Waiting for his usual slice of gossip.

That old man was as predictable as Christmas.

"So," Jep said in his raspy voice. Always tried to sound rougher than he really was, which totally cracked Nathan up. "Sit. What happened?"

Nathan took a seat on the top step. "What, do you want full details?"

"Hell, yes, I want full details," Jep answered. "Damn, son. What do you think I'm sittin' out here for all this time?"

Nathan shook his head. "I took her to the island," he started. "We ate. Talked. I showed her the Lost Boy tree."

"Ah," Jep crooned. "Got her with the old Lost Boy tree, eh?" He shook his head. "Good move, son. Good move."

Nathan laughed. "It wasn't a move, Gramps. We…connect." He met his grandfather's gaze in the darkness. "She's really special."

Jep watched him for a moment; long enough that Nathan recalled what it felt like to be ten years old again with an angry Jep staring him down for climbing the plum tree and knocking off the new buds. He almost squirmed before his grandfather spoke again.

"That she is, son," he said, his raspy voice quieter in the shadows than Nathan expected. Affection tinged his words. "So's that little girl of hers."

Nathan leaned his head against the post. "Yeah, I knew she'd have you wrapped around her little finger by the time we got back."

"Shoot," Jep grumbled. "She had me wrapped long before that."

They both chuckled in the darkness.

"Something's there, though," Jep added after a moment. "Can't quite put my finger on it. She has demons." He eyed Nathan. "Bad past? Ex?"

Nathan nodded. "Yeah, I get that, too." He

sighed, stretched his legs out straight and crossed them at the ankles. "I've got nothing, though. Other than my own observation. She is still packed up." When Jep cocked an eyebrow, he continued. "As in I get the feeling Cassabaw is just a stop along whatever journey she's on. I'm hoping she'll trust me enough to open up. Let me in. Let me help."

Jep nodded in approval. "Yep. That's my boy."

Nathan pushed up and stretched. "I'm hittin' the sack, Jep. See you in the morning."

"Did you at least kiss her?" Jep pushed.

At the screen door, Nathan stopped and grinned. "That, you nosy, old man, is none of your business."

"I'll take that as a yes," Jep concluded, nodding. He gave his rocker a push, and it creaked under his weight. Another familiar sound to Nathan. "Night, son."

With a shake of his head, Nathan left Jep on the porch with his thoughts and headed upstairs. He brushed his teeth and stared hard into the mirror. Turning his head side to side, he inspected his beard. Maybe a little trim wouldn't be such a bad thing. He didn't want to look like a thug. *The pirate look isn't so had. Maybe just not such an unruly one.* He stroked the beard he'd let grow a little wild, then dug his clippers out of the vanity drawer and set to work.

WHAT ARE YOU DOING, Sean?

She lay in bed, the covers pushed off, the soft whir of the ceiling fan going round and round above her. She'd started counting the rotations, since the fan was on low speed. She'd made it to 1,032. She could count no more.

Nathan Malone.

Why hadn't she met him years ago? Why now?

When she couldn't really and truly have him?

She'd been on the run for a long, long time. Somehow she'd managed to keep one step ahead of getting caught. Well, except in Norfolk. She'd had the distinct feeling she was being watched. There was no way possible that Willa's father knew she even existed, unless he'd been able to get a photo of Willa. If that was the case, then there'd be no question who her father was. Willa had his eyes. She looked just like him. Yet, she had her own look, too. The look that made her exclusively Willa.

Still, if Sean had been found in Norfolk, there was a chance she'd be found in Cassabaw.

And no way did Sean want the Malones to be any part of that. So, knowing all of what she knew, of consequences, of the secrets she kept buried, how could she fully let herself keep what she'd found in Nathan and his family? It wasn't fair to them. It wasn't fair to Willa.

Sean was being about as selfish as she'd ever been in her life.

Closing her eyes, she sighed, opened her eyes again, rolled onto her side, tucked her folded hands beneath her head and stared out the window that looked over the marsh. The moon hung low, like a giant yellow ball suspended in the night sky. Its light bathed a path over the dock, across the backyard and onto the deck.

She sighed once more, a gusty sigh. The way Nathan made her feel with just a single, profound look. Those green eyes held so much pain, and now so much hope. He looked at her as if she were…special. Worthy.

He didn't know her. Not at all.

And he never, ever could. It left her frustrated. Angry. Did she deserve it? This self-imposed purgatory? Maybe she did. Yet, she couldn't help but fall under the lure of normalcy. Of a guy and a girl. Of raging attraction. Of a connection.

A vision of his features bathed in shadows as he strode directly up to her, not even slowing down, bounding up the steps to grasp her face and kiss her senseless. It was like a movie inside her mind, one that ran on an endless reel. She'd have to remember it, just like that. Just as it was. A perfect memory to keep her company on lonely nights. When she felt as though the world was closing in on her. It'd be a balm of sorts. When she felt overcome by secrets, by running away. He'd be there, kept safe in yet another secret. A secret place only she knew about. A place for which she could fetch the key and let his memory out, and it would soothe her. She'd carry that memory of him for the rest of her life.

Her fingertips grazed her lips where he'd kissed her. Tasted her. She'd fallen under his touch, and could still sense the wobbliness of her knees as his hands had caressed her skin. The closeness of his body to hers, and the way he'd crowded her possessively. God, she wished it could last. Wished she could be free to be the woman who would forever make it less painful for Nathan to talk about his past, about his loss. She wished she had the freedom to spend evenings with the Malone family, laughing and teasing with such affection. Or that she could be the woman who could offer her child a family. A great-grandfather in Jep, and a grandparent in Owen. Aunts, uncles—an entire unit. Something she'd never had, either. Why couldn't she make it different for Willa?

And the way Nathan had taken to her daughter? The way his whole family had taken to her and Willa? Never in a thousand years would Sean have ever predicted stumbling upon such a treasure as the Malones when she'd set her and Willa's course for Cassabaw Station.

Was it a mistake? Coincidence? Luck?

Fate?

Sean rolled onto her stomach, punched her pillow a few times, then flopped against it, considering her questions. Mistake? More than likely, yes. Because when the day came that she and Willa had to pack up and leave again, it was going to kill her. This time, it'd hurt Willa, too, because she'd grown quite fond of Jep in a very short time. So yes. Probably a mistake.

Luck? No way. Sean never had luck. Ever.

Coincidence? Well, she simply didn't believe in coincidence. She believed in black and white. Not that mystical gray area in between. Did coincidence lean closer to the gray? How could it? So what was black and what was white? Decision? Choice? She'd made decisions. She'd made choices. There had been consequences. Not coincidence. Everything she'd done reflected in the dilemma she faced now. The past that chased her and Willa.

She rolled onto her back, her eyes focused on the whirling fan once again. That left fate. Fate could possibly be just as mystical and far-fetched as coincidence. Fate was like Santa Claus and the Tooth Fairy.

Right?

Did she dare to believe in fate? Coincidence, in Sean's book, had more substance. More science. Fate, on the other hand, seemed…magical.

If only she believed in that.

Sean wanted her brain to stop moving and shuffling, just for a moment. Just for once, let her and Willa simply…*be.*

Thump.

The unexpected noise coughed through the stillness of the room, and Sean all but jumped out of her skin. She bolted upright, staring into the moonlit room, straining her ears. What was that? A pinecone dropping onto the roof? Quietly, she climbed from bed, padded over to the window and stared out.

There were at least a gazillion squirrels living in the canopy above their river house. Maybe one had dropped a pinecone. Or a branch had fallen. It sounded faint, yet connected to the house. Close enough to make her jump out of bed.

Sean's eyes scanned the yard and marsh beyond.

Creak.

Her heart leaped to her throat. That sound she knew. It came from the front porch. *Three boards from the top step.*

She moved then. From behind her bedroom door she grabbed the baseball bat she always had hidden there, and crept into the hallway. Easing to the front door, she listened, scanning the darkness. Was someone here? Trying to break in?

Was it *them*?

With her heart slamming against her chest, she lifted the white lace curtain that covered the living room window and peered out onto the porch.

Nothing. No one was there.

Scanning everywhere—beneath the magnolias, the yard beyond—Sean searched. It couldn't have been Nathan. Or any other Malone for that matter. Had they taken the time to come over, each and every one of them would have knocked on the door.

Thwack.

She gasped and gripped her bat, and her insides went cold as a raccoon jumped down from one of the porch chairs, just on the edge of her view. Another soon waddled into sight. She sighed in relief. Slowly, she padded to the door. Her fingers slipped around the bolt lock, and she cracked open the door.

"Hey! Psst. Go home, you two!" Sean startled the raccoons, and they took off down the porch, running in their funny, inch-worm, cat-like canter. She watched them scurry down the drive, out of the porch light's circle, then into the shadows where the darkness swallowed them up.

River raccoons. Like to have scared her to death.

She really, really needed to get a grip.

Not everything was sinister.

Especially in Cassabaw.

And no way could any of Chase Black's men have tracked her to this reclusive barrier island. No way. She'd chosen the location completely randomly. Had leased it using a burner phone she'd discarded in Virginia. She'd not picked up a new phone until South Carolina. Another burner. Untraceable. There was simply no possible way she'd been found again. She'd learned to be careful.

It was her overactive mind playing mean, awful tricks on her.

With a heavy sigh, she made her way down the hall. She peeked in on Willa, who was sound asleep with her arms stretched out wide like angel wings, and that made Sean smile. She set her weapon behind the door and climbed into bed.

Regardless of luck, or fate, or mistakes or coincidences, she and Willa had a date later with a handsome pirate.

And for once in her life, Sean would push her past and fears behind her and just enjoy being on a date with a handsome, sweet man who thought she was, indeed, something else.

And as slumber finally closed in on her, she prayed Nathan would never find out the truth about her.

CHAPTER ELEVEN

Houston, Texas

"ARE YOU SURE this time, Mitchell?"

"I am, Mr. Black," the voice said. "I told you I'd catch up with her. I admit, it wasn't easy. She's a slippery one. She's changed her hair color, chopped it all off, too. But it's her. And the kid's still with her."

"How old is the kid?" Chase was curious about this kid, had had time to think about it.

"I don't know," Mitchell said. "Four, three maybe? Hard to tell. She's pretty small."

Chase Black leaned back into the plush leather chair and grasped a silver-tipped fountain pen between his fingers. Didn't really fit his timeline. She must have hooked up with someone along the way. "I want you to watch them for now. Be discreet. I don't want her alerted. Or anyone else for that matter."

"I know discreet."

"Make sure that you do," Black stated. "I'm leaving the country for business. I'll contact you."

"Yes, sir—"

Black ended the call abruptly. He'd said what he needed to say. Setting the pen carefully on his desk, he leaned back, steepled his fingertips and swiveled his chair to stare over the dark Houston night. Lights flickered like a pulse, as though the people down below were plugged in somehow. Like drones, maybe? All running, running, always on the move.

So, little Sara had tried to change herself. Obviously, she'd changed her name. She should know by now that when Chase Black wanted something, Chase Black got it. Despite where she came from. He'd cleaned her up, had given her a damned good life. Got her out of that bar, put a rock on her finger. He'd taken a street orphan and turned her life around. Gave her things she'd only dreamed of. And she'd taken off.

His eyes narrowed as he stared out into the night.

No gratitude.

Reaching over, Chase clicked off his desk lamp and sat in the shadows.

She would come to appreciate him again. She was the kind of woman, despite her roots, whom he just couldn't shake. She had fire. Determination. Despite her petite size, she was fearless. And smart.

Moreover, she knew a little too much about his business.

Again, he smiled. Besides, no doubt she'd want only the very best for the child.

She'd just need convincing.

He was exceptional at convincing.

Cassabaw Station

"MAMA, HOW MUCH LONGER before we go home?"

Sean peered through her sunglasses at her daughter as they walked along the boardwalk. She bent close and half turned Willa's narrow shoulders to face the ocean. "Well," Sean said, pointing with her finger, "we have to wait until Captain Nathan and Mr. Owen haul in their shrimp. See way out there? They are on the *Tiger Lily* right now catching lots of shrimp to sell. It kind of takes a while to go all the way out there and back."

Willa shielded her eyes and stared off toward the sea. "Yeah, I guess so." She looked at Sean. "So how many hours?"

Sean grinned. "Why? Excited about tonight?"

Willa squinted as she grinned against the sunlight. "I am! We get to go in the lighthouse!" She jumped up and down with excitement, clapping her small hands together. She pointed behind them. "It's just right there, too, Mama. Do you think we'll get to go all the way to the top?"

Sean peered at the black-and-white giant Willa pointed to. It almost seemed to disappear into the clouds, it was so tall. "All the way, Willa." She grasped Willa's hand. "Let's finish our walk and head home to get ready. Captain Nathan will be by to pick us up in a couple hours."

"Yay!" Willa exclaimed, and held tightly onto Sean's hand. They started down the wooden boardwalk, retracing their steps, passing tourists as they strolled in and out of the shops, with their colorful awnings, lining the waterfront.

Just as they neared the end, a cheerful voice called out. "Sean! Willa!"

They turned to find Nathan's sister-in-law, Emily, waddling down the steps of her café, the Windchimer. Dozens of sea-themed chimes clanked and tinkled in the wind where they hung from the outdoor sitting pavilion. Wearing white shorts and a blue-and-white-striped tank top, Emily approached. She had a white bandanna pulling back her long auburn hair. She looked like she'd stepped right out of the 1940s.

Emily beamed with joy. Sean recalled feeling that same joy when she'd carried Willa. Although she'd been scared at what being a single mom meant, she'd reveled in the little life that had grown inside her. It was a feeling she'd never forget.

"What are you two up to?" Emily asked, smiling.

"We're going on a date with Captain Nathan in two hours!" Willa exclaimed. "He's going to take us into the lighthouse when nobody else is there." She leaned toward Emily, motioning for her to lower her head. Emily bent, her ear close to Willa's cupped hand. "It's a secret tour," Willa whispered loudly.

Emily rose. "Is that so?"

Willa's head bobbed in agreement.

"Well," Emily said, shifting her gaze between Sean and Willa. "You two must be very important to Captain Nathan." She winked at Sean. "He doesn't just take any ole body up in the lighthouse after hours."

"Really?" Willa asked.

"Really," Emily said solemnly.

Sean felt her cheeks grow warm. "We're…" she started to say, and glanced at Willa. "We're really grateful that all of you have been so kind."

A knowing smile lifted Emily's lips. "The Malones are a very special family. Hey, do you guys want a sandwich? We can get Anna to whip us up something at the Windchimer before she leaves for the day. The Irish Club is my favorite lately," she said. She grinned at Willa. "I'm *always* hungry these days."

"Me, too! Can we, Mama?" Willa asked.

"Thank you," Sean accepted. "That'd be great."

They followed Emily into the café. The colors were darker inside, with polished wood, and the space was decorated with Gatsby-type antiques. Prints of mermaids and mermen hung here and there, and even the hanging lampshades had mystical sea scenes. Old tinny music played softly through the speaker system, and Sean felt as though she'd stepped back in time.

"Pull up a stool," Emily invited at the bar.

As Sean helped Willa scoot up, she noticed

the bar top had a penny top that stretched the length of the café.

"This is an amazing place, Emily," Sean commented, running her hand over the bar top then pulling up a stool. "Did you do all this?"

Emily gave a soft laugh as she settled onto a stool. "Not without gobs of help," she admitted. "The Beasts of Utah Beach helped nearly every day, and more than half of the pennies here came from them," she said, and there was love in her voice. Love and admiration.

"Who are they?" Sean asked.

"You'll find them here most mornings, sitting outside having their coffee and retelling tales of the old days and baseball, mostly. World War II vets and their wives. All in their nineties now. Four brothers, all in Normandy on D-Day. Quite an impressive group of guys." She brushed her fingertips over the bar top. "They helped put this bar together. There are quite a lot of pennies in here from the war. When we were renovating this place those old loves would sit in here with me for hours, setting the pennies in just so." She glanced lovingly at the pennies in front of her. "Matt, too. It was…an utterly extraordinary time in my life." She smiled at Sean. "I never thought I could be as happy as I am now."

Emily's joy seeped straight into Sean, and she couldn't help but return the smile wistfully. "It shows," she said. "You literally glow."

"Hey, Ms. Emily, what can I get you guys?" A young girl appeared from the kitchen.

"What would you like Ms. Anna to fix you, sweetie?" Emily asked, leaning forward to peer at Willa, who sat on the stool, swinging her little legs. "Anything you like."

Willa pondered the question. "Even a peanut butter and jelly sandwich?"

Emily laughed. "A girl after my own heart. How about you, Sean?"

"Whatever you're having."

"Ms. Anna, could we please have two Irish Clubs and one very special peanut butter and jelly?"

Anna grinned. "You got it, Mrs. M."

They chatted while Anna made their sandwiches, and despite her intentions of not getting too involved with this family, this place, it was unavoidable. The draw of the Malones, of Cassabaw, tugged at her insides like a physical vise. Their bond as a family—something Sean had lacked as a child—was the biggest enticement for her. How she would have loved to have a sister, or brothers. A grandfather. Parents. Things most people took for granted, perhaps. She, however, most certainly did not.

"How did you and Matt meet, Emily?" Sean asked.

"We grew up together," Emily said, her face beaming. "We were best friends. I spent more time at the Malones' than I did my own house, it seemed." Her expression fell a bit. "My parents were killed in a car accident, and my sister and I left to live with our grandparents in Maryland. Matt and I spent our entire teenage years and early twenties apart. I moved here when my aunt Cora passed away, leaving the Windchimer and our childhood home to Reagan and me." She shrugged. "The moment I saw Matthew Malone I knew I'd marry him." She winked. "Only, he needed a little convincing at first."

"Convincing about what?"

All three girls jumped at the deep, raspy voice that spoke from behind them. Matt sauntered up to his wife, wrapped his arms around her waist, then nuzzled her neck. "What stories are you fabricating about me, woman?"

Emily giggled and lifted her face to his, and

he rewarded her with a quick kiss on the lips.

"See?" Emily commented, leaning against her husband's chest. "When I first came back to Cassabaw, Mattinski here was a big fat Grinch."

Sean glanced at *Mattinski*, who merely shrugged.

"I worked super hard to drag my funny, lighthearted Matt out of his grumpy old shell." She patted the muscular arm that draped protectively around her belly. "It was worth every single second."

"Are you a pirate, too?" Willa asked. "Like Captain Nathan?"

Matt lifted one dark eyebrow. "Maybe."

Willa beamed. "Cool."

Matt gave Sean a wink then kissed his wife. "I've got that order you placed last week."

"Ooh, the part for the gramophone? Swell! You're going to fix it now?"

"I am," Matt confessed. "Thought you'd want it working properly for the Fourth."

"You thought exactly right," Emily said. "Thanks, darling."

Matt winked again. "See ya later."

"Not if I see you first," she teased back. The middle Malone brother walked out with a grin on his handsome face, shaking his head.

"What's a gramophone?" Willa asked, tracing pennies in the bar with her little finger.

"Well," Emily said, "it's a superold kind of music recorder. When Mr. Matt has it fixed, I'll let you see it."

"Oh, thank you!" Willa exclaimed.

Just then, Anna appeared with the sandwiches and a pitcher of tea, and they all dug in. The Irish Club was piled high with corned beef, slaw, Swiss cheese and some kind of delicious sauce, all on toasted rye bread, sliced thick. Willa's sandwich was made with homemade strawberry jam that Emily herself had canned. Sean had accepted a taste when Willa had offered it, and it was indeed superyummy, as her daughter had claimed.

"Good, huh?" Emily said with a mouth half-full, nodding in her own agreement. "This child is going to come out wanting corned beef instead of milk."

Sean smiled, noticing the small freckles across Emily's nose.

"You know, Nathan's changed," Emily said between bites. Her gaze darted to Willa, who was busy playing one of the little peg games that were scattered around the café. "Since he's met you two."

Sean took a sip of tea and dabbed her mouth with a napkin. "How so?" She was curious about Nathan's change. Was she truly responsible for it? The thought of carrying such heavy responsibility as another person's happiness—other than Willa's, that is—left a veil of fear inside. Yet, strangely, hearing the words gave her a thrill, as well.

"Well," Emily began, "after his fiancée died, he sort of...gave up. On life, on happiness." She held Sean's gaze. "On love. And it wasn't anything overt. He didn't brood, or mope around. At least, not since I've been back. But there was something missing inside him. Very noticeable to me, from the Nathan I knew before." Warmth and sincerity infused her eyes. "I see that old Nathan now. His spirit is lighter. His smile comes faster. And I really, really love that.

"I know for all those changes to happen within Nathan, something powerful stirs inside him. He doesn't make a change like this on a whim. He's sincere." She gave a soft laugh. "They all are. Sincere, protective and loyal... like you'll never encounter again. Ever. I swear it." She took a sip of tea, and nodded. "I just wanted you to know that."

In other words, don't break his heart.

It wasn't a warning, really. Sean knew Emily spoke from her heart, and she couldn't blame her. They were, indeed, a rare breed, the Malones. She had no intention of hurting any of them.

Especially Nathan.

Then again, she really hadn't meant to grow so fond of them, either.

"Thank you," Sean told Emily. "I feel grateful that Willa and I met all of you. Nathan is unlike anyone I've ever known."

"And we're just as happy to have met the two of you, as well." Emily grinned wide, showing off a dimple. "You fit right in."

Those four words wormed their way into Sean's brain and sat there for the rest of the day. Had she ever fit in with anyone? Yet, she truly did feel as though she and Willa belonged. It warmed her heart to think an entire family, strangers not so very long ago, felt that she and her daughter were worthy of their affection. Willa, sure—she could wiggle her way into anyone's heart without the least bit of trouble. But Sean Jacobs hadn't ever belonged.

For the first time, she felt she might. Despite that revelation, a feeling of weightiness lingered in her chest. Did she deserve a place here? What if she could never live up to the Malones? The very things she'd been hiding and running from might surface. That old self, her old life, was something the Malones didn't need. Right?

The rest of the afternoon went by quickly. And the closer the time came for Nathan to pick her and Willa up, the faster her heart beat and the more that silly feeling stirred inside her stomach. All at the mere thought of seeing him again.

By six o'clock, Willa was running around with her wings on, peeking out the window in hopes of catching the first sight of Nathan.

"Mama, can I wait for him on the porch?" she asked.

Sean smiled. "Sure. Just stay on the steps, okay?"

"Okay!" Willa exclaimed, dashing outside. The screen door creaked before it slammed shut, and Sean shook her head then checked her image in the hall mirror once more. She'd looked at least a dozen times since pulling on the little floral sundress and sandals. A plain dress. Plain brown sandals.

On her plain ole self.

She fingered her pixie-styled hair, the bangs just long enough to tuck behind her ears. Her hazel eyes, which seemed too wide for her face, stared from the depths of the mirror. At first glance, she simply appeared plain, average, just a young mother. Unfortunately, she knew the true person behind the image in the mirror. All the secrets she held. The life she once led. She used to not be so plain, that was for sure. Far from it. A vastly different image used to stare back at her. One she was…so very ashamed of.

What would the Malones think of her if they knew?

What would Nathan think?

Sean's heart sank. That feeling, as if something heavy sat upon her chest, assaulted her. She knew good and well what Nathan would think—what they'd all think. Even being nonjudgmental, loving and kind people, they'd only be able to judge the bare truth staring them in the face. A vision flashed of Nathan, of his expression of disgust at finding out how she used to make her living. Of how she'd lived on the streets, homeless. The times she'd steal. And…worse.

And that was why they must never, ever know.

“Knock, knock,” a deep, raspy voice called from the porch.

“Mama, Captain Nathan is here, and wait till you see him!” Willa called out through the screen door.

Sean turned, and her heart leaped when she saw the man staring back at her.

“Wow.” The word slipped from Sean’s mouth before she could stop it.

Nathan grinned, inspecting her from head to toe. “Took the word right out of my mouth. You look…” The smile on his mouth widened. “Beautiful.”

Words failed Sean. She felt the blush creep up her throat and settle into her cheeks, but still she couldn’t tear her eyes off him.

He’d shaven. Not clean-shaven, but he’d trimmed his beard down to a dark, well-groomed scruff on his jaw. He’d trimmed his hair, too. Still longish—longer in the front, perhaps, since he may have cut it by himself. It fell in sun-tousled waves to his collar, the bangs pulled back as was his usual fashion. He wore a long-sleeved white button-down shirt, sleeves rolled up, and a pair of well-worn jeans that clung easily to him.

He looked drop-dead gorgeous.

"Mama! Captain Nathan is still a pirate, just a clean one," Willa exclaimed, jumping around him.

Nathan grinned, and Sean smiled in return. "I see," Sean said softly, shyly examining his new cut. "A clean pirate, hmm? You look, well..." She shook her head in amazement. "You—"

Nathan was suddenly there, standing close, bending his head closer. "Literally take my breath away, Ms. Jacobs," he whispered, and grazed his lips across her cheek.

Sean's stomach dipped again, butterflies fluttering like crazy, and when Nathan pulled back, and those green eyes settled on hers with that merry, profound stare, her heart skipped a beat.

"Mama, why is your face turning so red? Captain Nathan, look at Mama's face," Willa said.

Willa.

The smile on Nathan's face stretched ear to ear, and he squatted beside Willa, rubbing his chin with thumb and forefinger. He leaned his head close to her daughter's, and the heat intensified in Sean's cheeks at his inspection.

"Would you look at that," he agreed with Willa, cocking his head to get a better look. "Why do you think that is, Princess Willa?"

Willa took the same inquisitive stance that Nathan had, rubbing her pointed chin in a similar manner. "Probably because she thinks you're handsome, Captain Nathan," she finally said.

"How do you know that?" Nathan asked.

Willa turned to him. "I don't know. Just probably, is all."

"Willa!" Sean laughed. "Honestly."

"What did she say exactly?" Nathan urged the five-year-old.

"We should be going," Sean exclaimed, guiding her daughter to the door, sufficiently quieting the loveable little tattletale. "Time to go to the lighthouse."

Willa started to jump up and down. "Yes! The lighthouse! Let's go, Captain Nathan."

Nathan rose, Sean gave him a mock frown, then together they headed outside to climb into the truck's cab.

As Sean tucked her legs inside, Nathan shut the truck door, grinning at her through the window.

Her heart fluttered as he got in on his side and started the engine, and they drove out onto the river road, toward the lighthouse.

Sean didn't want this feeling to ever end.

And as they traveled along the narrow two-lane road, with the sun dropping over the salt marsh, the light flickering as it shot through moss-draped live oak branches, she sighed in contentment.

Contentment? She'd only ever experienced a similar feeling the moment she'd held Willa in her arms for the very first time. This was different, though. A different sort of contentment. And for the very first time in her life, Sean felt as though she'd found a place in the world. A place where she and her daughter belonged, fit in.

Felt at home.

She felt as though she might have a shot at true love. Which was the absolute worst thing that could happen to her. Being happy, possibly sharing a life with Nathan, would do nothing but bring danger to them all. That danger was a very real threat.

Then again, perhaps she'd finally escaped the danger. Maybe, just maybe, she and Willa had become the ghosts she'd wanted to be all along. She'd covered her tracks. Backtracked, covered them again. How could her past, so many years behind her, still be such a threat? Had she become so paranoid? Had she built up the threat to be way, way larger than it truly was? Had she done so because she'd had nothing better to do than run?

Willa's safety had always been at the forefront of Sean's concerns. But how much damage was she causing her daughter by running? By not providing a safe, secure home. In one place. With family.

To Sean, a loving family had once been nothing more than fiction.

Was it much closer, much more obtainable than she'd truly believed?

And as Nathan and Willa started singing together to a Phil Collins song from the Disney movie *Tarzan*, she prayed fiercely fate was real.

And she prayed that fate wouldn't take away this extraordinary gift.

CHAPTER TWELVE

BY THE TIME Nathan parked the truck and they climbed out, the sky over Cassabaw had shifted from sky blue to lavender, striped with hues of sienna and rose as the sun sank into the horizon. The constant sea breeze caressed Sean's face and tousled her hair, and Nathan, walking beside her in the alabaster sand, slipped his hand into hers, winding their fingers together. For the hundredth time that day, Sean's heart surged.

He glanced down, a smile dancing in his eyes as he led her and Willa to the old lighthouse keeper's cottage. Around back, close to the dunes covered with wispy sea oats waving in the wind, a wooden swing hanging from a wooden frame faced the lighthouse.

Sean and Nathan sat close on it, hands clasped, and watched Willa as she ran along the dunes like a whimsical sea fairy, with her delicate wings flapping in the breeze behind her. They waited for the last tour to finish in the lighthouse, and it was so easy just being with Nathan. They connected. He didn't ask questions, never imposed demands. He simply…was there. All of him, there for her and Willa. Never had Sean encountered such ease and comfort in another human being, other than Willa. It completely astounded her. She liked the feeling. A lot.

"So tell me," Sean started to say, turning slightly to Nathan. He sat tall beside her, his muscular thighs taking up a good portion of the swing as he reclined in that easy way guys reclined, with legs spread just so, casual and carefree. The breeze lifted his hair from his collar, and his profile shined bronze in the fading sun. It was all Sean could do to keep her concentration. She cleared her throat. "Jep used to run around here as a little boy?"

Nathan laughed softly and nodded, pointing to the keeper's cottage. "There are photographs of Jep running with a kite—" he nudged his arm toward her "—much like this one, running around the dunes. Head full of crazy curls."

"Much like yours," Sean commented. "I can't wait to see."

Nathan's eyes were shining. His fingers

squeezed hers. "I like that you've taken to my family," he said. "To that crazy old man."

Sean laughed, and the breeze swallowed it up. "It's kind of impossible not to fall for that crazy old man." Sean dared to glance at their clasped hands, and again noticed the ring on his finger. It brought to mind an image of a young Jep, and how the sea influenced not only his own life, but the lives of his son, his grandsons. She wondered briefly what Jep had been like as a rescue swimmer. As a young man.

Sean focused again on Nathan's ring, silver in color, with a blue background on its face, decorated with gold anchors and engraved with the insignia. Sean scraped it gently with her finger. "You should be extremely proud of this," she said cautiously. "I don't want to unearth the hurt you bear, Nathan. I just want you to know what I think." She squeezed their fingers together tighter. "And I think you should be very, very proud."

Nathan's weighty stare lasted long enough to make Sean squirm, but she refused to look away. She hated the thought that he held himself responsible for his fiancée's death. Finally, his eyes softened.

"Thank you," he said, and held their hands up

to inspect the ring. "I've worn this for so long, it's became more of a habit than a conscious act of pride, like it used to be." He smiled. "I am proud of it. Thanks for the reminder."

It made Sean feel good to bring attention to something Nathan used to hold so special. She was glad he'd found it again. "You're very welcome."

"Hey, Captain Nathan, why are you holding Mama's hand?" Willa asked. She stood before them now, her bare feet sinking into the sand. The thoughtful expression lifted her eyebrows and scrunched her little nose. "Are you scared she's gonna fall or something?"

Nathan inspected Sean closely. "Yeah, maybe," he answered Willa. "I just want your mama to know I'm here to catch her," he said without breaking his gaze, "if she falls."

Sean's breath quickened.

"Did you hear that, Mama?" Willa said. "You don't have to be scared of falling. Captain Nathan will catch you!"

Sean nodded. "I know." And really, she couldn't think of another thing to say with Nathan looking at her the way he was. It'd been just Sean and Willa for so long. The thought of having someone—having Nathan—there to catch her if she fell? It almost seemed unfathomable to have a champion. Of having support, of having someone in her corner.

Just then a horn blasted, and Willa squealed.

"Last tour has ended," Nathan announced, and stopped the swing with his foot. "Are you girls ready for the personal tour?"

"Yes!" Willa exclaimed.

Together they walked, Willa between them, hand in hand, and entered the lighthouse by a side door marked Employees Only. Inside, Nathan led them through the main floor. Black-and-white photographs hugged the walls—pictures of a family, of a man and a woman, and their little boy, obviously adored. Some of the photos were a bit grainy, but there were a few of little Jep up close. Sean bent close to one showcasing a grinning little boy missing a front tooth. As they progressed farther around the circular wall, the photos showed Jep growing up. She spied a photo of him as a teen, standing next to his parents. She drew close and couldn't help the smile.

"Oh, my gosh, Nathan," she said, and he bent beside her. She turned her head and met his green gaze. "You do look just like him."

"Crazy, huh?" he said, and Sean could see the pride in his expression.

"That's King Jep?" Willa said, rising on her tiptoes to get a better view.

Nathan picked her up so she could look closely. "Yep. When he was just a young man."

They continued around the circular wall of photos, and as Jep Malone grew older, his parents did, as well. Soon Jep had a family, and a little boy of his own.

"Owen." Sean grinned.

"Yep," Nathan agreed. "The one and only."

Soon, Owen began to grow, have his own wife, then a son. Sean pulled close to the photograph. "Oh, my goodness," she said, and gave a soft chuckle. "Weren't you just adorable?"

Nathan chuckled. "I certainly was."

"Can we climb to the top now?" Willa said.

"Absolutely," Nathan agreed. He set her down then led them to a single door. He opened it and gave a bow. "Ladies first."

Willa squealed and darted through, and began the long ascent to the top, Sean close behind her with Nathan bringing up the rear. The stairwell was damp, somewhat musty, a lot salty and dimly lit. Finally, at the top,

Willa waited for Nathan to open the door with his key, then they walked out to the platform. The sun was nothing more than a fireball now, dropping inland behind them. Gulls cried and soared right by them, and Willa's little fingers wrapped around the iron rail as she squealed with delight.

"Mama, look. The birds are right there!" she said in amazement, and reached out as if to touch one. When a gull landed on the railing not five feet away, Willa's gape-mouthed expression made Sean and Nathan laugh.

"It must be really something," Sean said a few moments later as they watched the sky grow darker, and the faintest of stars emerged.

"What's that?" Nathan asked, and draped his arm over her shoulder, pulling her close to him.

"To know your family's history for generations," she admitted. She noticed the diamonds in the water, shimmering their last few sparkles of the evening. "To know where you come from, so far back." She looked at Nathan, only to find he was watching her closely. "To know who you are. Who your family is." She turned back to the sea. "To be proud of your lineage." Her thoughts skipped through her own childhood. She'd had lots of foster parents. Foster siblings. They'd not been bad. She, though, had been. She'd rebelled. Run away. Many, many times. She had no lineage. No heritage. Nothing substantial, anyway.

Nathan studied her for several moments. She could feel the weight of his stare, as though he could see through her skull and into her thoughts, before hitting a wall. "Some folks are lucky that way, I suppose," he said. "You know, long family history. But some..." He kissed the top of her head. "Some folks have to be the first. Be the ones who start the lineage. And that's something to be proud of, too, Sean." He turned her in his arms, and she allowed it. His head descended toward hers. "You've already started the cycle, right? Look at this amazing kid you've brought into the world." His lips found hers, and he kissed her gently, but the urgency was there, and Sean sank deeper into his arms.

Nathan ended the kiss and tucked her head beneath his chin. "I'm awfully glad you found Cassabaw Station, Ms. Jacobs," he said quietly.

Sean closed her eyes and simply breathed. The salty air mixed with Nathan's woodsy scent caused her to inhale deeper. "I am, too," she confessed.

And she meant it. Clear down to her bones. Just as fiercely as she knew that Nathan, his family, represented just as large, if not larger, a threat as her past. Despite the safety Nathan made her feel, she knew deep down how dangerous it was to remain. To keep…growing fonder. *To keep falling...*

Nathan had said she should be proud of the new lineage she'd started with Willa. Perhaps he was right. Maybe she had the right to start over, after all.

And be proud of the life she had now. Yet the ever-present underlying fear that someone would find them, would take Willa away, or hurt those she loved, clawed at her. Constantly. It was like a headache that wouldn't go away. It could fade, but it was still there. God, how she hated it. She wanted to barter for time. For just a small slice of happiness, without fear. *Just a little longer...*

After Nathan showed Sean and Willa the big nine-foot first-order Fresnel lens, they descended the station, and with Nathan holding her hand tightly, they walked the oceanfront boardwalk, lined with twinkling lights, to the small amusement park at the far end. There, Nathan helped them climb aboard a shining blue car on the Ferris wheel. With Willa between them, the wheel began its rotation, and Sean couldn't stop the smile as she watched the light shining in her daughter's eyes, and the admiration in Nathan's that made the emeralds sparkle. She noticed he spoke with his eyes—they'd soften, or turn a steely gray-green when he grew intense. He grazed her chin with his forefinger, his gaze lowered to her lips, and her heart did a flip. "I can't believe we're here. That I'm here. That…this is really happening."

"It is," Nathan said, his deep voice blending in the summer air.

Sean held his intense stare, stunned that she'd made such a confession. "I'm glad," she said. "Because if this is a dream, it's the best one I've ever had."

"Me, too!" chimed in Willa.

Sean laughed, and Nathan pulled her close.

It was a lot to take in.

She didn't want to let it go. Despite her paranoia, her fears of discovery, her past. She selfishly didn't want to let any of it go.

"Now you can see the whole of Cassabaw," Nathan said once their bucket reached the top of the wheel.

Sean looked out, so high up, amid the fall

of darkness. “It’s almost like we’re mingling with the stars,” she said, and noticed how many more had emerged. “This night was perfect, Nathan,” she said over Willa’s head. “Thank you.”

Nathan’s gaze stayed on hers. “It’s far from over, darlin’.”

The stain of heat hit her cheeks before she could turn her head.

Don’t let this end. God, please, don’t let it end.

CHAPTER THIRTEEN

"I'LL BE RIGHT BACK," Sean whispered as she cradled her daughter in her arms.

Nathan gave a nod and watched her disappear into the shadowy hallway, taking Willa to bed. Sean moved like a fairy herself. Her steps seemed effortless, and her body glided. Elegant, like a ballerina or something.

God, she's so pretty.

Inadvertently, Nathan's eyes moved to the boxes still sitting against the wall, and a slight fear gnawed in his gut. Even now, would she bolt? Would she leave Cassabaw in her dust, after he'd let her in? Jesus, he hoped not.

Rising from the sofa, he walked to the side door and let himself out onto the small deck that faced the marsh. The moon hung over the saw grass and oyster shoals, and the night crawlers and marsh birds rivaled in chorus. The evening had been perfect. Fun. They'd walked the amusement park, eating cotton candy and playing games after the Ferris wheel ride, and Willa's squeals of delight at winning a big stuffed bumblebee still pinched his heartstrings. What a cute kid. He couldn't remember when he'd had so much fun.

"Hey, here you are," Sean's soft voice sounded as she joined him. Nathan continued to stare out across the river, forearms resting on the old wooden railing of the deck. Finally, he straightened, turned to Sean.

The gentle expression on her face, bathed in moonlight, stopped whatever words he'd had dead in his throat. She stepped into his embrace, and he threaded his fingers through her hair and held her head with his hands, tilting it to just the right angle, then he closed his mouth over hers. Her hands slid up his chest and slipped around his neck as she rose on her toes, and Nathan let one hand drop to the small of her back, pressing her against him. Her sigh was audible, tangible, and he swallowed it whole.

When he deepened the kiss, Sean's mouth moved fiercer against his, and her lips parted. He tasted her, and she was sweet, soft, and when the slightest of moans escaped her throat, he hardened against her, breathed her in, then turned her in his arms so that her back was to the rail of the deck. In the still night air their breathing broke the silence, ragged, heavy, and he braced his weight on his hands placed on each side of her and dropped his mouth to her throat, kissing the hollow space at her collarbone, feeling her pulse there. His hands went to her hips, easing up her sides to cup her face and kiss her more deeply. Her hands quivered as she clung to him, and Nathan suckled first her bottom lip, then the corner. Finally, he pulled back, resting his forehead against hers.

Together, they caught their breath.

They stood there like that in the shadows, immersed in the sounds of the balmy summer night for several moments. Downriver, the faint voice of Ella Fitzgerald drifted through the marsh, and Sean's eyes turned up in the corners as she smiled. "Ella Fitzgerald," he said. "Em's playing her records." They listened for a moment, before another great song began. He smiled. "Billie Holiday. Big stuff." He shrugged. "We all grew up on the superoldies, blues, big bands of the thirties and forties. Some older."

"I love it," Sean admitted quietly. "There's something comforting about it, don't you think?"

Nathan's eyes searched hers. "Yeah, I do." He lowered his head again, and her mouth was there, and her lips so soft under his. He kissed and tasted her, but again pulled back. They listened to the old music, faint in the air.

"Why did you stop, Nathan?" she asked quietly, breaking their spell. "Did…I do something wrong?"

Nathan framed her face with his hands, and tilted her head until her gaze met his. He studied her, trying to find answers without asking, without seeking. He couldn't.

"Are you leaving here, Sean?" he asked quietly. Her brow furrowed slightly in confusion. "The boxes in your living room," he said by way of explanation. "I just keep wondering when you might actually unpack and settle in."

Sean's wide gaze, liquid in the darkness, stared at him. "Well, I…" She swallowed, seemingly fishing for words. "It's…a lot to consider, Nathan." She pressed her hand to her forehead, as though to smash the thoughts back into place. Clearly, he'd caught her off guard, and she didn't know what to do about it. "I've leased this place for the summer," she admitted. "When we arrived, that's all it would be. A summer escape. But then I met you—"

Nathan silenced her with his mouth. Holding her jaw firm with his hands, his mouth descending on hers with a fury, a fierceness, almost...a brand. She clutched his shirt in her fists, then slipped her hands around his neck and kissed him back, and again, Nathan stopped before he came unglued. He wanted her so bad, he hurt. He literally felt physical pain in his gut. But this wasn't the time. Wasn't the place.

He wanted it to be as perfect as the woman.

Sean's sexy gaze held his in the moonlight, and he dragged his lips over hers once more. "I don't want you to leave, Sean Jacobs," he whispered against her mouth. He kissed her again, slowly, and she groaned against his lips. "I really—" he kissed her lightly "—really—" he nipped her bottom lip "—want you to stay here."

When he finally lifted his head and stared at her, Sean's eyes were round, wet, and a timid smile tilted the corners of her beautiful mouth. "Really?"

He knew it was fast. All of it. Knew he'd

sound like a crazy man if he started making promises to Sean right now. Would telling her how just the thought of touching her, kissing her, kept him up at night make her turn tail and run? How about if he confessed that he recalled their conversations, their interactions, in his mind throughout the day? That his father had caught him smiling like an idiot? No, hell, no. He couldn't tell Sean any of that. It'd send her packing. It'd send any person with a lick of sense packing. Those confessions were too fast. He didn't want to push her away. He wanted to take time with her. Let her discover things on her own.

All he knew was that he wanted her to stay. Wanted her to be right here, just up the river, in Cassabaw Station. And he wanted her to not leave. Because he knew this thing they had was special.

It was meant to be.

Only, he couldn't tell her that, either.

Or could he?

He ducked his head and swept his lips gently over hers, settling there, and simply breathed. "I want you to stay, Sean," he mumbled against her, and tasted her lips once more. He lifted his head, staring down at her beautiful, surprised face. "Lease this place for a few more months. Let's see where this goes. Because the thought of you leaving?" He kissed her again. "It really, really doesn't seem like an option now."

The moon shone on Sean's face, giving everything a silvery glow, and to him, her features looked carved straight from marble. When she smiled? God and Jesus, he felt like someone had sapped all of his strength away. Like he'd been sucker punched in the gut. Like he did now.

"I can't think of a better place to stay," she said in the sweetest of voices. When she blinked it was as though everything had slowed down in time, like the effect a big, doe-eyed cartoon character had, only not comical. Sean Jacobs made him have hearts in his damned eyes, that was what.

Scary? Hell, yes. He wasn't sure why, but there was something telling him he needed to hold on to her tightly. That there was something that could make her run, despite her assurances. Unintentionally, he was positive.

She was just so damned sweet.

He grazed her cheek with his knuckle. "That's a good thing," he replied in as quiet a voice as he could muster. Because he wanted to punch the air and yell into the night. Shout as loudly as he could, release the excitement that had built inside him. But he didn't. Instead, he breathed. Smiled. "That's…a really good thing."

Sean leaned her head against his chest, and the intimate movement made Nathan's blood surge in his veins. He kissed the top of her head, and she snuggled closer. "Yes, it is," she replied.

Nathan lowered his head close, brushing his lips across her ear. "I'll talk to you tomorrow," he said quietly. "I've got to be on the water with Owen in a few hours." He kissed her cheek. "The next few days will be busy for us. Gearing up for the Fourth of July." He kissed her lightly on her forehead. "Can I call you?" He nipped her ear. Felt her shiver. Or was it him?

"Yes, call," Sean answered, and her voice came out a sigh.

One long kiss later, Nathan pulled back and looked down at her, grasped her hand in his, and they walked close, in silence, with only the night air and night creatures stirring. At his truck he swept her mouth with his once more, inhaling her scent, tasting the softness of her lips, her mouth. Her response to his kiss made that weak feeling come over him. Finally, he tore his mouth from hers and hugged her tightly.

"I'm forcing myself to leave now," he said with a chuckle, and climbed into the cab of his truck before he couldn't. He rolled the window down, and their eyes met in the darkness, a shy smile appearing on her mouth as she stepped back, folded her slender arms over her chest and waved. As Nathan drove away, he watched Sean graze her lips with her fingertips, and she lifted her hand once more to wave, and his heart skipped a beat at the entire scenario. Of the river, of the mournful words coming from an old blues singer, of the woman who now occupied his every waking thought.

He'd have to remember to thank his sister-in-law for the unintentional mood music.

The Malone house was quiet—even Jep had given up on getting any date gossip from him and gone to sleep—and Nathan climbed the stairs, brushed his teeth then fell into bed. He rolled off the mattress and walked to the window. Despite the heavy warm July air, he cracked his window until the voice of Ella Fitzgerald, coming from Emily's record player, drifted across the marsh and crept into his room. He dropped back into bed and lay there for several moments, and had to laugh at the irony of the song "If You Ever Leave."

Sean was staying. True, the house was a lease, but still. It was a start. Maybe she had finally found a home for her and Willa. A place they felt safe from whatever it was that had kept her on the run for so long. Hopefully, she'd one day open up and tell him what that threat was. He wanted more than anything for Sean to trust him. More than she did now.

Completely trust him.

Nathan smiled as his eyes closed, and contentment filled him, and sleep claimed him.

THE NEXT FEW days dragged slow and long as Nathan and Owen shrimped both tides. The fishing panned out. They caught more shrimp than they'd expected, and had even picked up an extra deckhand from the harbor—a young kid named Banjo—to help out. Nathan called Sean every day, usually at night before he crashed, and each afternoon when they'd head out for their second tide, Sean and Willa would be on their dock, Willa wearing her fairy wings, to wave them by. The sight stuck in

Nathan's head each day. It was just so damned cute, that little girl and her mama, waiting on the dock. For him. Waiting to wave. To *him*.

"Penny for your thoughts."

Nathan sat, perched on the side of the *Tiger Lily*, as they dredged the nets. He glanced up to a perfect, cloudless blue sky, listened to the dozens of gulls cry out for scraps, inhaled the salty air, then looked at his dad through his shades. "There's this girl," Nathan said. "She's kind of amazing."

Owen grinned, showing off the creases and lines he'd gathered over the past few years. "So I've noticed."

"You're a fairly good-looking Irishman, Owen Malone," Nathan said, studying his dad. "You've got all your hair, and aren't in bad shape for an old guy." Nathan patted his dad's abs, which luckily still had plenty of muscle. "Gives me hope for my own advanced years." He couldn't help but laugh as Owen shook his head.

"Thank you, Nathaniel, that's awfully kind of you to notice," his dad replied. "I'm happy my appearance suits you, and settles your fears of getting thin-haired and potbellied."

Nathan chuckled, and so did Banjo, who was

eating a sandwich he'd brought along as they waited to pull shrimp.

"You got something else to talk about, other than my physique?" Owen asked, leaning against the vessel's wheel.

Nathan's eyes shot to Banjo, who awaited his answer, then turned unashamedly to Owen.

"I asked Sean to stay on Cassabaw," Nathan admitted. "She said she would." He rubbed his jaw, only slightly missing the longer beard he'd trimmed. "But I have this feeling that, I don't know. Like it's going to be taken away from me. It's like some kind of unexpected miracle dropped in my lap. One day, I'm just going along, minding my own business of just accepting life as is, you know?" He shrugged. "Life without Addie. Life with the knowledge that I couldn't save her."

He stared at the deck below his feet, then across the sea. He stared so long, the gray water blurred. "Going through life seeing her standing there in the middle of that damned storm, waving at me, trusting me to save her. Then..." He turned his gaze to Owen. "Not seeing her at all. Ever again." Nathan took a deep breath. Let it out in a gusty sigh. "I'd really just resigned myself to accepting my life as it had become. Here, on the island, with my family. Then came along those two sweet girls. They just sort of…happened."

"Yeah," Owen said, walking over to stand before him. He clapped him on the shoulder and gave a firm squeeze. "I'm happy for you, son. You deserve it. But you can't spend your time worrying if Sean will change her mind. You have to either trust her, talk to her or… just accept whatever comes along."

Nathan nodded. "You're right, Dad. You're absolutely right." And he kicked off his worn white All-Stars. Already shirtless, he threw his leg up onto the rail and lifted up, standing, facing the sea. He threw a glance over his shoulder, at Owen and Banjo, who watched with wide smiles.

Then Nathan crowed, crowed like Peter Pan at his finest, and he did it again and again, louder and louder, the cawing sound echoing over the water until Owen joined him with his own crow, laughing. Then Nathan dived off the *Tiger Lily* and into the sea, amid the whitecaps and swooping gulls. The water closed over him as he dived in, warm and salty and familiar. Kicking to the surface, he turned onto his back and floated, and watched the blue sky above, and thought how lucky he was to feel so content. Happy. He'd trust her. If anything else came along, any kind of barrier? He'd deal with it then.

In his mind, and to his way of thinking, things could only get better.

"MAMA, MAMA, LOOK at that!" Willa exclaimed, her dark bob swinging as her head turned here and there. "Just look."

Sean took in the view. "I see, baby, I see." The four o'clock beachfront was packed with tourists and locals alike, gathering for the Cassabaw Fourth of July festivities. Large red, white and blue banners stretched between two long wooden poles at the entrance to the beach. A jazz band played at the end of the pier, the strains of bygone music wafting on the warm breeze. The storefronts were all festooned with something patriotic—banners, balloons, wind socks. Each store had pulled merchandise onto the boardwalk, selling their products with special Fourth of July prices. Food stands were set up along the beachfront offering everything from funnel cakes to Hendrik's hot dogs, from a chili pot cart to a snow cone vendor. The afternoon breeze picked up, coming in from the ocean, and the salty air settled into her lungs, and when she licked her lips, she could taste the salt there, too.

As well as the memory of Nathan's mouth against hers.

That thought left a slight shiver behind, despite the warmth of the day.

"Mama, where's Captain Nathan?" Willa asked, tugging on Sean's hand.

Willa was adorably dressed in white shorts, blue Keds and a red tank top covered with blue and white stars. And, of course, her fairy wings. They'd stopped at the first face-painting station they'd seen, and Willa now sported a small fireworks display on her cheek.

"Let's look for him, okay? He said he'd meet us at the Windchimer at five, so let's turn around and head that way."

When Sean turned, she collided with a solid body. She looked up into the face of a stranger. A tourist, she guessed, judging by the short-sleeved Hawaiian button-down shirt, khaki shorts and straw hat he wore. Around his neck hung a rather large camera. Dark shades covered his eyes.

A flash of panic gripped Sean. So unexpected, so sudden. Her eyes darted elsewhere, looking for…something. She knew not what. That familiar feeling of unsettledness fell over her, and her hand shot out to grab Willa's.

"Sorry there, missy," he said, and his gravelly voice carried many years of cigarette smoking. "Didn't see you." He glanced at Willa and tipped his hat. "Well, look at you, all decked out for the Fourth."

"Thank you," Willa said. "So are you."

He chuckled, and looked at Sean. "You wouldn't happen to know the best place to get a dog, would you?"

Sean was already pulling Willa along. "Sorry, no," she said, and shuffled her daughter through the throng of people milling about the boardwalk.

"Thanks anyway," he called after her. "Happy Fourth!"

"Mama, where are we going so fast?" Willa asked as Sean pulled her along.

She didn't know. She just knew she had to… go.

"Well, if you two aren't the prettiest things on the beach today."

Sean stopped abruptly and turned to face Nathan. His smile quickly changed to a worried expression as he seemed to read her panic. "Hey, is something wrong?"

Sean felt silly all of a sudden. There were dozens and dozens of strangers here. It was the Fourth. She'd overreacted. Taking a calming breath, she smiled. "No," she said. "Just… caught in the crowd, trying to escape."

"Hey, Captain Nathan!" Willa cried, and Nathan lifted her.

"There's my little beach fairy," Nathan said, grinning at Willa. "I like your face paint."

"Thanks!" Willa replied, and cocked her head. "I kinda miss your big beard."

Nathan laughed. "Do you want me to grow it back?"

Willa's hands grasped his chin, and turned his head from side to side. She again cocked hers, inspecting. "Hmm, no. I kinda like your face."

Nathan laughed. "Well, that's good to hear, since it's the only one I've got." He looked at Sean, and his presence calmed her.

"I think I kinda like it, too," she confessed quietly.

"Okay, you three stop gawkin' at one another and let's eat," a grumpy voice said from behind Sean. "My stomach's gnawin' on my backbone already." Jep, wearing his customary baby-blue jumpsuit, his navy Coast Guard hat and a pair of dark shades, was accompanied by Owen, who also wore his navy Coast Guard hat. Matt, Emily, Eric and Reagan were making their way toward them, not too far behind on the boardwalk.

"Why am I not surprised?" Nathan said with a chuckle. "The stomach speaks!"

"Hey, King Jep!" Willa said, waving at the older Malone.

"Well, hey yourself, darlin'," he said, and a grin pulled at his mouth. "I see you got your wings on."

"Yes, sir," Willa agreed.

"Nathaniel, where are your wings, bro?" Eric teased.

"I'll wear 'em anytime, squirt," Nathan remarked. "I'll get you a pair, too."

Eric grinned. "You're on."

Reagan, wearing dark shades and looking as lovely as ever in a pair of cutoff jean shorts and a white tank top, wore her blond hair pulled back into a ponytail. "I'm getting a vision of that," she said. "Might be painting-worthy."

"You gotta paint it," Matt urged, egging it on.

Sean knew who the prankster of the family

was. Well, she glanced at Jep. There was more than one, so it seemed.

"We can discuss it over food," Jep added.

"Dad, one would think you'd never eaten before." Owen laughed.

Sean took it all in; the family before her, joking and hugging and just...being together as the band played on the pier, and the wind socks whipped, and the gulls chimed in with their screeches, and the waves broke against the shore.

She knew then she never wanted to leave Cassabaw.

Never wanted to leave the Malones.

Especially the one holding her daughter.

In order to accomplish any of those things, she was going to have to figure out a way to remove the threat that never left her. The very one that caused her to react earlier with the stranger. She needed to face her past. Resolve the danger. Somehow. Presently, she had no plan. All she knew was that to stay on Cassabaw, to be free of her past, to be able to give herself freely to Nathan, she had to eliminate the threat. She couldn't continue to jump to conclusions every time a stranger approached her. She couldn't allow her daughter to be uprooted and yanked around.

She couldn't allow the fear to consume her any longer. And for that to happen, she had to face who she was.

The thought of confessing her past—her full past—to Nathan terrified her. Not only for the humiliation factor, but the fear of what that confession might bring to Cassabaw. But if she wanted a real life here, with these people, she'd have to do it.

It was a gamble.

It might be one she'd have to chance.

CHAPTER FOURTEEN

THEY SPENT THE last of the Fourth's afternoon rays settled on the deck of the Windchimer, joined by the aging yet engaging Beasts of Utah Beach.

Nathan had introduced Sean to the entire group. Mr. Wimpy, wearing his blue bucket hat, and his sweet-faced wife, Ms. Frances, who wore a pair of white gloves, a flowery dress and hat like in days gone by. The boisterous Mr. Ted, who still sported a flattop from the navy, and his wife, Ms. Leila, whose voice shook from a stroke she'd suffered long ago. Mr. Sydney, with his searing baby-blue eyes and white hair, and his spunky little wife, Ms. Evelyn, whose fake-scowling at the husband she obviously adored cracked Sean up. Dub, wearing his Atlanta Braves baseball hat, and his slender wife, Ms. Myrtle, who admitted her hair had turned from a dark chestnut to its current lovely snow white at age twenty-six.

And Ms. Frances's brother, Putt, who reminded Sean of the seventies actor Tim Conway, and his petite but feisty little wife, Anita, aka Pee Wee, all charmed her.

And, it was quite obvious how much the Malones loved this group. They all sat together, facing the sea, and it astounded Sean that not only were these folks still alive, but that they'd shared so many years—decades—of memories. They'd gone through a war together, and amazingly the brothers had all survived it. She couldn't imagine that all of them had been at Utah Beach on D-Day—it was unheard of to send that many brothers to war. And although Nathan said they'd all grown a bit frailer over the past year, they still managed remarkably well, even with the oldest, Mr. Wimpy, being ninety-four. It was a fast-dying era, those from World War II, and it saddened Sean to think that within a handful of years, they could be gone. They'd all known the Malone boys since birth—or in Jep's case, since childhood. It made Sean realize the history of this family extended well beyond even what she could see. Well beyond the photos in the lighthouse.

Life, she realized, was so very precious.

Together they ate delicious Cajun fried shrimp

cakes, barbecue shrimp and hush puppies. They wrapped up their feast with a big funnel cake—a delicious batter fried and rolled in powdered sugar.

Willa sat between Nathan and Jep, and Sean watched them all stuff funnel cake into their mouths. She wasn't sure who had more powdered sugar on their chin—Willa or the guys or Emily. Now, that girl could eat, and according to Nathan, it wasn't just a pregnancy affliction. Her appetite made Sean smile.

"Em, describe that funnel cake to Sean," Nathan said to his sister-in-law.

"It's a gooey, fricd, sugary, gilded coaster of pure rapture," Emily said without missing a beat. She winked at Sean. "How's that?"

"Sounds perfect to me," Sean answered, licking the sugar from her fingers.

Soon Willa finished up, wiping her mouth with a napkin.

"Mama, can I run in the sand?" she asked. "With my bare feet?"

Sean laughed. "Sure, baby."

Willa kicked off her Keds and took off down the steps, running through the dunes, fairy wings flapping as several people on the beach flew bright red, white and blue kites.

"Well, that's a damn sight, ain't it?" Jep exclaimed.

"Here it comes," Eric said with a chuckle. "Wait for it..."

"Why, I used to run up and down this very same beach, back before all this—" Jep waved his hand toward the boardwalk "—fancy stuff was here. With a homemade kite my da made me out of—"

"An old linen apron," Eric, Matt and Nathan all said in unison.

Everyone laughed.

"Well, he did," Jep said, and turned to Sean directly. "That thing would soar the skies, I tell ya." His hand waved toward the clouds. "I'd unwind that string so far you'd lose sight of the kite." He winked at her. "Them's the good ole days, darlin'."

Sean smiled. "I believe it."

"And weren't you just the cutest little thing, Jep," Emily stated. "Wearing knickers and suspenders."

"And the most comfy, soft hat you could imagine," Jep added. "Yep. Good old days, indeed. And you bet your sweet patootie, I was some kind of cute."

His lack of modesty tickled everyone.

"Tell me what you see, sweetie," Reagan said to Eric, leaning against him.

Eric's gaze leveled the beach, and as he studied the scene before him, his mouth quirked into an astonishingly handsome way. "Well, beautiful, the sun is just setting. The sky is turning all shades of reds and oranges and purples, and Willa is running around, jumping in the air trying to catch dragonflies. She's wearing those cute fairy wings strapped to her back, so it looks like she's about to fly. There are colorful kites flying in the air. One is blue and shaped like a star. The wind is blowing, so the sea oats are swaying back and forth on the dunes, like ocean wheat. Seagulls are flying low overhead, hoping for a scrap. And those little brown sandpiper birds are scurrying at top speed across the sand, just out of reach of the water." He draped an arm around Reagan, pulling her close to him, then kissed the top of her head. "How's that, gorgeous?"

Reagan had removed her shades, and although she was mostly blind, you couldn't tell it if you didn't know. She had the most brilliant blue eyes.

And the love in Eric's green ones—trademarks of the Malone men—shone so bright, it was unmistakable. Anyone could tell how much Eric loved Reagan, and that he was not only used to describing things to her, but enjoyed it, and took great effort in getting the smallest details correct.

Nathan slipped his hand into Sean's then, and his fingers squeezed hers lightly. She shifted her gaze to his. Those eyes twinkled and spoke words to her no one else could hear and that she was almost positive she made up in her head. Affection. Attraction.

"Em, tell Sean that little story," Reagan suggested. "The dragonfly one."

Emily gave Sean a smile then pointed toward the sea, and Sean noticed a thick cluster of dragonflies had gathered and were flying and darting in sync.

"I adore dragonflies," Emily stated. "Isn't it lovely how the sun shoots through their wings, like colorful stained glass in a chapel? They're so magical." She waved her fingers in the air. "I can imagine fierce little warrior fairy knights in full fairy armor, riding on the fireflies' backs and fighting the evil Raven King who's come to take over their secret kingdom in the dunes. That's why they're all over the place, the dragonflies." She wiggled her eyebrows at Sean. "A battle ensues."

Matt laughed softly, pulling Emily close. "I keep telling her to write that stuff down," he said lovingly. "Kids would love it."

Emily smiled at her husband. "Maybe for our kid."

Sean's thoughts clamored at the desire to tell the Malones her occupation. To talk dragonflies and fairy kings and queens with Emily. How…natural it seemed. She wished it could happen now. She wanted it to. Maybe soon?

A quiet, comfortable silence set upon the whole group then, and Sean looked between the Beasts of Utah Beach, who carried on their own conversations about baseball and the good old days, to Owen and Jep, talking shrimp among themselves, to Nathan's brothers and their quiet, secret words meant only for their loved ones' ears.

It was the most contentedness that Sean had ever felt.

"Captain Nathan! Mama! Come chase me!" Willa hollered over the breeze.

Nathan grinned and pulled Sean to her feet. They headed for the sand, where they kicked off their shoes. Nathan chased her little girl around the dunes as Willa's squeals of delight rose over the cries of the gulls, and Sean couldn't stop laughing—especially when Nathan turned from Willa to her, and she became the hunted. Sean ran, laughing, as Willa and Nathan scurried after her, until Nathan feigned exhaustion and threw himself down into the sand. Willa fell on top of him, doing whatever he did. He was good with her. Natural. Like he'd been there all along…

Suddenly, Sean noticed that stranger from the boardwalk, the one with the straw hat and camera. He was in the sand, near the water, camera pointed toward the kites. He gave a wave and a wide smile, and she waved in return. He pointed his lens toward the kites once more, and continued along the beach.

It was all surreal. Cassabaw was surreal.

When her gaze found Nathan's, he was already looking at her, a smile lifting his mouth upward in the cutest of tilts. Willa scooped sand and covered his legs with it, while he patiently sat there as though it was the most natural thing in the world, getting sand dumped on your body by a five-year-old.

Sean's heart surged in her chest.

Nathan Malone was surreal.

Soon after, the sun completely dropped out of sight, and darkness settled over the sky, and the first stars emerged, twinkling and winking where they hung. The Cassabaw Station Police Department put on the fireworks show from a barge in the water. Sean and Nathan, with Willa nestled between them and Jep, sat in chairs Owen had set up on the beach and watched the colorful display overhead. Multicolored streams of sparkles and fire shot through the sky like meteors, preceded by the loud boom, and Willa cupped her ears.

"Here it comes!" she hollered. "Mama, here it comes!"

Just before the firework exploded into the night sky.

After nearly thirty minutes of spectacular fireworks, the light of the last sparkle illuminated the faces of all spectators. Willa climbed onto Jep's lap, and as he showed her the various stars in the sky she drifted off to sleep against the old Coast Guardsman. He glanced at Sean over the top of Willa's head.

"Looks like we wore her slap out," he said with a grin.

Sean moved to get up. "Oh, I'll take her—"

"You got plans to attend to, missy," Jep said, patting Willa on the back. "Owen, come help me and the little Cassabaw fairy up, will ya?"

"Yes, Dad."

Owen winked at Sean, and as the Malones moved about in military fashion, gathering up chairs and cups, Emily waddled over to her.

"I hope you don't mind," she said, grasping Sean's hand. "Nathan is a wily boy. He has what I expect is a most romantic tryst set up for the two of you." She sighed, glancing at the stars, then back to meet Sean's eyes. "Do you mind if Willa spends the night with us?"

Sean glanced at Nathan, who grinned and shrugged.

"She'll be fine," Matt chimed in, standing next to his wife. He'd already gathered Willa from Jep's arms, and she snuggled against the width of Matt's muscular chest. Her little legs dangled down, lost to exhaustion.

"That's…great. Thank you," Sean said. "Thank you both. You've all been so kind to us. To Willa."

Matt patted Willa's back gently. "She's a sweetheart," he confessed. "Won the heart of old Jep there faster than anyone I know, other than this one." He inclined his head to his wife. "I'll watch after her," Matt assured her. "She'll be fine. Go have fun."

"I'll take her crabbing on the first morning

tide," Jep announced, coming to stand beside them. "I promised her breakfast with the porpoises," he confessed. "Alfresco."

Sean took Jep's weathered hand in hers. "She'll love that. Thank you." She glanced at all of the Malones. "Thank you all. For… everything."

"Let's go," Nathan whispered against her neck, and Sean felt the blush heat her throat.

Nathan slipped her hand in his, and with a wave, Sean left Willa in the care of the Malone family, leaving on an unknown nighttime adventure with the eldest son. The feelings of assuredness, of trust that her daughter was in good hands, stunned her. It was another first. Never had she entrusted her daughter's care to someone else before meeting the Malones.

Butterflies beat furiously inside her belly as Nathan led her down the beach to just under the boardwalk, where the music sounded near. Nathan gave her a spin and pulled her close, and they danced in the sand to an old blues song. He twirled her once more then swept his lips over hers, and then held her head still and kissed her deeply.

The sound of a motorboat disrupted their kiss, and Sean turned just as the driver of the boat killed the engine, skidding it onto the sand. He was blond and well-built, with a Coast Guard cap on.

Nathan gave her a sly look. "Your sea chariot," he said with a grin, and helped Sean into the skiff, and as the other man climbed out, Nathan clapped him on the back. "Jake, meet Sean," he said. "My girl."

Jake grinned. "Nice to meet you, Sean."

"I owe you one, Jake," Nathan said.

"No prob, Malone," Jake said. "Nice haircut, man." He glanced at Sean. "You must really be something, for Malone here to have chopped off the beard. Have fun, you two."

Once in the boat, Jake shoved them off, and Sean looked at Nathan in the moonlight. "What are you up to?"

His mouth lifted upward in one corner. "You'll see. Now come here."

With the moon bathing the sea in a swath of silver, Sean nestled against Nathan's chest as he navigated the skiff across the water, and the warmth of his body blended with hers. Before long, the small island Nathan had taken her to before loomed ahead. A small fire flickered in the darkness.

"Neverland," Sean said, and Nathan kissed the top of her head.

"Neverland," he confirmed. His mouth grazed her cheek. "Or, Foreverland." He smiled, and she felt it against her skin. "Whichever suits best."

Foreverland?

She couldn't even begin to hope.

Just enjoy the now, Sean. Enjoy this man, and this time now.

It might, just might, become yours and Willa's forever.

"Are you always so…"

"Sappy?" Nathan helped her from the skiff. Sean's bare feet landed in the water, and its warmth lapped her bare thighs, wetting the hem of her dress. "Yeah, I've a sappy bone, Ms. Jacobs." He pulled her with him onto the beach, where he dropped the anchor behind a fallen tree. His eyes shone as his gaze found hers. "Strangely enough, I get this romantic bone from my grandfather," he confessed, and guided Sean along to the small campfire, already snapping and crackling, sending sparks flying up into the night. A large blanket lay on the sand near the fire, and a small cooler sat atop it and a large sleeping bag opened with two pillows. Next to the cooler, a big vase and a handful of wildflowers sat waving in the breeze. “He took my grandmother here, once upon a time.”

Sean smiled, because the sweetness of it, the nostalgia, sank into her bones. “I love that,” she confessed, then she smiled. “Thank you, Nathan Malone. I—”

Nathan pulled her to him, his hands sliding up her throat, grasping the back of her neck as his eyes searched hers. He lowered his head, his mouth moving against hers.

“Thank you,” he corrected, and kissed her deeply, one hand moving down her back, over her hip.

Sean moved her hands over Nathan’s chest, around his neck, and kissed him back. Her nerve endings fired, humming just beneath her skin. “For what?” she asked, nipping his bottom lip. She slipped her hands into his hair, loosened the band then tossed it to the ground. Nathan’s hair fell in waves around his face. Shorter now, but still…pirate-like.

“You saved me, Sean Jacobs,” he said quietly. In his eyes, Sean saw the firelight’s reflection. Intense pools of dark green stared down at her. “Before you came into my life, I’d given up on, well—" He shrugged, seemingly struggling with words. "Let's just say I'd become complacent. With the island. With my family. I got so used to it average seemed…okay with me. I kept my guilt over Addie's death hidden, and never thought of forgiving myself. I have now. I never thought, though, that I'd find someone. Someone like you."

Sean's heart surged, and Nathan grazed her mouth with his thumb. "It's like you and Willa," he began to say then lowered his mouth to her ear, holding her tightly against him. "It's like you two were meant just for me."

Sean's heart melted then, and she breathed, closed her eyes, breathed some more. "Nathan," she began. *Should I tell him? If I do, will it crush his newfound forgiveness? Confirm I'm not to be trusted?*

"Open your eyes, Sean," he said quietly. She did, pushing her thoughts aside, and that penetrating gaze that seemed to see past everything studied her. She closed her eyes again, and this time felt the slightly rough caress of his thumb against her lips. "Look at me."

Slowly, Sean opened her eyes, and the darkness filtered in, and all she saw was the man standing before her, holding her head still, forcing her gaze to his.

Nathan's eyes searched hers for a moment, seeking, studying. The sounds of waves rolling against the shore of the small Foreverland island, and the salty, warm air, filled Sean's senses. Their faces were so close—close enough to breathe the same air, swallow the same gasp.

"Just…trust me," Nathan said softly.

Just trust me.

The words sank into her bones, and Sean inhaled, exhaled. Then she gave Nathan the slightest of nods.

She'd trust him. With some things.

He couldn't know everything. It would be dangerous if he did. And the thought of something happening to Nathan, or his family, made her physically ill. She couldn't let that happen. She'd have to figure out a way to resolve the threats, her past, on her own.

But tonight, she'd trust him with some of her secrets.

Enough to warn him of just what and just who it was he was falling for.

Slowly and without a word, Sean led Nathan to the fire, and together they sat, and with a cleansing breath, Sean looked at this man who'd risked more than she'd ever meant for him to risk, and began to tell the story that could very well scare him away.

She prayed it wouldn't.

CHAPTER FIFTEEN

NATHAN WATCHED THE fire play over Sean's features, and his heart surged for her. He knew she felt fear. He could see it in the lines now furrowing her brow. Could hear it in the quaver of her voice. She was scared.

Scared that she was going to run him off.

Little did she know, it'd take a hell of a lot to accomplish that.

He'd fallen for her. Hard. For her and Willa. Package deal. Bad past and all.

He tried to envision the next day, the next week, without them, and the vision wouldn't come. Didn't want it to. He wanted them on their little dock, waving as he and Owen sailed by after a day of shrimping. Waiting for him on the front porch after he'd showered and hurried over. His girls.

No way could she scare him off.

Yet, she obviously thought she would. So Nathan prepared to listen closely as she sat, her knees pulled up beneath her sundress, arms wrapped around her legs tightly, hanging on.

She didn't say anything for some time. Just stared into the darkness, beyond the firelight, just…staring. Finally, she looked at him.

"Nathan," she began to say, her eyes wide. "I'm…not who you think I am."

He said nothing; simply held her gaze, hoping to assure her he could take whatever she dished out.

"I come from…nowhere," she continued. "Orphaned, and I have no idea who my parents were. All I know is they were on the streets. And my mother left me at the hospital, right in the room she had me in." She stared again, possibly caught up in some memory. "I, of course, don't remember that," she said, "so there isn't any sadness that accompanies that loss. It's…just a fact. I was abandoned. Why, I'll never know. The first thing I do remember, though, is sitting in some office, wearing a pair of thin *Star Wars* pajama pants and waiting there for—" she shook her head "—hours. I suppose I had either been dumped by one foster family, or was waiting for another one. I don't know." She looked at him then. "I was in and out of homes, some okay, some not.

Most were okay." She dug a line in the sand with one finger.

"But I thought I could do better on my own, so I ran away. To the streets, to a group of older teens who had befriended me. I thought they would have my back." She smiled, but it wasn't happy. "They didn't. I really fell into the streets then, Nathan." She met his gaze. "Alcohol. Drugs. Theft. It's how I lived my life, until..." She sighed. "I met a guy in a bar. A really nice, wealthy, decent guy. I...believed him when he made promises. I thought he loved me, thought...he'd rescue me.

"I was so young, thinking I deserved whatever heaven he was promising. I was dead wrong about that, too."

"Willa's father?" Nathan asked.

Sean nodded then seemed to ponder her next words carefully, for a long time. "I was already pregnant when I realized how wrong I was, so—" she gave an acerbic laugh "—I did what I did best. Ran. To another city, states away. And I've been running, with Willa, ever since. I've...not been with anyone—another man—since I got pregnant with her. And...I never finished high school. I have a GED—I got that just a few years ago." Tears welled in her eyes, and she looked away, but Nathan grasped her chin and made her stay focused. On him. Through her tears, she smiled. "Ever since Willa was born, I've made up stories to tell her. Fairy-tale stories. I created a safe world, a safe place, and Willa became the strong, feisty little fairy in my stories. One day, I decided to write one down. I had a pretty decent savings account. From…before. From Willa's father. But I knew I had to do something to make more money for Willa and me to live on. I didn't want to leave her with anyone else, didn't want anyone taking care of her. So I did a little research, took a chance and submitted my story to a literary agency. That ultimately led to a rather nice contract with a children's book publisher."

Nathan said nothing at first. He was completely fascinated that one woman could have so much courage. "You're a writer? That's what you meant when you said you do freelance writing?"

Sean nodded. "It was a great way to make money while still being able to care for Willa by myself," she said. "I write under a pseudonym. Completely random."

"And now you're in Cassabaw," Nathan encouraged.

"Yes. I…just…was trying to fit in. To find a decent home for Willa, while staying one step ahead of—" She paused after her voice trembled. "Willa's father is…possessive. In a psychotic way. I never wanted him to find out about Willa. So…that's me in a nutshell. A mess." Then she let the tears fall, and Nathan pulled her into his lap and, with his thumb, wiped the tears from her cheeks.

Five years. She's been alone for five years. Longer.

No more.

"All of that was before, Sean." He tilted her beautiful face upward to see him, to look in his eyes when he spoke. "Important, because it made who you are today, and darlin', that's what matters to me." He smiled. "I think you've found what you've been searching for." She buried her face into his neck and sobbed. He held her, ran his fingers through her hair, kissed her temple, then forced her to look at him once more. Her wide hazel eyes stared into his, waiting. "You don't have to run anymore. You belong here, Sean. You and Willa both. With me."

Those wide eyes searched his for several seconds, as though trying to see if he was bluffing, or if he'd change his mind. He saw the moment in the wet depths when she believed him, trusted him, and she grasped his face in her hands and pressed her mouth to his. She kissed him, long, lingering against him, her lips trembling as they sought his, and without words, he knew Sean accepted him, accepted the fact that she hadn't scared him away. She clung to him so tightly, it nearly made his breath come short.

He laid her down, his arms still wound around her, and kissed her deeply, tasting her mouth, swiping her tongue with his, not getting enough of her. She'd bared her hurt, her past to him, and it'd been nothing but a past to Nathan, one he wanted her to put behind her if it caused her pain. He wanted her to live in the now, on Cassabaw, to begin her new life, void of bad memories. Filled with good ones.

Bracing his weight on one elbow, he rose above her, staring into her face. He traced along her temple, down her cheek, her jaw, her chin.

"You're perfect, Sean Jacobs," he said quietly. "Perfect for me."

Sean's hand stilled his, the one he'd been tracing her features with, and she brought it to her lips, closed her eyes, and kissed his fingertips. "Thank you," she said, and her voice quavered, and when she opened her eyes they were filled with tears again. Then, she smiled. Slightly. Timidly. Shyly.

The gesture made his heart surge, and Nathan lowered his mouth to hers, kissing her slowly at first, but then she sat up and faced him bravely. And when she reached for his shirt, he allowed it, trying with all his damn strength to give her time to undo each button when he wanted to rip the thing apart. When she had it off she sat back, her eyes on his, and pulled her white sundress with little blue flowers over her head, never breaking his gaze, and dropped it beside them. When her fingers went to the clasp between her breasts, holding her bra together, and let the garment fall over her shoulders, Nathan's intake of air fell on the night air, and Sean took his hands, placed them against her skin, her breasts. She was so soft. They fell together, their mouths fused, their tongues tasting, and they were one. It felt right. It felt good.

And Nathan wanted to touch, taste every inch of her.

Her willingness to trust his touch made his heart beat hard against his ribs, and he kicked off his jeans, pulled her against him, and they rolled until Nathan was on his back, and Sean lay against him, looking down. It was her turn to explore every scar, every flaw, every contour of his face. She traced his throat and Adam's apple, and she fell atop him, his arms around her body, their mouths searching, exploring. His hands moved over her hips, her buttocks, pushing her panties down until they were skin to skin, nothing left between them but body, and Nathan's pulsed with desire. He rolled Sean gently onto her back, his hands exploring her collarbone, her breasts, trailing down her narrow, flat stomach, and when his gaze rose to meet hers, her eyes were wet with need. She grasped his hands in hers and pulled him down to her, and wriggled the slightest bit beneath him. Nathan nearly exploded at her actions.

But her thighs fell open, and she welcomed him, kissing him, sliding her tongue along the rim of his bottom lip, releasing the slightest of groans, and Nathan moved, filled her and stayed completely still until she grew used to him there, taking up space in a place that she'd trusted to no one in so long. She trusted him, now, and he gently caressed her lips with his, pushed her silky fairy hair from her face, kissed each eye, the tip of her nose, the corners of her mouth, her top lip, then the bottom one.

Then, Sean's legs wrapped around his hips, pulling him completely inside, and Nathan couldn't help the groan that escaped him. He kissed Sean as he began to move, to rock, and she moved with him, and their mouths and tongues mimicked their sensual movements, until Sean pulled back, her eyes closed, and she bit her lip as a moan tore from her throat and she convulsed as pleasure rocked her. And only then did Nathan turn himself loose, and the orgasm that racked his body pulsed through him over and over, going from his groin to behind his eyes, to his brain. He felt Sean's hands caressing his back, his hips, and he moved his mouth from her shoulder as the remnants of ecstasy left his body, and he kissed her slow, long, leaving not an inch untouched.

Finally, he propped his weight on one elbow,

and he stared at Sean in wonder, and watched as firelight and moonlight merged on the planes and angles of her face. Having come from a close-knit family, the thought of never knowing a loving bond, of never having siblings, parents, grandparents stunned him. Even in his darkest moments, after Addie's death, he still had his family, his home, to come back to. To heal, as best he could. He didn't know what it felt like to truly be alone. With no family.

"Hey," he finally said.

A slow smile curved Sean's sexy mouth. "Hey back," she said sweetly.

Nathan lifted his hand, holding it out to her until she grasped it. He shook, grinning. "Evening, Ms. Jacobs. My name's Nathan Jebidiah Malone." His grin widened. "And I'm the last guy you'll ever need to meet."

NATHAN MALONE STOLE her breath away.

Never in her life had she felt like this.

Sean's smile deepened at his gesture. "Is that so?"

Nathan's head bobbed, those sun-bleached curls falling around his face, and his lips curved into the sexiest of grins. "Yes, ma'am, it is."

She didn't even know what to say to that.

"Shy? No, can't be shy," Nathan teased, playing with the shell of her ear. "I think we've just kissed those days goodbye."

Sean giggled as Nathan tickled her ear. "Not hardly," she confessed. "I'll probably be eternally shy."

"Well. Even better," Nathan confessed, continuing to explore her face with his fingertip. "It will be my ongoing pleasure to attempt to break you from eternal shyness."

"Good luck," Sean advised. "I'm a hard nut to crack."

"That sounds like a challenge," Nathan said, then nodded. "I accept."

Together, they smiled, and a joy sank deep into Sean, a feeling that had been absent from her life in...forever. She felt protected. Wanted. Desired.

Even knowing her past. At least, some of it. Willa's father had been the first and last male figure Sean had trusted. That trust had shattered in the most horrific of ways. Although Nathan didn't know every single detail of her past, he knew a lot more than anyone else did. Yet, he still accepted her. Chalked every bit of it up to experience, leading her to be who she was now. That fascinated her. Humbled her.

A lingering fear gnawed at Sean as Nathan pulled on his jeans and moved around their little camp, humming some old blues song, putting together a plate of meats and cheeses and sweets from the cooler, and Sean squished the fear. Pushed it back. Way back.

She'd told Nathan all he'd ever need to know. The rest? Well, that could stay in the dark place it was meant to be in. Knowing any more could potentially put Nathan and his family in danger. It was best left alone.

He'd accepted what she'd told him, and it hadn't scared him away. In fact, he'd pushed it away, turned around all those bad memories Sean had and claimed that they'd molded her into the person she was now, and that he preferred it that way. That was then. This was now.

He threw a look over his shoulder, his bare back and muscles catching the fire's light as he knelt by the cooler, chewing on something he'd popped into his mouth. A long curl fell across his forehead, and he grinned through it, and Sean's heart melted even more.

Just trust me.

I'm the last guy you'll ever need to meet.

She eased her dress over her head, found her panties and slid them on, too. Nathan plopped down beside her and spread his legs wide, holding the plate above his head in one hand, then he pulled her to rest between his thighs. Reaching behind him, he pulled two colas from the cooler and handed her one, then set the plate in her lap. Together they ate. Laughed.

They simply…were. Nathan at her back, his chin resting atop her shoulder. His lips caressing her ear, her jaw, the back of her neck, until she squealed.

Sean had never felt such joy in her entire life.

Aside from having Willa.

Nathan now represented a new joy.

The prospect of a future on the island, with Nathan, maybe? The Malones?

That was more than she could have ever dreamed of having.

AFTER THAT NIGHT, the fears inside Sean subsided almost completely. She and Willa began to decorate their little river rental, and, with Nathan's help, hung twinkling fairy lights along the dock and dock house. They'd sit by the river at night, listening to the marsh creatures settle in, watching fireflies blink in the darkness, and would hear the occasional porpoise blow close by. Not a day went by that Nathan and his family weren't a part of their lives, and Sean reveled in it. She didn't believe in luck, or else she'd claim to be the luckiest girl alive. Instead, she felt fate had intervened, had waited all this time to gently shove her and Willa in Cassabaw's direction, to find the most caring, warm and funny man in Nathan Malone. Luck, Sean thought, was for gamblers. Fate? That came from a much higher power. One out of her control. And her being in Cassabaw had to have come from something other than a random, blind finger pointing at a spot on a map. She'd lived in dozens of cities before finding Cassabaw. She'd encountered other people. Other men. It was her decision, she thought, to get to know Nathan and his family that had brought such happiness. Perhaps she'd never been open to knowing anyone before. She'd chosen to stay cut off from the world, from others. To not get to know anyone.

How glad she was that she'd convinced herself to join Nathan on that first date. Had she not, would she have closed him out, too?

She thought about her relationship with Nathan now, and still, it baffled her, the easy connection of their personalities. At night, after Sean or Nathan put Willa to bed, they'd fall into each other, and Nathan made love to her as though they were both on their last living breath, and each time was a bigger miracle than the last. Not just for her, but for Nathan. That fact shone in his eyes, in the gentle way he touched her, in the excitement on his face each time he looked at her. Sean couldn't get enough of it.

She never wanted it to end, these new feelings that Nathan had stirred within her. She wondered if, should they stay together, it would stop? Slow down? If his brothers were proof, these feelings could only get stronger.

That thought fascinated her, and one evening, while she and Nathan and Willa were on their backs on the floating dock, watching the stars and searching for falling ones, and after Willa had drifted off to sleep, Sean had the desire to speak her mind.

"So," she questioned. "This…romance. Does it ever wind down?"

"Just so you know," he said, turning over onto his side, propping his head up with his hand, "when a Malone finds the woman of his dreams, it's forever. It only gets stronger. Better." He wiggled his eyebrows.

Sean blinked, grinning. "Kind of like a turtledove?"

"Or a dolphin. Whale." He grinned, squinting one eye at her as though he truly were a pirate. "Can you handle that kind of affection, Ms. Jacobs?" He laughed, rolled onto his back. "It really doesn't slow down. Ever."

"Huh," Sean said, and pulled her arms back, resting her head in her hands. "Is that so?'

Then, Nathan was over her, and his lips swept hers, lingered there, until that ache only he could create began to well up inside her. He pulled back, and Sean noticed he had that same pained look of desire. "Yes, ma'am," he confirmed. "That's so." He winked. "Just so you know."

As the days went by, and days turned into weeks, Sean found those words and that night on the dock kept coming back to her. Haunted her in a very, very good way.

She could handle that kind of affection. For that amount of time.

Forever? He'd implied it, but hadn't said it.

And neither one of them had confessed the *L* word, either.

Time. They had time for that. She knew how she felt in her heart. It was larger and more powerful than anything she'd ever felt for anyone, save Willa.

She'd gladly and patiently wait for Nathan to utter the words.

She was astounded by how thrilled she was at the thought of hearing them.

It was a couple of weeks later, and Nathan and Owen were out on the *Tiger Lily*, while Willa was with Jep having a chess marathon, that a knock sounded at Sean's door. Padding over, she peered out of the lace curtain to see Matt's wife, Emily, standing there.

"Hey! Do you feel like an adventure?" Emily asked.

Sean studied her. "Sure."

"Great! Do you mind driving?" She patted her belly. "It's kind of hard to fit all of this wonderful magic behind the steering wheel anymore." She laughed.

"Where are we going?" Sean said, grabbing her bag. She met Emily at the door, and cocked her head, inspecting her. "Are you sure we should be going anywhere at all?"

Emily waved a hand at her. "Pshh! It's fine. I'm not due for another two weeks or so, give or take a day." Again, she patted her belly. "I just had a checkup yesterday. Doctor says I'm right on time. I wouldn't bother you, but everyone's tied up, including my beloved. I've already asked Jep if he was okay having Willa staying with him. They were quite heavily involved in their game. I hope you don't mind."

"Of course not. Sounds like fun, actually. Do you want to take my car? I've hardly driven it since we got here."

"Hmm. Your car's small, and I may need the space in my Jeep for the haul," Emily said, and her eyes glittered with mischievousness. "See, there's this box of 1930s treasures I bid on and won, and they're in Piper's Cove, just up the way," she said, motioning with her hand. "Won't take long at all!"

"Well, then, I'm ready," Sean said, and headed outside in the sunlight that was somewhat filtered by a few gray clouds and a few white ones. Another fine coastal day on the island.

With that, she and Emily climbed into the Jeep and headed toward Piper's Cove.

CHAPTER SIXTEEN

Houston, Texas

"SIR," DOMINICK, CHASE BLACK'S steward, said from the door of the dining hall. Chase lifted his gaze from his meal and waited for the steward to finish. "A Mr. Mitchell is here to see you."

Chase wiped his mouth. "Send him in."

Dominick, a thin older man who had been with the Black family since before Chase was born, and had stayed on even after the deaths of first Chase's mother, then his father, gave a curt nod. "Sir." He disappeared to retrieve the guest, and moments later, Mitchell walked through the door.

Chase leveled his gaze at Dominick. "Thank you, Dominick. Leave us, and close the doors."

Another silent nod as Dominick did what he'd been asked to do. Chase beckoned Mitchell with a flick of his wrist. Mitchell approached, looking like his usual pudgy, unrefined self. His double chin had grown larger, almost looking like he wore a tire's inner tube around his neck. His skin was burned and peeling in patches. For as long as Chase had known him, he could say he hadn't been more thoroughly disgusted by the man than he was now.

"Sit," he told Mitchell, who pulled the dining chair back and stuffed himself into it. He handed Chase a large manila envelope, and sighed.

"If you think it's hot here, damn," he said, and he wiped his already-sweaty brow. "It's hot as shit there."

Black said nothing. He'd been in Tokyo for almost a month now, and he'd only just arrived home the day before. He was tired and didn't have much patience for Mitchell—except that he'd brought news. Chase nimbly opened the envelope and retrieved a healthy stack of photographs. He was good at his job, Mitchell was. And that was about it.

"She's gone and found herself a family," Mitchell said, pointing to the photographs. "Happy as a clam, that one. And she's unpacked."

"When did you find this out?" Chase demanded.

"A few weeks ago maybe. You said you'd be out of the country, right? I texted you."

"I didn't get any texts from you," Chase accused.

He looked at the first photograph.

His insides turned icy.

There she was, sitting at the beach, on the steps of some café. She had changed her appearance, just like Mitchell had said. Dark short hair replaced what once used to be fiery red and nearly to her waist. A modest little dress with flowers and plain brown sandals had replaced the skin-tight designer jeans, silk blouse with plunging neckline and impossibly high heels. He stared at her, fascinated.

She easily passed for a respectable lady.

He'd have never believed it.

Continuing to inspect her features, he noticed she wore very little makeup, whereas before it was heavily applied, with brightly colored lipsticks and false lashes. And her hair—he could barely get over it. How it must have pained her to cut it.

He flipped to the next photo and it was of

Sara and the kid, who was wearing some sort of costumed wings and running through the sand. With short dark hair, almost black, the kid was…small. In the next photo, she was closer to the lens, and Chase stared hard. He stared, stared and shook his head.

He couldn't believe it.

The kid had his eyes. His same blue eyes.

Jesus Christ, the kid was *his*.

He flipped to the next photo, and the next, and the next. With each photograph, anger swelled inside him. So, she'd found a man. Not just an entire family, but a man, as well. An unsuspecting man, no doubt. He wondered what sort of lies Sara had come up with to hide her true identity. No way would she have told the guy the truth.

Studying the man, he looked…blue collar. Probably some type of laborious job, judging by his physique. Longish hair. No telling. Perhaps he sold surfboards at the beach. Maybe a construction worker.

Chase's blood began to boil beneath the surface of his skin as he perused the photographs. Yes, indeed, Sara had found herself a new life. With his child. A child she'd hidden from him for five damn years. He studied Sara's face in each photo, laughing, holding hands with that beach bum, and his arms around her—even kissing.

Sara was *his*. That kid was his, too.

If she thought she was going to forget him, her past, who she had been—rather, *was*?

She was painfully mistaken.

"Good shots, eh?" Mitchell finally said. "Kid looks like you," he said. "*Just* like you. Freaked me out when I saw her up close."

Chase leveled a hard gaze at Mitchell and pushed a smaller envelope toward him. "Take your money and leave." Chase pressed the call button beneath the tabletop. In seconds, Dominick appeared at the door.

"Sir?" he said to Chase.

"Show Mr. Mitchell the way out, Dominick."

"Yes, sir," Dominick said, and turned to wait for Mitchell.

"Text me the address to this place," Chase ordered Mitchell.

Mitchell, whose eyes had been solidly stuck on Chase's dinner plate, nodded. "Sure, sure."

"Now," Chase clarified. "Then leave."

Mitchell pulled out his phone, tapped the

face a few times, and in seconds Chase's cell vibrated in his pocket. He retrieved it and tapped the message, and when he was satisfied the directions were clear, he gave a nod. "Good work. Now leave."

Mitchell's face turned red, indicating he'd hoped for a bit more praise. Or perhaps an offer to dine. He'd get neither. He'd done his job, done it well, and Chase was paying him amply for it. He didn't want his company. Didn't want to be friends.

Mitchell, mumbling under his breath, grabbed the envelope, pushed the chair back and left.

Chase continued to stare at the photographs, well into the night.

He studied her flawless features, and the Black features he noticed on the little girl. *His* little girl.

A slow smile lifted the corners of his mouth as new thoughts invaded his brain. Sara would come back to him, and with very little influence. Zero resistance.

Chase shook his head in disbelief. He'd rescued Sara. She'd been homeless, living on the streets like a criminal, on the verge of being an alcoholic with a good head start in drugs. She'd been dancing at some seedy bar, and he'd stepped in and saved her. Gave her a good life. Cleaned her up. Pulled her from…those people, and that shit hole she'd called a life. And this was how she repaid him?

Sara James had run long and far enough. She'd hidden enough secrets, too. A rather large one. His daughter. His own flesh and blood, for Christ's sake.

It was time she came home.

To him.

Besides, his daughter needed a real name. And he was going to give it to her.

Give it to them both.

Lifting his cell, he tapped an icon. A voice came over the other end.

"Get the plane ready," he said. "We leave in an hour."

"Yes, sir," the voice said.

And Chase Black smiled.

Cassabaw Station

"OH, MY WORD, Sean," Emily said, gently pulling items from the box she'd just purchased. Already, she'd pulled on one of the bucket-styled hats—a soft ivory color with an adorable rose-colored bloom affixed to the side. It completely suited her. She held up a pair of lace gloves. "Aren't these the best? Not dry-rotted or anything." She grinned. "Wearable! And oh, my lucky stars. Look." She held up a baby's gown, linen, with tiny roses embroidered on the front. It was so little. Emily's face glowed with delight. "How absolutely completely perfect is this?"

Sean smiled at how Emily marveled over her new old treasures. "Completely perfect, I'd say."

"Me, too," Emily agreed.

Piper's Cove hadn't taken too long to reach, but it was still nearly an hour up the coast from Cassabaw. Sean hoped Willa wasn't running Jep too ragged.

Or vice versa.

"Okay, I'm ready," Emily finally said, satisfied the box of clothes and jewelry, along with a few Depression-era pieces of glassware, were what she'd paid for.

"Let me get that," Sean insisted, and hoisted the box.

"Thank you," Emily said. As she opened the shop's door, a little bell tinkled, and they left. Clouds had gathered overhead. Dark ones, swirling madly about. A storm approached, and Sean wanted to get to Cassabaw before it hit them square on. At the Jeep, Emily opened the door, and Sean set the box in the backseat, then they climbed in just as the first big, fat raindrops fell.

"Phew! Just in time," Emily commented, pulling her seat belt over her large belly. "Thank you again, Sean." She laughed. "I get so excited over these buys."

Sean grinned and backed the Jeep out of their parking spot, then glanced at Emily. "I can see why," she commented. "The pieces are lovely, Emily. You pull them off well."

"Why, thank you kindly," Emily said, then peered out the windshield at the storm. "Wow, look at those palms," she noted. "This storm is a whopper for sure. Came up kind of fast, too."

Sean also noticed the palm trees lining the narrow, two-lane island road swaying in the wind. The rain fell heavily now, slashing sideways. "It sure did," she agreed, and lowered her speed to a crawl. It was difficult to see through the deluge, and lucky for them, the traffic was light to nil. Piper's Cove was a hole-in-the-wall little township on the coast, and right now they were in the middle of nowhere...

"Gosh, are you okay, Sean? I can hardly see a thing."

"Yeah." Sean gripped the wheel tighter. "It's pretty bad, huh?"

"It's a loo-loo," Emily added, and Sean grinned. Emily had an unusual way of speaking. It was endearing.

Sean really liked Emily. Liked her confidence. Her cheery disposition and her eagerness to please. She couldn't imagine what it'd be like to see Emily angry. It may very well be a nonexistent trait.

They'd driven ten miles at a snail's pace, through the worst downpour Sean had ever seen, when the Jeep jerked, and she gripped the wheel even tighter.

"Did I hit something?" she asked, trying to see out of the rearview mirror.

"Oh, boy," Emily said.

"I'm sorry," Sean said, and noticed the Jeep continued to be jerky to handle. "I'm going to pull over, Emily."

"Oh, boy," Emily said again.

Sean glanced at her as she pulled to the side of the road, with marsh and river on either side. She put the Jeep in Neutral and pulled the brake. Emily's face had paled, and the perpetual grin was no longer on her face.

"Emily, what's wrong?" Sean asked.

"Well," Emily said, and her face had paled even more. "Well…"

Sean blanched and noticed the way Emily was holding her belly. "Oh, Emily," she breathed. "Tell me no."

"Oh, boy!" Emily said, and she gave a sheepish smile.

Panic rose inside Sean. "Tell me you're not having that baby. You're two weeks away from your due date."

Emily shrugged then glanced at Sean. "Well—oh." Her hands went to her stomach. "Well, there's that."

Sean blinked. "Are you having this baby?"

The sheepish grin widened. "I…think my water just broke."

"Okay, okay." Sean tried to comfort Emily. This was not happening. They were not in the middle of some deserted island road with a squall surrounding them. "It's okay, Emily. It's your first baby. You won't give birth for hours."

"Oh…boy!" Emily said a little louder.

Sean breathed and undid her seat belt. She turned to Emily. "It's going to be okay, do you hear me? Just…breathe. Breathe like you do in birthing classes, okay?"

"Okay. There. It went away."

"I want to jump out and check the Jeep," Sean said. "I think we may have a flat."

Emily nodded and breathed, and Sean braced herself, then threw open the door, slammed it shut and went to the rear driver's side. In seconds, the pouring rain stung her skin and soaked her. Sure enough, the knobby tire was flat as a pancake. She didn't bother looking at anything else. She opened the door, dived inside the Jeep then slammed the door shut.

"It's definitely flat," Sean said. "I can change it," Sean assured Emily. "It won't take but a sec—"

"I'm sorry," Emily said. "What a predicament."

"Hey." She grabbed Emily's hand. "It'll be fine, don't you worry." Beneath the surface, though, Sean fought panic. Despite Emily being two weeks out, Sean knew as well as anyone who'd had a baby that any and everything could happen. She didn't want to convey her fear to Emily, though, so she took a deep, calming breath. *Get it together, girl*, she told herself. Get. It. Together. "Okay," she said. "Just to be on the safe side, I'll call 9-1-1, and then Matt."

Emily nodded, then leaned her head back against the seat's headrest, closed her eyes, held her belly with both hands and breathed.

Sean tapped her cell's screen and then the numbers, and waited for someone to pick up. Finally, they did.

"9-1-1, what's your emergency?" a man's voice asked.

"I have a pregnant mother and her water has broken," Sean said calmly. "Her due date is in two weeks. We have a flat tire, and we're stranded on an island road. In the rain. We, uh, need an ambulance. Please."

"What's your location, ma'am?" the voice said.

"Where are we?" she asked Emily, then tapped the speaker.

"On Island Marsh Road, ten miles out of Piper's Co—ove! Oh, boy," Emily wailed. "Whoa!"

"We'll send a bus out right away, ma'am," the dispatcher assured. "Until then, just set the phone down and keep me on the line. I'll talk you through."

"Okay," Sean agreed, and set the phone on the Jeep's dash. Glancing in the backseat, she noticed a woven throw sitting on the seat and grabbed it. "Emily, where's your cell?" Sean asked.

"In my bag."

Sean found Emily's cell, located Matt's icon and tapped it. He answered right away.

"Hey, gorgeous," his gravelly voice said with affection. "What are you up to—"

"Matt, it's Sean," she said. "Um, your wife is kind of in labor."

"What? Jesus!" he hollered. "I'll be right home."

"Wait!" Sean said.

"Ma'am, is everything okay?" the dispatcher asked over the phone's speaker.

"Peachy!" Emily called out. "Oh, I think another one's coming."

"Who's that?" Matt asked. His voice was now steely. Edgy.

"We're not in Cassabaw," Sean said. "We're ten miles south of Piper's Cove, on Island Marsh Road. Emily's water broke, Matt. I've called 9-1-1. EMS is on the way. We had a flat in the Jeep, and we're on the side of the road. And it's storming."

"Is that the father?" the dispatcher asked.

"Yes," Emily wailed. "Oh, boy!"

"Put me on speaker," Matt asked, and Sean

did so. "Em? Hold on, baby," he said. "I'm on my way."

"No!" Emily said. "Not in this weather. Meet us at the hospital. King's Fer-rrry!" she wailed again as another pain gripped her.

"Jesus Christ," Matt muttered.

Emily glanced at Sean once her pain passed. "What if I have to push?"

"Don't you dare!" Sean insisted.

"What?" Matt hollered.

"Sir, calm down," the dispatcher announced.

Meanwhile, the rain poured down, the humidity in the Jeep gathered and Sean had to swallow her concern. She'd given birth before. She could remain calm, for Emily's sake. She looked at Emily. "Do you want something to drink?"

Emily nodded. "I've a juice in my bag, thanks."

Sean found the bottle of juice, opened the top and handed it to Emily. She gave her a reassuring smile. "You're going to be fine, Emily. Okay?"

Emily nodded. "Thanks, Sean. Oh, boy, here comes another one."

"Em?" Matt said. "What's happening?"

"Ma'am, the bus will be there very shortly,"

the dispatcher announced. "Can you do some distraction techniques?"

"Distraction?" Matt hollered. "Christ, man!"

"Sing," Emily requested, her eyes closed. "Matthew, it's not too bad, but would you sing with me? It'll take my mind off of the fact that we're stranded on the side of the road."

"Godalmighty," Matt muttered, then cleared his throat. The sound of an engine turning over came through the speaker, then Matt cleared his throat again. "One, two now we're off, dear."

Emily smiled and joined him. "Say, you pretty soft, dear."

"Whoa! Don't hit the moon.

"No, dear, not yet, but soon.

"You for me. Oh gee! You're a fly kid.

"See I'm up in the air.

"About you for fair," they sang together.

Then a pain gripped Emily, and she winced, breathed and flashed a faint grin at Sean before continuing.

"Come, Josephine, in my flying machine.

"Going up she goes! Up she goes!"

"Whoa!" Emily exclaimed, and leaned forward, grasping her belly.

Matt's voice. The dispatcher's voice. Everyone was talking in the Jeep, and the windows had fogged, the air inside clammy and damp, and Sean felt a little queasy from it all.

Then Emily glanced at her and smiled, while Matt cursed, the dispatcher tried to calm him with meaningful words. Emily grasped Sean's hand and squeezed.

Sean held Emily's pleading gaze. She smiled. "We got this, Mrs. Malone. You're going to be fine."

Sirens sounded in the distance and grew louder, and with Matt yelling into the speaker, the dispatcher hollering back, Sean distracting Emily with anything she could think of. Baby names. The sweet little dress she'd found in a box of items from the 1930s, in the event the baby was a girl.

By the time the ambulance pulled up, Emily had squeezed all circulation out of Sean's hand and Matt was desperately hollering that he'd made it to King's Ferry General and would they hurry the hell up and bring his wife. Sean grabbed the cell phones, bags, a packed diaper bag that Emily had smartly carried in her Jeep for the past two months. As the EMTs loaded Emily, who through it all still wore that lovely hat from the box she'd purchased, into the back of the ambulance, Sean grabbed one more item from the Jeep, then joined Emily for their trip to the hospital.

And braced herself for a wild ride and more hand-squeezing.

CHAPTER SEVENTEEN

INDEED, IT WAS one crazy ride in the back of an ambulance, through a squall, with a wailing pregnant woman as she and her husband sang a century-old song together.

Sean had decided that Matt was one sweetheart of a guy.

Even though he liked to portray a tough guy.

Emily hadn't let go of Sean's hand the entire ride to the hospital, and although she sang with Matt, her bright eyes had found Sean's. It had all been quite…surreal for Sean. She remembered every second of her labor and birth with Willa. She knew Emily would long, long remember this day. The day she and Matt welcomed their baby into the world.

When the bus pulled up beneath the Emergency Department entrance awning, Matt was there, his face slightly pale, a scowl affixed to his handsome features. Sean climbed out as the EMTs unloaded Emily's stretcher, and Matt grasped Sean's shoulders.

His penetrating gaze bore into hers. "Thank you," he said, and his voice cracked.

Sean smiled at him. "Anytime. Now, go."

With a final squeeze of her shoulders, Matt did go, hurrying alongside his wife, their hands clasped. With Emily's baby bag and purse slung over her shoulder, Sean made her way to the waiting area on the labor and delivery floor.

She stood at the window in the vacant waiting room, watching the storm roll overhead. It had seemed to spring up out of nowhere, and then… She shook her head, continuing to stare at the bend of the trees in the parking lot below.

Matt and Emily's life was about to change. For the better.

Their sweet little baby would soon be here.

She prayed everything was okay.

She stayed by the window, remembering the day she'd had Willa. What a long night and day that had been, but it had been worth every pain, every breath. She'd been completely alone, with only the nurses assigned to her that shift to keep her company. They had, and they'd been nice. But often, Sean had wondered what it would be like to have a loving husband there, by her side, at the arrival of their baby.

Every single second since then, her precious daughter had brought her joy, and she'd been worth it all. When Sean looked deep inside and remembered that skinny, dirty little street kid she'd become, then everything after… It was hard to believe that person had, at one time, been her. *Sean.* Maybe Nathan was right. Maybe Sean had needed to experience life exactly the way she'd done it in order to get to where she was now. With Willa.

With him.

"Mama!"

Sean whirled at the sound of her daughter's voice.

It was the sight before her that made her breath catch.

Nathan stood in the doorway of the waiting room, Willa in his arms and hers wrapped tightly around his neck. The smile that lifted Nathan's generous lips seared Sean's heart, and Willa cupped her hands and spoke into Nathan's ear. Something private. Quiet. Something secret, between the two of them.

It was endearing, and it made Sean want to weep.

Nathan crossed the room and gathered Sean in his arms, with Willa squished between the two of them.

It felt…so real. So good.

As if it was meant to be—had been meant to be all along.

As if Nathan Malone was something she'd been waiting for her entire life.

"You're all wet, Mama," Willa noted, "and your hair is sticking all up." Willa giggled. "You look funny."

Sean poked her daughter's belly, making her giggle further. "Well, thanks a lot, you," she teased.

"You," Nathan said, and his green eyes swam with pride, "are something else."

Sean grinned at him. "Nah," she argued. "I didn't do anything. Emily," she stated, "is a champion. A strong, strong girl."

"You kept her from delivering my niece or nephew on the side of a road in a storm," Nathan argued. "I spoke to Matt. Briefly." He grinned. "In between bouts of pretty decent swear words and his and Em's song."

Sean laughed softly. "That was the absolute sweetest thing I've ever heard." She met his gaze. "In. My. Life."

Nathan's gaze searched hers, and he set Willa down, who ran over to the window to watch the storm. Nathan grasped Sean's face with his hands and gave her a lingering kiss. Her heart immediately reacted, skipping a beat.

"Whoa, now," a gravelly voice grumbled from the doorway. "Quite enough of that business."

"King Jep!" Willa cried.

Nathan and Sean turned to watch Jep, Owen, Eric and Reagan file into the waiting room. Eric walked up to Sean, a wide smile on his handsome face.

His eyes twinkled as he handed her a small duffel bag. "Reagan fetched some clothes for you," he said, covering his mouth as though trying not to laugh. "If they don't match, don't blame me." He inclined his head toward Reagan. "She's been known to wear different-colored shoes."

"Son," Owen said, "you do realize if you keep up that teasing, Reagan will get even with you."

"Don't worry," Reagan defended herself, smiling. "He'll pay for that."

"I can only hope," Eric said.

Reagan rolled her eyes. "Eric says you and I are close to the same size, so I grabbed what I thought would suit you best. I hope it's okay."

"Yes, thank you so much. They'll work fine. Willa, sit right there beside King Jep and behave while I go change."

"Yes, Mama," Willa assured.

Jep gave Sean a wink.

A few moments later, Sean returned wearing dry clothes that did indeed match. A pair of long denim cutoff shorts, a blue spaghetti-strapped tank, a pair of blue sandals and a white cardigan sweater that she'd slipped on to ward off the chill of the hospital. She'd run her fingers through her damp hair, trying to get it to lie down, and it had, somewhat.

In the waiting room, Sean sat with the Malones, awaiting news from Matt. Nathan sat beside her, holding her hand, or draping an arm over her shoulders. Jep and Willa kept each other entertained, and Owen flipped through the daily newspaper. Eric and Reagan talked among themselves, too quiet for Sean to hear.

How dumbfounded she was, to look back at how she used to stand on the outside of family—no matter how nice the foster families were—wishing she could really belong. Now she was part of it. Part of that sacred unit she'd always dreamed of. Before, she'd watch the interactions between foster parents and their own children, and wished she had that. The arguing. The love. The dinner table conversations. Now she did. She had it. It still amazed her.

Soon, Matt swaggered into the room, wearing a green gown and surgical hat. The smile that pulled at his mouth illuminated his painfully handsome features, turning what might be a scowl or a frown into…sheer Malone beauty. That was the only way Sean could describe it.

"Well, what do I have, boy?" Jep called out. "Don't just stand there, grinning."

"We have Miss Rose Katherine Malone," Matt said proudly, pulling his cell phone out and moving toward his family.

Nathan leaped up and gave a quiet *whoop!* He pulled his brother into a fierce bear hug. Eric joined them, doing the same, and they all hovered over Matt's phone, staring in awe at the newest Malone addition. Matt looked at Sean and grinned, ear to ear, and moved to her, showing her his new daughter.

Behind her, Eric was describing the baby in detail to Reagan. It was so sweet, tears filled

Sean's eyes. For a moment, sadness slipped in. She'd been alone in her joy when Willa was born. At the time, she'd felt overcome by the addition to her one-woman family. Sean may have been alone, but Willa had the chance to be enveloped by the Malones. And to think, despite her lean welcome into this world, Willa had emerged a gracious, enthusiastic child, ready to engage with people. It left Sean dumbfounded, and full of love for her daughter.

"She's named Rose, after Reagan," Matt said quietly. "And Katherine, after their mom, Katie," he said. He leaned over and surprised Sean by kissing her on the cheek. "Em wants to see you as soon as she gets in her own room."

Sean smiled. "She's beautiful, Matt," she said, studying the tiny little face, reddened from a good cry. Soft downy hair, light brown in color, covered her little head, and her perfect little lips pursed together as her eyes, unfocused, stared at her daddy's camera.

"Yeah, she kinda is, huh?" Matt replied, and his eyes remained fastened to the picture for several seconds before Jep interrupted them.

"Well, can you get over here and let me look at her, then?" Jep griped. "I'd rather see her myself, though."

Matt winked at Sean then hurried over to Jep and Owen to proudly show off his little girl.

It was indeed a happy day for the Malone family.

Sometime later, they all gathered in Emily's room, and the new Malone mother lay in her bed, propped by pillows, with tiny Rose, wrapped in a pretty pink swaddling blanket, snuggled against her. All the men turned to giant piles of mush at the introduction to the little Malone girl, and it was such a heart-warming thing, Sean could scarcely believe she and Willa were a part of it.

Emily smiled at her as she stroked the soft down of her baby's hair. "Thank you, Sean. You were…amazing."

Sean felt the blush steal up her throat. "No," she argued. "You guys, really." She glanced between Emily and Matt. "You make a great singing duo."

"Please tell me you recorded it," Eric said, eavesdropping. "They sang their song together, didn't they?" He looked between Emily and his brother. "The Josephine song?" He chuckled. "Oh, man. They used to sing it together when they were kids. Jep taught it to them. It's…

superold. I'd have paid good dollars to have heard it now."

"It was endearing," Sean added. "I loved it."

Matt, scowling, gave her a slight nod. "Thank you, Sean. Eric doesn't know good music when he hears it."

Eric just grinned.

By the time the room and excitement settled down, and visiting hours were over, Sean was exhausted. Odd, really, since she hadn't done all that much.

Her brain was exhausted.

Leaving the diaper bag with Matt, Sean and Willa left with Nathan, and the rest of the Malones followed suit, giving the new mommy and daddy some bonding time.

"Mama, I want to stay with King Jep," Willa crooned as they all climbed into the elevator.

"Oh, baby," Sean said. "King Jep probably wants to go home and rest." She bent close to Willa. "You're quite a busy bee, you know."

"King Jep wouldn't mind a bit if the little sea fairy wants to come try to beat me at chess," Jep chimed in. "Keeps me young."

"Please, Mama?" Willa begged. "I promise to be good."

"I know you'll be good." She looked at Jep. "Are you sure?"

"Positive," Jep answered. "You could come over later, too, if you feel like baking me something."

Owen shook his head and smiled at Sean. "Ignore him and his bottomless stomach."

Sean giggled, and her heart soared when Nathan's hand found hers and he threaded his fingers with hers. "Okay, then it's fine with me." She grinned at Jep. "And I'd love to come bake you something."

"Good. It's settled." He wiggled his eyebrows and winked. "Win, win."

Sean just smiled.

"What's that?" Nathan inclined his head to the bundle Sean carried. He nuzzled her neck as they stepped off the elevator.

"It's one of Emily's treasures," she commented. "It's why she'd asked me to go with her to Piper's Cove. She'd bought this box of things from the 1930s, and this—" she held up the tiny infant dressing gown, embroidered with roses "—was in the lot. I'm going to launder it and give it to her here. I think she'd love to bring Rose home in it."

"You are so damn cute," he said, and brushed

a kiss over her lips. When he pulled back, his eyes shone. "She'll love it."

"Hey, bro," Eric said, walking up to them. "Since the storm's blown over, how about you drop Sean off and ride with me to get Em's Jeep? We have to change the tire." He looked at Sean. "Can you stand to lose him for a couple hours?"

Sean met Nathan's gaze, and he gave her a conspirator's grin then shrugged.

"I suppose," she told Eric. "But hurry home."

"She can ride with us," Owen said. "Reagan, too. That way you boys can head out."

Nathan turned to Sean. "I'll be back before you know it."

Sean gave him a lazy smile. "I'll be waiting."

Nathan grabbed Eric's arm. "Move it, junior. Let's get out of here."

Sean could only laugh.

By the time Owen dropped Sean off at home, the rain and excitement had settled into her bones and made her weary. It had zapped the energy from her. With a wave, she paused at the steps to the porch, noticing the after-rain smell of the river, the scent of some sweet flower drifting on the salty breeze and the sound of the crickets and bullfrogs at the marsh battling for airtime. A slight wind shifted the moss hanging from the live oaks that formed a canopy over her rental home, and Sean briefly wondered what it would be like to call this home.

Truly, home.

She headed inside to take a long, soaking, hot bath. First, though, she'd launder the little gown and hang it up to dry.

With a light heart, Sean stepped inside the river house and went directly to the kitchen sink. All at once, the hairs stood up on her neck and arms, and a cold chill crept inside her. A feeling of unsettledness came over her, of fear, and she drew a deep breath, let it out.

"Get a grip, Sean," she told herself out loud. "Your imagination is running again."

"No," a voice said from the darkness. "It most certainly isn't your imagination."

Sean's heart leaped to her throat, and her eyes widened as she focused on a figure sitting in a corner chair. She dropped the gown.

"Sara." The figure stood then emerged into the light.

He hadn't needed to.

She knew that voice anywhere.

Cold fear pulsed through her veins as Chase Black stepped toward her.

"You look…different," he said in his refined, old-Houston accent.

Sheer panic moved through Sean's veins, and she wanted to run, escape.

There was nowhere to go.

Chase smiled at her. "Aren't you happy to see an old friend?"

Sean said nothing. Just stood frozen in disbelief.

Chase smiled, his painfully handsome face chiseled, shaven, perfectly groomed.

"More than friends, right?" he persisted. "Or has nearly six years made you forget?"

She couldn't speak. Couldn't move. How had she allowed this to happen? Dropped her guard for too long. Stayed in one town for too long.

Grew comfortable, settled, content, for too, too long.

Chase stood in his perfectly fitted tailored suit, widened his stance, crossed his arms over his chest then rubbed his jaw. He studied her. Hard.

"I never gave you enough credit, Sara," he said slowly, continuing his perusal. "I never thought you'd just…leave me. Particularly on the eve of our nuptials, which really, really hurt." He clicked his tongue. "I won't make that mistake again."

She had nowhere to run. And Willa. *Willa!* Oh, God, what was she going to do?

A slow smile transformed the handsome face of Chase Black into one of pure dominance, arrogance and manipulation. This was the Chase Black she knew.

And before he could even speak, her stomach plummeted. He knew. She could tell by his expression.

"What did you name her?" he asked. "Our daughter?"

"You stay away, Chase," Sean warned. "We are not a part of your life. I'll never be a part of it. Ever!" she growled, even as Chase rushed her and grabbed her arm. He jerked her to him and lowered his head to hers.

"You will," he said calmly, his large blue eyes—exactly like Willa's—staring at her. "You both will. And you'll do it willingly, Sara."

Fury replaced the fear in Sean's veins. "You stay away from her!" she warned, pleaded.

He cocked his head, inspecting her. "Look at you now. Little country mouse, with your little cardigan. The sea air has done you good, Sara. And even your new look?" His eyes scanned her hair. "Quite a change, but I could get used to it. You could completely pass for a respectable lady, Sara."

He was baiting her. Ignoring her. Trying to control her.

Just what he always did.

"You have no rights," Sean warned. "To me, or to her. Stay away, Chase."

That slow smile returned, and his gaze bore into hers. He drew closer.

"No, darling Sara," he said. "I really, really think I have rights. More than, say, you, wouldn't you agree?"

Cold settled into Sean's veins again.

"Now," he said, his smile widening. "I'd very much like to meet my daughter."

CHAPTER EIGHTEEN

WHEN NATHAN PULLED into Sean's drive, it was a little later than he'd expected.

Once he and Eric had made it to the Jeep, they'd discovered the flat tire had met its end by means of a nail, probably picked up in the parking lot of the thrift shop Sean and Emily had gone to. He and Eric had had a hell of a time getting the spare loose, but once they did, they threw the spare on and headed home.

Thoughts of Emily, Matt and little Rose came to mind, and Nathan couldn't help but smile. He'd never seen his brother so happy, so content.

For the first time in a long, long while, he could see himself having the very same thing.

With Sean and Willa.

Maybe, one day, even a new little person of their own.

He bound up the steps of Sean's porch, shaking his head. That sort of talk would probably scare Sean right out of Cassabaw.

The lights were off; the house was dark. Maybe she'd gone to bed? With a soft knock at the door, he waited, listened for movement inside. When he heard none, Nathan tried the door. It was uncharacteristically unlocked. Sean always locked the door. Despite the safety of Cassabaw, it was a habit, she'd said once.

Quietly, Nathan let himself in.

Standing in the living room, he glanced around. Only the light above the kitchen sink was on, and he could see the little dress that Sean had insisted on washing to take to the hospital for little Rose. It was lying on the floor by the sink. *Something's not right.* Crossing the room, he picked it up.

"Sean?" he called.

Nothing. Not a sound.

Making his way through the darkened house, he ducked inside Sean's room, and in the dim light filtering from the kitchen, he noticed the room was empty.

He switched on the lamp by the bed, and light flooded the empty room. The bed was made. And there was no sign of Sean.

Walking through the house, he absently

checked each room, calling her name, before stepping out onto the back deck that faced the marsh. All was empty.

No signs of Sean. Anywhere.

Until he walked back through the kitchen.

There, on the counter, was Sean's purse, along with her cell.

Nathan lifted each, for some odd reason, then set them back down.

Maybe she'd gone to his house to be with Willa.

Only, Sean's car was in the drive.

An unsettled feeling gnawed at Nathan and he hurried out of the house and jumped into the truck, making his way home. When he got there, Jep and Owen were in the living room, watching TV. They both turned when he came in.

"Where are Sean and Willa?" Nathan asked.

Jep frowned. "What do you mean, where are Sean and Willa?"

"They aren't with you?" Owen asked.

"No, and they're not home, either," Nathan offered. "House was unlocked. Her car is there. Purse and cell phone there." He met his father's and grandfather's worried gazes. "They aren't there."

"Sean came here not long after we got home," Owen said, rising from his recliner. "Said she and Willa were going to make you a special dinner."

Nathan ran his hand over the back of his neck. Worry struck him. "Something's not right, Dad."

"Well, what in hell's name could be wrong?" Jep asked, rising from his chair. "They couldn't have gone far, son. Not without her phone and car and purse. No female goes anywhere without her purse."

"I know," Nathan agreed, and he began pacing the room. He then pulled his cell out and called Matt. Maybe she'd gone back to the hospital, for whatever reason.

"Have you seen Sean?" Nathan asked Matt.

"Not since you all left here," he answered. "Why?"

Nathan gave a short laugh. "She seems to have vanished," he said. "I know it sounds crazy, but I can't find her."

"Take it easy, bro," Matt said. "You know how girls are. They get an idea and off they go."

Nathan breathed. "Yeah, you're right."

"Maybe she's with Reagan and Eric."

"I'll check," he said. "You guys rest."

"Let me know if you need me," Matt said. "I mean it."

"Will do," Nathan replied and hung up.

After a quick call to Eric, who confirmed he and Reagan were alone and hadn't seen Sean and Willa since the hospital, Nathan's concern grew.

"I'm going to take another look around Sean's house," he told Jep and Owen.

He took off out the door before either could reply.

When he pulled into Sean's drive, he cut to the side, parking just off the path. Grabbing a flashlight from the glove box, he hopped out and inspected the ground. Kneeling, he noticed the tracks leading in, then out, then in and out once more. Tracks other than his old pickup's tire marks.

Not Sean's, either.

Running up the drive, he took the steps two at a time and rushed into the house, ran straight to Willa's room and threw open her drawers. Clothes still filled them, and her little shoes were lined up by the closet.

He dashed into Sean's room, only to find

the same. Her clothes were untouched. Shoes lined up. And in the bathroom, her toothbrush, makeup, blow-dryer, perfume.

"Where are you?" Nathan said angrily.

How had they simply vanished? In a handful of hours?

More to the point, *why*?

Nathan stood in Sean's living room, frustrated, worried and stumped. He had zero idea where they'd gone, how they'd gone or why. He had nowhere to turn, didn't even begin to know where to look.

Had something happened to them?

Had an intruder kidnapped them?

"Now you're talking crazy," he told himself.

Cassabaw didn't have intruders, break-ins or kidnappings. It simply didn't exist here. So where did they go?

Walking out to the front porch, Nathan stood there, staring into the darkness. It was then he noticed a slip of paper, lying on the wood-planked floor. Reaching for it, he surmised it'd fallen from the door when he'd thrown it open.

His fingers fumbled the folded paper, and he dropped his head to better read the writing. It was Sean's.

How had he missed it before?

His gut seized as he read her words, scratched hastily and messy—so unlike her usual neat handwriting.

Nathan,

I know this is unexpected, and I'm sorry. For everything. This can't be undone, so don't try to find us. Just…forget you ever met me. I'm begging you, leave us alone. Trust me. It's better that way.

Sean

The words blurred as Nathan read and reread them, anger and hurt building each time. He crumpled the paper, smoothed it out again then squeezed it tightly in his fist.

She'd gone.

Sean had taken Willa and left him. Left Cassabaw.

But why?

It made zero sense. He'd been with her a handful of hours ago, and she'd been smiling, teasing. She was happy. Willa was happy.

They belonged here.

They belonged with *him*.

His gaze moved down the lane, where the

multiple sets of tire tracks led in and out of the property. Sitting down, he held the note and stared at the words once more. Hell, no. It made no sense at all.

He didn't know how, or why, but he felt in his heart Sean didn't just…leave. Not after everything they'd shared. No way had she faked it all. The feelings. The words. Every touch, every kiss—nobody could fake all of that.

So why had she gone?

Staring into the night, Nathan finally got up, walked to his truck and climbed in. He stared at the little river cottage for some time before turning the engine over and heading home. Once there, he parked the truck and sat some more.

What in the *hell* was he supposed to do now?

Black Hills Estates
Houston, Texas

SEAN STARED OUT the window, at the vast expanse of the estate. So much land, she couldn't even tell where the road leading out was.

Not that it'd do any good.

She couldn't leave.

She could never, ever leave. Her biggest fear had come true. She'd let her guard down, and the one thing she'd worked so hard to keep at bay had found her. Found her and Willa.

Nathan's face came to mind, and she closed her eyes in hopes of squelching the memory.

It'd been two weeks. Two weeks since little Rose had been nearly born on the side of an island road in the middle of a storm. Two weeks since she'd experienced joy deep in her bones. Two weeks since she'd felt Nathan's fingers entwined with hers, his lips caressing her mouth…

The door lock turned, and the door opened. "Oh, come now, Sara." Chase's voice startled her. "Please get that solemn look off your lovely face." He moved closer, lifted her chin to force her stare to meet his. "It's rather unbecoming."

His jabs no longer hurt. The only thing that did hurt was the threat he held over her. The threat of taking Willa away. He could do it. Legally. He could easily prove her unfit, simply using her past.

And he'd vowed to do just that, should she try to take Willa and run.

Not to mention what he'd promised to do to the folks in Cassabaw.

He kept her and Willa locked up like prized bunnies, just in case they tried to escape.

"I can see your wheels spinning, you know," Chase said. He quirked an eyebrow. "Since when did living in Houston's riches prove to be such a bad thing? Here, I can give my daughter the very best of everything. Better, for a certainty, than you could ever attempt to give her, hmm, Sara?"

"Not everything is money, Chase," Sean said. "And stop calling me Sara."

"It's your name." He smiled.

"No," she corrected. "It's the name *you* gave me."

Chase laughed. "So it is. Still. It becomes you. It's much more…refined than Sean. Don't you think? Now, what are you staring at so feverishly? Not plotting an escape, are you?" he said quietly. "There's nowhere to go, really." He dropped his head, caressed her cheek with his knuckle. "Even if you managed to get away, could you live with yourself knowing I'd make sure a certain shrimping vessel, along with the business, foundered? Or, that, I don't know—" he shrugged, rubbing his chin "—that a particular café burned to the ground?

And there'd be no telling if someone had been trapped inside."

Terror dug into the pit of her stomach at the thought of something happening to any of the Malones. "All these years, and I kept quiet," she whispered harshly. "I've never told a single soul about what I saw. Why do you think I'd start now?" Sean blew a sigh in frustration. "You don't need to threaten those innocent people. Your secret is…still safe with me."

That slow grin Chase had, which transformed his exceedingly handsome face into something horrible, spread across his features. "Yes. I know it is. And I'll make sure it stays that way. Now." He glanced around. "Where's my little girl?"

Anger rolled inside Sean. "She's napping."

Chase narrowed his gaze at her. "You know, it's really bad, bad parenting, in my humble opinion, to have kept her a secret from me all these years," he said. "What if…what if she'd developed some rare disease, and I was the only one who could help her—" he leaned close "—being her flesh-and-blood father?"

Sean could say nothing. She never knew when Chase would snap, and he had that spark in his eye that frightened her. She wouldn't put anything past him. She kept quiet.

"I've arranged for riding lessons for Willa," Chase announced. "I expect her to be ready in thirty minutes."

Sean stared at him as he swaggered to the door then turned his gaze on her. His mouth lifted in a knowing smile. "Dream all you want, little country mouse, of escaping with my daughter, to that backwoods, saltwater town," he said. "I know even you're not stupid enough to cross me twice. Oh." He snapped his fingers nonchalantly, as if discussing a grocery list. "I took the liberty of arranging a preacher to perform a ceremony," he announced, and Sean's stomach dropped. "Next Saturday. Very exclusive. Just us. And Dominick."

He turned and left, the resounding click of the lock echoing as he imprisoned them in the loft of Black Hills Estates.

A forced marriage. Captive in a loft. Kidnapping.

How could all this be happening?

Chase was going to force her to marry him then legally give Willa her rightful name. In a week.

It was a living, breathing nightmare.

He was even wilder now than he had been five years ago.

With a heavy heart, her thoughts returned briefly to Nathan, the Malones and Cassabaw Station. Squeezing her eyes tightly shut, she again tried to rid her mind of the memories. They hurt, tore at her gut, making her insides tight, her lungs robbed of breath. Jesus, she wanted it back, so bad. Wanted it all back.

Wanted Nathan Malone back.

But that was not going to happen. Chase Black was too powerful. He had connections, and he wasn't going to let her or Willa go. Ever.

For a brief moment, tears burned Sean's throat, scorched her eyelids. They seeped out and fell down her cheeks. She allowed herself a small cry, to let it out, and let the memories in. They were all she had of…

The man she loved.

She'd keep every single memory tucked away inside, forever.

Wiping her cheeks, patting her eyes dry, she made her way to Willa's room to prepare her for unwanted riding lessons.

She'd brace herself for Willa's questions—the same ones she asked every single, solitary day since their forced exit from the island.

Where's Captain Nathan, Mama? Why can't we go home? I miss King Jep. When can we leave?

With a heavy heart, she opened the door and made her way to her sleeping daughter.

She hated for her to ever know the ugly truth. That her father had been born into privilege, had been left a fortune when his parents had died with him the sole heir. And instead of using those resources for anything remotely good, he'd delved into a dark, dark world. A world of deceit, of illegal businesses, of threats. He was nothing more than a crook in a fancy suit.

Sean recalled the first time she'd laid eyes on Chase Black. God, she'd thought he was… exotic. So refined. So classy, cool, confident. They'd met in a bar, one she'd been dancing in. She hadn't even been eighteen. At the time, when he came on to her, she'd thought she was special. For a time, he had made her feel that way. Made her believe she was above seedy bars, above dancing half-nude for money. She'd thought him to be her prince. Her champion.

He'd been anything but.

One day, though, she knew her precious

daughter would find out. Find out everything. It terrified Sean.

She could only pray Willa wouldn't hate her for it.

CHAPTER NINETEEN

Cassabaw Station

"NATHANIEL," OWEN CALLED OUT.

At the wheel, Nathan turned to stare at his father. Another storm approached. It was the beginning of hurricane season on the Eastern Seaboard, and they were already in line for a tropical depression. They'd haul this load of shrimp in if it killed him. They were almost to the harbor, and the wind had picked up, tossing the *Tiger Lily* around like a rag doll.

His mind was on nothing, save Sean and Willa.

They plagued him. Night. Day. And all in between.

Like now.

They'd left, and not a scrap of news had arisen. He had no idea where they'd gone, could find no trail of evidence.

The names Sean and Willa Jacobs were fabricated.

Nothing legal about either.

Whom had he given his heart to, then?

"Yes, sir," he finally answered his dad.

Nathan heard his father speaking, even over the squall. He heard the wind, heard the rain splattering against the deck, felt it sting his skin.

"We need to get this haul in now, son," Owen yelled.

"Right!" Nathan agreed, and navigated through the storm. Inside his head, though, his thoughts were a myriad emotions.

His heart, his insides, felt twisted. Gutted. The constant sensation that he'd been punched in the stomach plagued him. Sean Jacobs had lied to him. Rather, she'd left something very important out. What, he didn't know, other than her name wasn't really Sean Jacobs, and Willa wasn't really Willa Jacobs.

He wanted to forget about her. It'd be easier that way. He'd exhausted every other avenue he knew to find them, but even if he did, what would he do? Force them to return to Cassabaw? Make her love him, like he loved her? Hell, yeah, it'd be a lot easier to hate her, even, but damn, he couldn't. His heart had a hole in it now. Sean was missing from his life. Willa was missing from his life.

His life…didn't mean much to him anymore.

They rode the rest of the way back to the harbor, fighting the rain. Once they made it to the docks and unloaded their coolers, they headed home. As they passed Morgan's old place, Nathan's heart squeezed a bit more. How easily the vision came to mind of Sean sitting on the dock, her long legs dangling in the water, and Willa, with her sweet little fairy wings strapped onto her back, jumping up and down. Both of them waving as Nathan navigated the *Tiger Lily* by.

The rain pounded down now, the sky nothing but a flat, gray blanket above, and Nathan pulled the boat up to the Malones' dock, and only then did Nathan realize his father was speaking. *Yelling.*

"Son," Owen said again, this time right in front of him. "It's killing me, Nathaniel, seeing you like this. It's…" His father rubbed his eyes, his jaw. "It's worse than when you lost Addie."

Nathan heaved a heavy sigh. "Yeah, Dad, probably so," Nathan agreed. He pushed his hair from his face, wiped the rain from his eyes. "Addie didn't run out on me or desert me. Not on purpose. Sean, or whoever she is, did." His throat caught, that ever-present lump pushing up, up, threatening to make him choke. "Made me love her, love her little girl, only to take off. No warning. No reason. Yeah." He wanted to punch something, hit something. Hurt something. "It's a hell of a lot worse. Addie just died. She didn't mean to."

Owen grabbed Nathan by the shoulders and shook. "What makes you think Sean did anything on purpose, son? Stop wallowing in your own pity and do something about it!"

Nathan stared at his father through the rain, the wind. Maybe water had gotten in his ear, settled in his brain. "Do what, Owen? I don't even know who the hell she is!"

Owen shoved away, just as angry as Nathan, or so it seemed. Water ran rivulets down the navy blue bill of his Coast Guard cap. "I don't know, son," he said. "I just know people, is all. And there's no way in hell anyone can convince me that girl and her little daughter didn't love the hell out of you. Out of us." He continued to shake his head. "I refuse."

Nathan blinked.

So did he. He honestly refused to believe Sean didn't love him.

Only, he didn't know what step to take.

He'd asked his brother Matt for help. Being ex-black ops, Matt knew people. Knew a lot of people. Some, the kind of people you wished you'd never encountered. All the had to go on was a hang-up call. Matt had people on that one, but so far, nothing.

"Look," Owen said.

Nathan looked, blinked hard.

Matt was standing there. In the rain. Waiting.

Owen glanced at Nathan then leaped onto the dock and secured the boat.

"We've got something," Matt said over the rain. "Or, might be nothing."

Nathan held his gaze. "I don't care. Let's go."

Black Hills Estate
Houston, Texas

SEAN'S HEART WAS in her throat.

How stupid could she be?

Watching her daughter sleep, she knew she had to escape this. Perhaps she deserved everything that Chase had in store for her, but Willa didn't. She deserved better. A better life.

A better mother.

One without a tarnished past. One Willa could be proud of.

This wasn't about herself anymore. It wasn't about how broken Sean's own heart was, that she'd had love in her grasp with Nathan—a man who'd fallen for her, and who'd treated Willa like his own—it was about Willa. She was all that mattered now. And growing up with Chase Black for a father could be nothing but bad.

Sean would not expose her child to his world.

Not if she could help it.

Sean stared out into the night. Chase was still in the city, at his office, late…blessedly, like he had been for the past few days. She and Willa had won the affection of Dominick, who, in Sean's opinion, thought just as little of Chase as she did. Only Dominick was…obligated. Probably scared. Knowing Chase, he'd threatened the old steward someway, somehow.

Sean knew the repercussions of her actions. She would more than likely lose Willa. But Willa would not have to become Willa Black, and everything that went along with the Black name.

At first, Sean had tried to look deep, hard, at

the interaction between Chase and Willa. Willa had been her typical charming self. Chase? He'd tried to pass off being a kind, funny guy, but Sean could see right through him.

This wasn't about him gaining his daughter.

It was about controlling Sean.

Sick-minded as it was, that was what it had always been about.

Sean knew something about Chase Black, though.

Had witnessed an exchange one night. A not-so-legal one. Chase knew she'd heard the exchange between him and one of his competitors, Will Chalmers of Chalmers Enterprises, late one night in Chase's study. She witnessed how Chase had blackmailed Will out of millions, simply by baiting him with picture-proof of infidelity—and not with just any high-priced escort. But one who wasn't quite seventeen years old. Chalmers, apparently, frequented one of Houston's underbelly clubs—one Sean herself had once worked at. He had a taste for underage girls. Chase had picked up on it and set one of his bulldogs to gather photos of Chalmers.

What Chase didn't know, though, was that Sean had discovered proof that he owned the underbelly club, knew where he kept the deed to the building, and could name him in more than one illegal gambling ring. Illegal fight-club boxing, in his building.

Chase was as illegal as they came.

Sean had never dared cross Chase, though. And once she'd discovered she was pregnant, Sean had thought the very best thing to do was to get out of his life for good.

She should have known, even six years later, it'd never, ever be that easy.

No matter how far away she'd run.

Now the only thing she wanted to do was… run again. This time west, not east. She'd have to stay as far away from Cassabaw as possible. Once Chase discovered she'd run in another direction? He'd leave her beloved Malones alone.

Wouldn't he?

She fell against the bed, dropped her head in her hands and just…shook. She didn't know what to do. Useless information that could help put away a crooked businessman. One who, if she ran, could possibly do harm to the people she loved most. If she stayed? She subject her daughter to a maniac father who'd been raised in a fake world of money and possessions and dirty, dirty secrets.

Who was she kidding? She couldn't do a thing. Chase had her trapped at all angles. She'd be forced to marry him. Forced to stay at Black Hills. Forced to watch her daughter be manipulated, just like she'd been.

God, what was she going to do?

Sometime later, a noise jolted Sean out of a restless slumber. She sat upright in her bed. Peering through the darkness, she stared at the illuminated numbers on her clock. It was after 1:00 a.m.

Please, don't let it be Chase again...

Padding quietly to her door, Sean stood there, her ear to the cool wood. Listening. The doorknob turned. The door cracked open.

All at once, a figure stepped in, dressed all in black, and grabbed her, pulled her against him tightly and placed a hand tightly over her mouth.

Just as fast, he turned her around, forced her to look at him.

To see him.

It was Nathan! He placed two fingers to his lips to hush her. Then, a second and a third figure stepped into the room. All in black, with black face paint, black skully, just like Nathan.

Matt! Eric!

Sean's heart lurched so hard, she thought it would pound out of her chest. Her insides weakened at the sight of him. Her brain couldn't register it. Others were present, too. Men she didn't know.

"Where's Willa?" Matt said quietly.

Sean pointed to the adjoining room, and Matt disappeared into the shadows. Moments later, he appeared, her sleeping daughter hanging onto his neck.

Sean moved her gaze to Nathan's, and her heart froze. Those expressive green eyes held hers, but they seemed…cold. Unresponsive.

She'd hurt him. He was still in pain, and angry.

Her thoughts whirled as they made to leave. Sean regained her senses and vehemently shook her head.

"No," she whispered to Nathan and Matt. "We can't leave!"

"Why the hell not?" Nathan said. "Don't tell me you *want* to stay?"

The jab shot through Sean. "You don't know who he is," she pleaded. She'd worry about her sore heart later. She gripped Nathan's shoulders and stared between him and his brother.

They'd broken into Black Hills Estate and

rescued her and Willa. Black ops kind of rescue. How had they even known where to find her?

"He's made threats," Sean confessed. "If he finds us gone, he'll sink the *Tiger Lily.* And burn the Windchimer. He's been to Cassabaw. He knows where you live." Her knees weakened at the thought of it all. "He'll *do* it. Please. I don't want you hurt."

"He has something on you," Nathan said, close to her. "What is it?"

Sean shook her head. "Please, just go," she begged.

"Hey." Matt slid a glance out the window. "No time for chitchat. We'll get this sorted out later." He looked at Sean. "Do you want out?"

Sean couldn't find her voice.

"Sean," Nathan said close to her, and his gloved hand squeezed hers then gave her a firm shake. "Do you want *out*?"

Tears welled in Sean's eyes. Fear clutched at her. She did. God, how she did.

But what would the price be?

This is about Willa, she thought. *Only Willa.*

Didn't matter now what the Malones found out about her past.

As long as her daughter had a fighting chance.

Taking a deep breath, she nodded.

Nathan took not another second. They turned and, hand in hand, followed Matt and the other man down the stairs and out the side entrance they'd come through. Once outside, there were no vehicles waiting. On foot, they crossed the estate, until they came upon a wall that Matt, after passing Willa to Nathan, quickly scaled with the help of a few ropes he'd thrown. It all happened so fast, it was like a movie.

Was this Matt's secret life?

Nathan shoved Sean toward the rope and boosted her up to Matt. Nathan followed, carrying Willa, then the guys Matt had brought along. Soon, they were hurrying through the adjoining woods, until they met the four-lane road leading to Black Hills. A Tahoe awaited them, and Nathan hustled Sean inside then climbed in with Willa in his arms, and they took off.

The interior of the Tahoe was completely silent as they made their way to the main interstate leading to George W. Bush International Airport. Sean's pulse never would slow down. She could only stare out the window, watch the shadows dance across their faces as they passed streetlights and try to swallow the fear.

Fear of what was now to come.

"He's going to come after us," she finally said quietly to Nathan.

He didn't answer at first. Instead, he sat there, silent.

"Let him," Nathan finally said. "Let him come."

"Mama," Willa crooned sleepily, tucked, as she was, between Sean and Nathan. He'd buckled Willa in, and her head had slumped over as she'd slept against his shoulder.

Her eyes blinked open, and she looked around. "Mama, where are we going?"

"Hey, you," Nathan said quietly.

"Captain Nathan!" Willa cried out, and threw her arms around him. "Mama, it's Captain Nathan!"

"I know, sweetie," Sean said, fighting tears as she watched the exchange.

Willa rubbed her eyes and turned her face to Nathan. "Did you see my daddy?"

NATHAN'S STOMACH LURCHED at the thought.

"No, baby," he said softly, and chucked her under the chin.

"Are we going back home?" she asked. "I miss King Jep."

"He misses you, too," Nathan assured her. "Do you want to go back home?"

She nodded. "I do! Mama, don't you want to?"

Nathan's gaze slid to Sean's in the darkness. He'd been unable to read anything from her, other than the sheer and absolute terror in her voice. Even now, her eyes were wide, unsure.

"I do, sweetie," Sean answered, and her gaze lifted to Nathan's. "I do."

Then Sean turned her head and continued to stare out into the darkness.

What had happened to her?

Willa fell asleep once again, and Nathan could do nothing but keep his gaze trained on Sean. He hadn't seen her in nearly a month, and he ached to hold her, to kiss her. He wanted to ask her everything. Ask her nothing.

He wanted to know who she really was.

He wanted to know only the Sean he'd been introduced to.

After Jep had received a hang-up call the week before, it had made Owen suspicious, and Matt had checked out the number. It had originated from Houston, and on further investigation, he discovered it was the estate phone of Chase Black, a big-shot developer. They'd thought it was nothing, at first. Until Nathan had done a Google search on Chase Black, and once he'd laid eyes on his photograph, from the cover of one of Houston's city magazines, Nathan had immediately recognized Willa's face in his features. Same nose. Same brilliant blue eyes. Same mouth. Had Sean gone to him willfully? Or had she been forced? Nathan still didn't have those answers. Maybe he didn't want them.

Maybe he would not like what she'd have to say after all.

Maybe all would have been better left as it was.

They made it to the airport in record time, and thanks to Matt's acquaintances, ex-black ops guys, they boarded a private plane without incident and started for Cassabaw.

Once settled, with Willa fast asleep—as well as the guys, save Matt—Sean finally turned to Nathan, tears in her eyes.

"I'll tell you everything. I'm warning you, though," she said, and pain laced her words, shook her voice as she spoke. "You're going to have a very different opinion of me, once I'm finished."

He stared at her. "It's only fair to let me be the judge of that."

She nodded and looked fully at him.

Nathan braced himself.

"My name isn't Sean Jacobs."

CHAPTER TWENTY

SEAN STARED AT the man she loved.

She hadn't told him as much. She was too scared.

Scared of a lot of things.

Mainly, that they'd all jeopardized the safety of the people she loved in Cassabaw.

She saw the question in Nathan's eyes, and she continued.

"The name I grew up with on the streets was Sean Anderson. Everything I told you before—that night on the island—was true," she confessed. "I was abandoned as an infant. I'm not sure from who and when I obtained the name, but I can remember it as long as I have memories...seven, maybe? I was raised in foster care. Ran away. Alcohol. Gang. Drugs. Bars. Theft." She looked at him, and his expression was emotionless as he waited for more. "What people perceive to be a textbook, messed-up foster kid, I was. All that's true, Nathan. I led a very rough life, not because of bad foster parents. But because I was rebellious. Hard-headed. Without leadership.

"I was..." She swallowed, so ashamed. "I didn't have anyone to tell me quitting school was a terrible thing. I just knew I didn't want to go anymore, and when the foster family I was with at the time disagreed, I ran. I...was dancing at an escort's bar when Chase Black first saw me," she admitted. "He, for whatever reason, liked me. Became almost infatuated with me. I was a month away from turning eighteen. So, I admit I was infatuated with him, too. He had money—lots of it. Gave me... everything. Jewelry. A car. He took me out of the bar, cleaned me up, so to speak. Got me off the streets." She sighed, threaded her fingers together. "He bought me an apartment, set me up there in the city. Most nights, he stayed. He...had me dance for executives. Private dances." She looked at him, and his jaw clenched. "Not sex. Dance. And back then, that seemed fine with me. I'd get paid a ridiculous amount of money. I saved it. I saved nearly all of it.

"Chase asked me to marry him. To this day, I have no idea why, other than..." The shame she felt roiled to the surface of her skin, but she kept on going. "His…sexual appetite isn't—" she chanced a glance at Nathan and could see the pain, the disbelief in his eyes "—normal. The things he'd do, have me do…" She sighed, looked out the window. "I agreed to marry him. I thought it was my way to stay off the streets. He promised me a good life. One where I'd never have to scrounge through Dumpsters to find a meal, ever again." She looked at her nails, twisted her hands together.

"It wasn't until the eve of our wedding that fear and pride got the best of me. I'd found out that day I was pregnant, and decided to do something special. I'd gone to his office to surprise him with a wedding gift—the test, wrapped in a glittery gold box. What I walked in on was Chase blackmailing one of his competitors. I hid and listened, learning things I didn't want to know, didn't want to be a part of, didn't want my unborn child to ever, ever be a part of." She laughed acerbically. "But I inadvertently was.

"He threatened the man—chairman of another large Houston developing firm—with photographic proof of infidelity with a minor," she said. "He claimed to have proof of not only that man, but several others, all participants at his underage escort bars. He kept the names, photographs, in a safe-deposit box—along with the deeds to the buildings in his name.

"I hid until the man left. I was going to steal the photos and proof, but didn't get the chance. Instead," she confessed, "I left. I emptied my bank account, chopped off my long red hair and dyed it dark brown, changed my name with a fake ID and ran as far away as possible. I just…kept moving, town after town, for fear he'd find me." She leaned forward, holding Nathan's steely, silent gaze. "He told me he'd send photos of me to your family," she admitted. "And…other things. He recorded our personal sex life, and I had no idea, but Nathan, please," she pleaded. "He's going to come after us. He'll know it was you." Tears rolled down her cheek. "I can stand a lot of things, Nathan. Pain. Humiliation. Starvation—I've done it all. But I can't stand the thought of my daughter or your family being hurt. Not because of me."

NATHAN FELT LIKE an absolute ass.

His heart broke for Sean. For the pain she'd suffered for so long. For her fear.

Fears he was determined to put to rest once and for all.

Chase Black of Houston, Texas, wasn't the only person with *connections*.

He grasped Sean's hand and tucked it against his chest. Her eyes widened when he leaned close.

"Remember that night on the island? Foreverland?"

Tears welled in Sean's large hazel eyes. She nodded.

"I meant what I said, Sean," he continued. "I don't care about…before. Before is what made you this selfless, beautiful person you are now. Trust me." He repeated his words from that night on the island in a hushed whisper. "I'm the last man you'll ever have to meet."

Tears spilled over her cheeks, and so much emotion built inside Nathan, he could hardly contain it.

"I love you, Sean," he said harshly—almost angrily. "Do you hear me? I'm crazy in love with you, and nothing—especially some *idiot ass* like Black—will change that. He's not scaring me off. Neither are you. *Do you understand?*"

Sean nodded, tears rolling down her face,

and Nathan could still feel hesitation, shyness, shame in her gaze.

Reaching down, he flipped her seat belt off, yanked her onto his lap and wrapped his arms around her. She buried her face in his neck and sobbed, and it was all Nathan could do, in the company of his brother and four black-ops marines on a secret civilian mission, not to *crow*.

Pushing Sean back, he dried her tears with his thumb. "I'm going out on a limb here, but it's customary when someone tells you they're in love with you, that you—"

Sean fell against him, pushed her lips to his and wrapped her arms completely around his neck. "I love you, Nathaniel Jebidiah Malone," she whispered for only him to hear, to feel the vibrations against his mouth. She pulled back, just far enough so that they weren't looking cross-eyed at one another. "I'm crazy in love with you," she said, and a stray tear escaped. "I want to stay on Cassabaw. Me and Willa. If you'll have us."

Nathan's heart turned to liquid at the request, and he couldn't stop staring at this strong woman before him. The one who'd been through hell and back, then back again. She'd stayed in the company of a sadistic ass who wanted to control her, all for fear he'd harm Nathan's family.

Chase Black wasn't going to hurt anyone. Ever.

He situated Sean in his lap, and together they held hands, staring out the window, and soon Sean's even breathing indicated she'd fallen asleep. As much as Nathan wanted to, he couldn't. This woman loved him.

And he loved her with his whole heart.

He'd do anything it took to keep her and Willa safe.

"Nice, bro," Matt said, leaning over the seat. "You must've learned all that smooth talking from Jep."

Nathan smiled, wanting to swat his brother but not wanting to disrupt Sean's sleep. "Shut up," he said. "We have some work to do. This guy's not going to leave Sean alone, Matt."

Matt's gaze turned hard. "I know." He patted Nathan's shoulder. "We'll figure it out. You can bet your ass we'll do that."

Nathan continued to stare at his little brother. "You're…pretty impressive, you know that?"

Matt grinned with pride. "Ooh-rah," he said, and the other ex-marines quietly repeated the same.

Nathan gave a respectful nod.

Soon, they landed in Savannah, and made the journey to Cassabaw. It was nearly 7:00 a.m. by the time they pulled into the Malones' drive, and Sean's eyes welled with tears at the sight of Jep on the porch, waiting with Owen.

"King Jep!" little Willa said sleepily, climbing from the Tahoe and hurrying over to the old man, who pulled her onto his lap and hugged her tightly.

Sean turned to Matt, threw her arms around him tightly. "Thank you," she said. "You left your wife and baby Rose to come for us. I have no other words."

Matt winked. "You get rested. Take your time. But Em's dying to see you," he said. "And so's Rose."

"Tell her I'll be over soon," she said.

Nathan led Sean up the porch, where Owen, then Jep, pulled her into tight embraces. They accompanied her and Willa inside, and while Willa had breakfast, they all discussed issues in the living room.

Nathan told Owen and Jep all they needed to know.

The very private and humiliating facts that Sean had shared with him? She need not ever feel that way again. They'd take care of Chase Black without that knowledge.

"So," Jep said, rising from the chair he'd sat in while Nathan filled him and Owen in on Chase Black, his power over Sean and Willa, and the very real threats he made toward this family. He started for his room.

"Dad, where are you off to?" Owen asked.

"Well," he said, and glanced over his shoulder, "you don't expect I can keep track of all the numbers I need, do ya? I'm ninety years old, son." He winked at Sean and disappeared up the hall, and Sean turned a questioning gaze at Nathan, who could only smile.

Minutes later, Jep ambled into the room, sat down, put his glasses on and flipped open a small black book. Grasping his cell phone, he tapped in a number, took his glasses off and cleared his throat.

"It's me," he grumbled into the phone. "And I'm here to collect that favor you owe me."

Nathan, Sean and Owen all exchanged looks, while Jep, looking like a wolf in a chicken coop, wiggled his eyebrows and continued his conversation.

Nathan could only sit in sheer awe.

He'd always known his grandfather knew some highly powerful people.

He'd had no idea just how powerful, apparently.

Jep gave a speedy recap of the conversation they'd just had with Nathan on Sean's behalf. The man on the other end had apparently asked Jep if Sean was with them, because Jep looked right at her, winked and nodded. "Yep. Chase Black. Black Hills Estates. Black Enterprises, Houston. And she ain't goin' anywhere. Not until that jackal is in cuffs, Gabe. Only then, and I'm serious."

Everyone exchanged looks, and Nathan's hand squeezed Sean's.

Her eyes were full of gratitude as she looked at him, and his heart felt like it would explode.

Nathan couldn't wait for this nightmare to be completely over.

So they could get back to their very ordinary, extraordinary lives on Cassabaw.

"HEY THERE."

Sean's eyes fluttered open to stare into Nathan Malone's emerald gaze. He grinned at her, kneeling by her bed.

He hadn't left her side for a solid second since they'd returned to Cassabaw.

Now he grinned. "Black's in custody," he said. "FBI took him in this morning."

Relief swamped her, and she threw her arms around Nathan's neck, burying her face in the warmth of his throat. His strong hands pulled her close, nearly out of the bed. He kissed the top of her head.

"Go back to bed," he said softly. "I'm going to help Dad on the boat this morning, now that I know Black's in cuffs." He smiled at her, looking boyish with his long curly waves falling across his forehead. "Can you stand being without me for a bit?"

"Only for a bit," Sean teased, and stretched across the bed. "But hurry back."

"We'll celebrate tonight," he said.

"You got it."

After Nathan left, Sean lay there in the early-morning hours, and her mind raced over the events of the past couple of months. Everything from the day she and Willa first saw Nathan sailing by, to the night Nathan and his brother broke into Chase Black's estate and rescued her. Had it all really happened? In such a short time? It seemed more like a dream. One she wanted to be real so very badly.

How the FBI had gained access to Chase's secret documents and photos stunned her. It had seemed almost…too easy. He'd fallen, in a very short time. And fallen hard.

An envelope had arrived at the Malones', post-stamped in Houston. Owen had brought it directly to Sean. She'd peeked, and true enough, Chase had tried his last hand at controlling Sean by mailing the photos of her. Provocative, half-nude photos of an almost-woman thinking she was making it in the world. Sean had promptly burned them in the fireplace. She wanted those memories to go up in smoke so badly.

Now? Now Chase was in custody. His property had been seized, and he was at long last beaten.

Sean could hardly believe it was true.

As the days passed, Sean laid her fears to rest and resumed the idyllic life she and Willa had discovered on Cassabaw. The only difference was Nathan stayed with them at their cottage. He was…so funny. So chivalrous. He insisted on sleeping on the sofa, for Willa's sake. When she was older and looked back on him, he'd said, he didn't want her feeling he had disrespected Sean in any way, shape or form.

A true hero, in Sean's eyes.

And she was crazy in love with him.

Even crazier, he was in love with her, as well.

Two things she'd not expected to happen when she'd driven to Morgan's river cottage back in June.

Sean spent time with Emily and little baby Rose, and a sweeter pair she'd never encountered. Em was a born pro at mommy-hood, and she sang the Josephine song to the infant. Nine times out of ten the song put her to rights if she was fussy. Even now, as Sean sat on the back deck, she could hear the sound of Emily's old record player, the mournful songs of Ella Fitzgerald wafting over the marsh.

So many things, noises, scents, sounds, had become home to her. And to Willa.

It was the following week, midafternoon, when Willa was visiting Jep for a day of cracking pecans and playing chess that Sean was alone. Nathan was out on the *Tiger Lily* with Owen, and the faintest dregs of a storm appeared over the river. She decided to walk to the floating dock to write some notes.

In all actuality, Sean had wondered if she'd be able to return to her work. Now that she felt safe for her and Willa, a wash of inspiration filled her mind. Nathan's accounts of his boyhood adventures with his brothers on their own private Neverland island? Of Irish diamonds in the sea, merfolk and magical moonbeams across the water? She'd decided to put a few ideas together for a new children's book. Now that she no longer had to run, to hide, perhaps it wouldn't be as difficult. And, although the trial in Houston could take months—maybe even years—her mind would be 100 percent at ease. Chase would remain in jail, though. His bail had been denied because he'd been seen as a flight risk with the means to leave the country. The relief Sean felt as that awful part of her life came to an end was overwhelming. In a good way, though. At last, she could stop running.

A smile touched her lips as she grabbed a pad of paper and a pen from her kitchen drawer, then trotted down the dock to take notes.

Ideas for a new children's book came to her

mind—the first in quite some time—and she tucked herself into the dock house and waited for the storm to approach, and furiously began writing notes.

NATHAN NAVIGATED THE *Tiger Lily* through the inlet and made his way toward Morgan's Creek. When he neared Morgan's place, he searched for Sean and Willa. The dock was empty. Probably the storm clouds spurred them to head inside. A light drizzle had kicked up since they'd dragged anchor. He'd dock the *Tiger Lily* and head over to their place.

Once docked, Nathan took off. He'd been hungry to see Sean all day, and a smile touched his mouth as he pulled into their drive. Jumping out of the truck, he leaped up the steps and let himself in.

"Sean?" he called, and walked through the house.

An uneasy feeling grabbed him.

It was just like before.

He took off, only to be met by Matt and Eric outside.

Nathan's eyes widened. "What?"

"He made bail and although given instruction not to leave, he left Houston," Matt said.

"Apparently, he's friends with the judge. Jep's contact just called."

"Sean's gone," Nathan said.

"Willa's with Jep," Eric added. "Let me make some calls." He turned and pulled his cell out.

Nathan scoured the ground and saw Sean's footprints leading down to the dock. He took off running, and once at the end, found a small notebook and a pen, lying on the floater, the pages whipping in the wind. Her blue Keds were kicked off to the side. There was no sign of her. Anywhere.

"He took her, Matt," Nathan said, panic setting in. "I shouldn't have left her."

"This isn't you, bro," he said and grabbed Nathan by the shoulders. "It's him. All him."

"Hey," Eric said, jogging to meet them. "He rented a boat. Gerald just ID'd him."

Nathan said nothing. He pushed past his brothers then took off running.

He saw red.

He'd kill Black. If one hair was out of place on Sean, he'd kill the man.

"Whoa, Nathan," Matt said, catching up and grabbing him by the arm to stop him. Thunder rolled gently overhead, and the gray sky had dropped, making everything surreal, gloomy.

"We go together," Eric said. "Jake's bringing a boat around to Dad's."

Nathan headed for his truck, his brothers climbed in and he took off down the drive, skidding out onto the river road and up to his own drive. The engine hadn't died before Eric and Matt were out, running to the dock.

Nathan was right behind them.

Within minutes, Jake, the rescue swimmer Nathan had introduced to Sean at the Fourth of July celebration, pulled up to the dock in his private skiff. The three Malone brothers jumped in and Jake took off toward the inlet at top speed.

"Captain has the chopper," Jake hollered over the wind and engine. "He sees them first, we'll know it."

Nathan barely heard Jake's voice. His brain hummed with anger, fear and something he couldn't quite define. So much fury built inside him, he all but shook where he stood, holding on to the rail. His eyes scanned the horizon, searching.

"No way he knows our waterways," Matt hollered. "We'll find him."

The storm pierced the air with thunder, and the rain picked up, slashing sideways, stinging Nathan's skin. He didn't care. All he cared about was finding Sean.

Minutes later, Jake rounded the first barrier island, and a crackle came over the radio.

"Two islands down," the voice stated. "In a small skiff, just on the Atlantic side."

Jake turned the wheel and the skiff lurched forward, flying over the choppy water as they maneuvered the small barrier islands.

The rain poured down now, a deluge nearly as fierce as the one the day Rose was born. There, ahead, the skiff was in the water, on its side, and Nathan's throat nearly closed. He scanned the water for Sean, any signs of her.

Then he saw Black, just as he pulled himself onto the island's shore.

"There she is!" Matt hollered.

Jake turned the boat and raced toward where Sean was, clutching a seat cushion.

Nathan clamored to the skiff's side and turned to Jake as they closed in on Sean. "Slow down!" he hollered, and when Jake did, Nathan dived in. He swam hard against the current and grabbed Sean under the arms and pulled her against his chest. Swimming backward, he stopped, treading water, as Matt and Eric leaned over the skiff's rail.

Nathan pushed the water from Sean's eyes and kissed her. "I'll be right back," he said, and handed her up toward his brothers' outreaching arms.

Then Nathan, blinded by fury, took off toward the shore. His arms cut through the water as fast and as hard as he'd ever swum before, and finally, his feet found sand beneath them. He dragged up onto the beach. He knew these islands. He knew all of them.

Black didn't.

And Nathan wasn't leaving until he had him.

Just then, through the downpour, Nathan caught sight of Black's blue shirt, heading into the small bit of wood. He took off after him, cutting sideways, and caught up with him.

Black turned and held a pistol, pointing it right at Nathan.

"She doesn't belong to you!" Chase screamed against the wind. He looked wild. Feral. Out of his mind. Maybe he was.

Nathan lunged at him, just as a shot rang out.

Fire seared Nathan's shoulder, but he ignored it and threw his arms around Black's legs. Nathan's left arm didn't seem to want to do much, so he grabbed the pistol with his right and threw it, then cocked Black with his fist. They went down in the sand, and Nathan came out on top, and he beat Black until he stopped moving, and until Matt pulled him off. Only then did Nathan feel the weakness take over him, and although he'd risen to his feet, he now dropped to his knees.

Nathan felt the sand as his face collided with the ground, but before blackness filled his eyes, he saw Eric give Black a good kick in the gut. Heard Black groan. Heard Matt swear.

Then, Nathan saw and heard nothing at all.

CHAPTER TWENTY-ONE

"HEY THERE, HANDSOME." Sean's voice broke through the haze and fog of his fuzzy mind. "How are you feeling?"

Nathan blinked several times, trying to clear his blurry vision. "I'm good," Nathan said. "Only, I think I'm in some weird dream."

Sean giggled. "Why do you think that?"

"Because," Nathan said, blinking some more, "I think a fairy is hovering over me. She's cute, don't gct me wrong. Shiny dark hair, cut just so," he said, wiggling his fingers toward Sean's head. "Giant gorgcous eyes and cute pointy cars."

Sean leaned over and gently pressed her lips to Nathan's, and he breathed her in.

"I don't have pointy ears," Sean whispered.

He stared hard at her, and her face came into clear view.

Worry lined her eyes, and dark circles sat beneath those beautiful orbs.

"You saved me," she said, and rewarded him with another kiss. "Again."

Nathan found Sean's hands and threaded their fingers together. "He won't bother you again, darlin'. I promise."

"I know," Sean said softly. "Thank you for coming after me. He came out of nowhere, took me completely off guard—"

"Shh," Nathan crooned, and pressed a finger over her lips to shush her. "He's gone, baby. He won't cut into our lives again."

"Jep says he's going to jail for long time now," she said. "He won't have a judge friend post his bail this time. They've added another kidnapping charge, and attempted murder." Her voice caught, and tears welled in her eyes. "Nathan, he could have killed you."

Nathan gave her a gentle tug. "He didn't. I'm here, and I'm fine, and I'm not going anywhere," he promised.

"The shot was a clean one," Sean said, and her face blanched a little as she nodded toward his shoulder, wrapped in white gauze. "Through and through. You lost a lot of blood, though," she said. "You need to rest."

"Stay?" Nathan asked.

"I wouldn't dream of leaving."

He stared at her for several moments, searching. "I love you, Sean Jacobs."

Sean smiled, gave a soft laugh and wiped her eyes. "I love you back, Nathan Malone."

"Good," he said, and closed his eyes. "Good."

"Well, it's about time you woke," Jep's gruff voice called from the hospital's doorway. "You all right, son?"

Nathan reached out with his working hand, and his grandfather took it, wrapping his old one around it. Jep squeezed. "Damn hospitals. I spend more time in 'em with you young'uns than I do for my ninety-year-old self."

Nathan gave a soft laugh.

"I'm glad you're all right, son. Gave me a hell of a scare." He looked at Sean. "You too, missy."

Sean grinned. "Yes, sir."

"Captain Nathan!"

Willa darted in from the doorway, Owen close behind. She pulled to a stop at the hospital bed, inspecting Nathan's shoulder. Her wide blue eyes found his, and she smiled.

"Does it hurt, Captain Nathan?"

"Nah," Nathan said. "Just a little."

Willa nodded then inspected the rest of Nathan, and she slowly walked around the bed to come to stand close. She leaned over, looking into his eyes. "Are you sick?"

Nathan grinned and tapped Willa on the nose. "No, baby, my shoulder's sore. I'll be okay and back home soon enough."

"Home to your home? Or home to mine and Mama's home?" Willa asked.

Nathan's gaze moved to Sean's and held it steady, and a slow smile lifted his mouth. "We'll see," Nathan said.

"Okay," Willa announced, and slipped her hand into Jep's. "Let's go, King Jep."

Jep looked at Sean and Nathan and shrugged. "Wrapped," he announced. "That's all I'm saying."

Nathan and Sean laughed as Jep and Willa left the room.

Sean sat beside him and threaded her fingers through his. She laid her head on his chest, and Nathan's heart surged with love.

Would he ever get used to his girls?

A thought finally struck him, and he tugged on Sean until she looked up at him.

"I found your notebook on the floating dock. Who is Nathaniel, Fairy King?" he asked with a smirk. "Please tell me I'm the witty, handsome Fairy King. Brave, too. Did I mention handsome?"

Sean grinned. "You're not too shy, are you?"

Nathan pulled her closer. "Nary a shy bone in my Fairy King body."

"Well, then. Let me run a few ideas by you. See how well you can manage being Nathaniel, Fairy King."

"Only if you'll be Sean, Fairy Queen."

At her expression, his heart soared.

He wanted to tell her that, at last, she could stop running. For good.

She had her prince.

Her champion.

A family for her and Willa.

He would tell her. Soon.

EPILOGUE

THE LONG DOG days of summer rolled to a balmy end on Cassabaw, and September settled over the barrier island.

The past couple of months had been pretty remarkable.

At least, in Nathan's eyes.

In the short span of a summer, Nathan had discovered who he truly was, what he wanted out of life and that he *mattered*.

He hadn't been responsible for Addie's death.

He'd stayed in that furious Bering Sea until he could barely keep his head above the bobbing waves, searching for his fiancée. Then later, in the chopper, he'd searched and searched. He'd done all he could to find her, and hadn't been able to rescue her. Hell, he hadn't even been able to find her body. The sea had, indeed, swallowed her.

But he'd done his best. He knew that now.

It'd taken a while for him to get it.

And it had taken a pair of sweet fairies to make him understand it.

The sun began its descent over Cassabaw as he and Owen navigated the *Tiger Lily* through the inlet, and the salty breeze lifted Nathan's hair and left that familiar, tangy grit on his skin. He loved the sea. While he'd never go back to the Coast Guard—because he'd made his life now running the Malones' shrimping business—he no longer shrugged away memories of the Guard. He'd been a good rescue swimmer. It'd taught him a lot. His captain, his mates—he'd learned valuable lessons from them all. It was a part of his past, and now, it was a past he could be proud of. He'd hold on to those memories, be proud of the lives he'd saved. There'd been a hell of a lot.

He remembered each one, too.

As the *Tiger Lily* chugged along, Nathan looked up, watched the fading sun spear through the mossy canopy above, and he smiled. His life had been saved, too.

Sean Jacobs and her daughter, Willa, had saved it.

Fate had sent those two fairy angels his way, and he'd be grateful for it till the day he died.

As Morgan's place came into view, so did his girls. An automatic smile pulled at his face. Everything had fallen into place. Matt and Em's little Rose was thriving and healthy. Eric and Reagan were planning their wedding for the spring. And now, Nathan had met the love of his life, and she came with the most engaging little daughter. Every time he looked at them, joy filled his heart. It was all he'd ever wanted in life.

Chase Black was incarcerated while awaiting trial. This time, there'd be no judge to award Black bail. Sean had agreed to testify, and they'd go to Houston together to see it done. He'd be glad to finally be rid of Black and the threats he'd held over Sean's head for so long.

And despite being Willa's biological father, he'd never gain rights to the little girl. Jep had made sure of that by way of another phone call.

A federal judge.

The depths of Jep's well of friends in high places never ceased to amaze Nathan.

The trawler grew closer now, and Willa jumped up and down on the dock, her little wings flapping with each leap. Her mama had a pair on, too. The girls his girls waved as he passed, and Nathan blasted the horn.

Willa's squeals of delight echoed down the river.

"I never thought I'd see such joy on your face, son," Owen said, giving Nathan's shoulder a squeeze. "Makes my heart feel good. She's one of us, whether she realizes it yet or not."

Nathan grinned at his father as he docked the *Tiger Lily*, and together they leaped out, tied the boat off, and Nathan headed inside to shower then pick up his girls for supper.

After throwing on a blue button-down shirt and a pair of jeans, Nathan pulled his damp hair back and secured it with a leather tie then hurried to Sean and Willa's.

When he pulled up in the drive, they were both there, sitting on the porch, waiting for him.

His girls. Waiting.

For *him*.

Willa ran to him and leaped into his arms, and grasped him hard around his neck, being careful not to squeeze his injured shoulder too hard.

For such a little kid, Willa was a gracious, kind old soul.

He tucked her into the cab of the truck, and she pulled her seat belt on.

Nathan then turned to the other woman in his life.

Sean sauntered up to him, inspecting him with a twinkle in her wide eyes. “You take my breath away,” she said, rising onto her tiptoes and pressing a kiss to Nathan’s lips.

His arm went around her waist and he held her there, close to him, and deepened the kiss. Then he pulled back, and his eyes searched hers, and he could see nothing but trust and love there.

They hadn’t known each other a terribly long time, but they’d connected. They’d reached a level of intimacy that went beyond physical. When they talked, they listened. They encouraged. They inspired. He’d felt a connection once before, to Addie, and he’d always hold her in a special place—a locked treasure box inside his heart. At first, after Black had finally been caught and imprisoned, Nathan and Sean had many long talks. Some lasting well into the early morning on days Nathan wasn’t out on the *Tiger Lily* with his father. He’d told Sean how he’d met Addie, and how he’d loved her. The devastation he’d felt as she’d disappeared from his sight in the raging sea. Sean had listened carefully, without offense. Without judging. She'd let Nathan get things off his chest, and ever since, Addie had found a place to rest inside his heart. Thoughts of Addie rarely crossed his mind anymore. They'd loved, and they'd lost. He and Addie hadn't been the only ones.

Sean had lost, too. Never could Nathan have imagined such loneliness as the life Sean had led before having Willa. Growing up with such a loving family, it was hard for him to grasp the fact that Sean's mother had literally abandoned her in the hospital. Her father had been nonexistent, apparently. No one had ever claimed baby Sean. From that moment of being abandoned on, she'd gone from one foster home to the next. It was a comfort to know Sean recalled nice foster families. Yet, despite the kindness, she'd ended up on the streets. Living a life no kid—no person—should ever have to endure.

Nathan recalled birthdays, Christmas mornings when he and his younger brothers would creep down and hide on the stairs, just to try to catch a glimpse of Santa leaving gifts under the tree. Had Sean ever experienced a truly happy Christmas? Had she ever hunted Easter eggs? Or dressed up for Halloween? Image after image of his childhood flashed, and with them happy, magical times. It pained him to think of Sean on the streets on Christmas Eve, alone. No tree. No gifts. No family to love.

Things would be different for Sean now. She'd know all of those wonderful and magical childhood dreams. So she'd discover them as an adult? It was never too late to start, to his way of thinking.

Sean had divulged every sordid detail of her life on the streets, and Nathan had a difficult time putting that young kid inside the Sean he knew now. Going hungry. Eating out of Dumpsters. Drinking. Drugs.

In a way, she, too, had been swallowed up. By the system. By the streets. But unlike Addie, Sean had kicked her way to the surface. She'd found a way to breathe. She'd survived.

No, more than that, she'd thrived.

Despite that lonely childhood, despite the controlling environment Black had forced her into, Sean had risen above it all. She'd escaped. Had obtained her GED. Had raised a sweet, bright, witty little girl. And Sean was just as bright, just as brilliant, and had more love in her heart than anyone Nathan had ever met.

In some ways, she reminded Nathan of his mom. Funny, how that went sometimes.

Nathan knew he wanted Sean to be his wife, and Willa to be his daughter. He wanted to adopt Willa, give them both his name. The Malone name. And with that name came an entire family. A tightly woven unit of love.

And he'd ask Sean and Willa both, when the time was not just merely right.

But absolutely, unforgettably *perfect.*

Sean was grinning now, the softest of curves lifting the corners of her lips, and she reached for his hand, sliding hers into it. She gave it a firm yet ladylike shake. He liked the feel of her small hand in his. Slender fingers, a feather-light touch. She was delicate, strong, fierce all at once.

"My name's Sean," she said sweetly. "I'm the very last woman you'll ever need to meet."

Nathan's heart surged as Sean looked at him, those eyes filled with trust.

"Is that so?" Nathan asked, shaking her hand. He lifted it to his mouth, brushed a kiss over her knuckles. "Well, I'm Nathan Malone," he said, "and I'm the very last man you'll ever need to meet."

Sean grinned, and pressed another kiss to his lips, and she smiled against them. "I know," she whispered.

Nathan pulled back, watched the last of the sun's rays play across her skin, warming her cheeks to a pink, and making her pixie-like hair shine.

Yeah, it'd be perfect. When he'd ask Sean to marry him, he'd ask not only Sean, but Willa, too. He'd ask them both to be a family. His family.

Become a Malone. *Forever.*

"What is going on in that noggin of yours?" Sean asked, nuzzling his neck. "I think I see smoke."

Nathan stared at her, grinning.

"You know? From your brain's wheels spinning round and round?"

Nathan pulled her close once more, pressing a kiss to her neck, her collarbone, her ear. "Oh, you know," he whispered. "I love you," he said against her skin.

Sean leaned back, and those large hazel eyes turned wet. The corners of her mouth lifted, and she was the most perfect girl.

Perfect for him in every way.

"I love you, Nathaniel Malone," she said, smiling. Her fingers twined in with his.

"Oh, you two," Willa called from the cab. "I'm starving over here!"

Sean's gaze turned bright as she giggled, and Nathan smiled. He saw Sean to her side of the truck and settled her in, then as he rounded the hood he drew a deep breath and looked out over the marsh.

His girls had saved him.

He'd spend the rest of his life protecting them.

A smile tugged at his mouth as he climbed in, and an old blues song wafted over the river from Emily's record player as they ambled down the drive.

He'd be the last man Sean and Willa Jacobs would ever need to meet.

"How do you know where we're going, Captain Nathan?" Willa asked as they drove along the river road, watching the sun sink over the water. A few stars had already popped out, and they twinkled in the fading dusk.

Nathan pointed to one particular bright one. "First star to the right then straight on till morning," he said, and Willa squealed and laughed, and Nathan's heart surged once more.

He'd found his Neverland.

Rather his *Foreverland*.

With his two girls.

He'd forever be grateful to fate for that one.

* * * * *